THEREFORE
BE
BOLD

Books by *Herbert Gold*

BIRTH OF A HERO
THE PROSPECT BEFORE US
THE MAN WHO WAS NOT WITH IT
THE OPTIMIST
LOVE AND LIKE
THEREFORE BE BOLD

THEREFORE
BE
BOLD

A Novel by
HERBERT GOLD

THE DIAL PRESS   1960   NEW YORK

Copyright © 1960 by Herbert Gold
All rights reserved

Library of Congress Catalog Card Number: 60-13431

To
    Seymour A. Slater
    —this has been reserved
    for you.

ULYSSES: Therefore be bold; we will be just hereafter.

—Sophocles, *Philoctetes*

Cast

THE BOYS

DAN BERMAN: Our Hero. Skinny, argumentative, nosy, poetico-philosophical, four-eyed, and fleet on his feet.

JUICER MONTAGUE: Fat, bullheaded, amorous, and genial. A hero to our hero. A hero to himself (he wishes).

TOM MOSS: Intelligent and discreet as a pig, who never looks at the sky. But the pig is much maligned, and so is Tom.

RED MASTERS: A bamboozling little genius of fourteen, too smart to spit into the wind but too brave to shirk spitting merely because of an adverse wind.

OTHERS: Chuck Hastings, a wandering scholar without a brain in his head; Lewis Snyder, a star left end who will not be left out; various humorists, squirmers, grinds, extras; Cast of Dozens!

THE GIRLS

EVA MASTERS: Plump, poetic, hyperthyroid, desperate, careful, with sidelong ambles and unusually triste musings.

9

LUCILLE LAKE: A much amused harpist (though amusement does not prevent a harpist's being unstrung).

PATTIE DONAHUE: A bestial beauty, with eyes too close together.

ROSALIE FALLON: Pattie's friend, with eyes too far apart.

OTHERS: Jean Thompson, who wants to do good on people; other willing or unwilling suburban ladies; Cast of Several!

THE PARENTS

MRS. BERMAN: When the cradle rocks, she will mourn. Who stole her baby? Her baby.

MR. BERMAN: He knew what he thought he wanted. What he wanted: the other thing.

MR. MASTERS: Oh, ow, ouch, the villain. An ideologue.

MRS. MASTERS: Stupidity won't kill you, but it will put that look of death in the eye.

MRS. LAKE: A benevolent laughing lady who wears high heels and is nobody's Earth Mother.

NON-PARENTAL ADULTS

Mr. Welch, a high school teacher with a head full of fuzz; a lady of difficult virtue named Black Lil; T. S. Eliot, an English gentleman; Omar Khayyam, a Persian gentleman; Roosevelt, Stalin, Neville Chamberlain, Adolf Hitler; barkers, streetcar conductors, repairmen, suburban animals, counselors-at-lawlessness, the author.

1. *Fireflies, a harpist, and her ice cream*

IN SPRING A FANCY YOUNG MAN turns to light thoughts of love and other promises. Age was not laid upon us. We were introduced into it, as visitors to a wedding are caught up in the dance, taken toward rhythmic joggings under solemn sweating jowls and astonished by unsuspected desires to kiss the bride. We entered this dance without knowing the music, but we entered with musical blood.

"Yes, why?"

"Oh I tell you," Juicer said, listening.

"Oh yes I'm listening," I said, talking.

Our angel sat on a stool in the front parlor of her house, noncommittally strumming a harp, while we descended like June bugs to loll unseen on the surburban grass outside. We rested amid the sweet damp and linked dreams. I would be the greatest lawyer in the world. Juicer would be the greatest detective in the world. We would work together, Juicer and I, to make the greatest team in the world. Watch out for the greatest friends in the world, the Greatest Law-Enforcement Team in the world.

Or maybe I would be a poet, Juicer a novelist. Or Berman and Montague, All-American end and halfback for Ohio State, carried out on parallel stretchers after their historic Rose Bowl aerial attack. The worlds of If danced on a string in those days, and our changing voices came echoing back to us from strange vistas (vocational aptitudes). We could do anything. Our fingers, scrabbling with shared reveries in the damp evening grass, touched bugs.

Pluck-pluckety-pluck. Lucille, the busy-eyed harpist inside, sometimes diamond-eyed, grabbed the strings and stroked them, milking thoughts that she would be the greatest in the world.

"Greatest what?" Juicer asked me.

"Just the greatest," I promised, dogmatic in itchy socks, corduroy pants, and my father's Florida silk shirt with the sleeves cut off. I was imitating some legal eagle I had once heard about, but I was right. "The greatest," I said, "past the very end."

Since we both adored her, Lucille already was. Sometimes I still worshiped Pattie Donahue, but mostly I adored Lucille Lake. Anyway, two inspirations are better than one. (Occasionally I even gave a look to Miss Eva Masters, whom I had *really* always loved.)

Lucille Lake wore red slacks in the ninth grade class play and, later, black slacks in the senior one. Ordinary girls in Lakewood, Ohio, didn't do that. Someone would have spoken with her mother, except that Mrs. Lake stopped going to church after her divorce. Lucille had a busy face, as I have said: the colors of her eyes whirling with their contained energy like that of a barber pole, twining forever inward upon its absent self while you expected it to go sailing off to penetrate the heavens. When she smiled a crinkle of fuss appeared in two taut harpstrings between her eyes; the remainder of her fatherless face protested cutely at amusement above the tomboy shirt with its lining of the first female buttons; the lean rump, quick as a firefly, dodged and leaped in athletics designed to avoid laughter. She was our gorgeous agile firefly, our super deluxe V-8 cricket with its tail ablaze, possessed by light and a deep squeaking.

Juicer and I held her image—and that alone—in our cupped palms in order to extract the cold light and wonder at its distant brilliance. Could this jeweled stinger burn? Would it sing or singe? "I can't make her out, what she's thinking," Juicer said. "How about you, Dan? Is that music she's playing or scales?" We held her morally, analytically, tightly, but in brutal fact we did not hold her at all. We may or may not have existed—as she chose.

Once, years before, three children, Tom Moss, Lucille, and I had danced about a fountain in Lakewood Park. Lucille, even then a musician, sang out: "The next person who drinks this water, it will be filled with snakes and snails, but the third person, it will be clean and nice."

"Snakes and snails and puppydogs' tails. Drink!"

Nobody sipped, nobody dared. Then, obedient to her music, I drank.

"Snakes and snails and puppydogs' tails! Daniel drank!"

"All right for you, Lucille Lake," Tom Moss said. He nudged her with his fiddling elbow. She did not stir. He shrugged. He drank. And then she leaped into the air and her lovely knees caught the light and, pouncing, her voice thrilled out:

"But the third person, it will be clean and nice and ev-ver-ry-thing that Loo-cille likes."

She lapped up the water in silence while Tom and I worried each other away. She wiped her sweet mouth with her sweet forearm. Even then I loved purpose and pattern, though it be the child Lucille's purpose, who began her career of flirtation with suave and deadly song.

"What you thinking about?" Juicer asked me on the grass seven years later.

"Nothing. Tom Moss and me, we used to play with Lucille before she had her development."

"You mean her harp lessons?"

"She was always talented. I mean her bosoms."

"You mean gifted, Dan," he reproached me.

"I mean even before her harp lessons and the class play. I mean way back there when Tom Moss and I knew her very well. I recognized her talent, Juicer."

Juicer begrudged me my prescience and early acquaintanceship. "That music I said, or scales? Whyn't you answer?"

This Daniel Berman, although a carrier of my will to be done, the skinny twiddler to whom I refer as "I," is not always dear to me and was certainly not dear to Juicer, his friend, at that moment. That earlier self which is a favored son to us—the black sheep in our family of fates— was now being a pest on the grass with Juicer Montague. "Maybe music," Daniel Berman replied. "Maybe scales," he negligently added.

We lay on the lawn and listened to the harp. Pluckpluckety-pluck. Sublime flotations of music to us who were impatient of all but the purest song, kety-pluck.

Lucille, our evening firefly, had a thin, energetic, bony face, pretty because of a teasing generosity in the mouth and in the quickness. Her beauty was limited by the spectacular: a husky voice even at that age, a dangerously long stride, a sufficiency unto herself. "Lots of personality," my mother commented when she met her. "Lovely girl. Peppy. Very nice."

At what cost peppiness?

Juicer felt his responsibility to self-doubt in the disembodied eyes of fireflies teasing the night air, coming for no purpose but their own, going for the same. "Do you think maybe she's in love with Chuck Hastings the genius?"

"Naw," I said, "I don't think he's such a genius."

Juicer's priestly hands pinched and kneaded the milk from a dandelion stem; I sympathized.

This lumbering Ronald Montague, bearded at thirteen, a drinker of whiskey in high school, a perspirer-under-the-armpits and a depositor-there-of-salt, a man among boys, a wielder of his Adam's apple and his meat-loving belly in laughter, known as The Juicer—he washed his father's collars on Saturday morning instead of hiking with me or warily patrolling before Lucille's house on bicycles under the pale elms of Hiawatha Avenue. His father was a man with an extra wife in France left over from '17, a heavy car, an onyx ring with his initials in diamonds, and obscure bad habits. He obliged his eldest son to wash his collars of a fine Saturday morning. "Juicer! Don't do it, Juicer," I had warned him.

"My mother says I should," he said, trying logic on me. "Always do what Dad says."

"Don't."

"I could get a licking."

"Don't. I don't, Juicer," I said.

"Dad says I should," the man among boys replied, his belly hanging soft in a college-boy football sweater: rolls of fat and rolls of wool.

"He's taking advantage"—this a phrase learned from my mother. "Your good nature. Why should he wear that kind of collar, the kind a son washes?"

"They're more dignified, they're cleaner. I suppose your father wears attached collars."

"Well"—evasively—"that's not what I'm saying. Your father, he has a slave, you. Am I right? That's what it looks like to me. What good's a detached collar anyway? Not one of the important things about life."

"You got to starch it specially. First you put in the bluing, then you put in the starch. Stir it good. Dip the collar. Wring it out. Dip it again. Funny where all that grease comes from, from my father's neck. You could scrape it off with a knife. . . ."

"Use mine."

"Guess he wants to show me where to get off," Juicer admitted. "Dad's always showing people where to get off."

"Don't do it," I darkly warned him.

"Oh, I don't mind. Ma says it gives me something to do."

"Keeps you out of mischief," I suggested sarcastically. I felt it a sign of servility to use the word *Ma,* although *Dad* seemed manly enough. "Give 'em an inch—parents—and they'll take a mile."

"Oh, I don't know," Juicer argued. "Six-seven collars is the limit. If you keep'm in the hamper too long they begin to stink."

"What'd Lucille say if she only knew? I'm just suggesting as a friend, Juicer. Do you want to lose your independence?"

"Sometimes they stink anyway, if you smell'm close."

Secretly I envied him in my Saturday morning disuse. Why couldn't my father wear detachable collars? I reasoned that Juicer looked like his father (fierce, hairy, booming in laughter), drank and gambled like his father, scowled, smoked, and slapped his thigh; therefore the collar laundry offered an apprenticeship from which he would graduate a *real man,* one of the greatest, like his father.

I measured my own father, who only worked, who merely slept, who simply moved on his way and never asked his son to wash the detachable collars he did not wear. I mourned my collarless heredity and dreamed of imperial ancestors in ruffles and pantaloons. (This prince passed with his guitar under my mother's window, see. . . .) My stomach turned with fault-finding and desire. Once I tried washing one of Mr. Montague's collars.

"Not like that," Juicer said, scrubbing with his beefy hands in the basement washtub; "like this."

"Here"—and I gave him the soapy mess—"you do it then, you're the expert." Both of us would have drunk the suds in order to partake of the mysteries of a parent's power. And the bluing. And the starch.

I wasn't a collar-washer, me, Daniel Berman. I was smaller than Juicer, wiry or scrawny, take your pick. I did not have a deep laugh like his; I could make jokes, but the laugh is the important thing to humor. Sly, pimply, poetic, fifteen, I dreamed his ruin while he dreamed mine; we were friends. We shared our candy bars and calamine lotion. We loved Lucille together, he with moans and choked cries in the street on Friday evening after the movie, I with listenings and secret scraps of paper. "Dan," he would say, "this is a fine little poem you wrote here. This is a great little poem. I especially like where you say, You-in-the-darkness-of-my-heart. . . . *Darkness* is very good, not to speak of what a profound thought. Metaphorical. That's a nice style you have there, with metaphors. Let's go piss in Lucille's back yard."

"Maybe I shouldn't dedicate it to Lucille. What do you think of Pattie Donahue and Eva Masters?"

We would then go piss in the darkness of Lucille's back yard. The darkness was good, while we tampered with the chickweed which flourished about Lucille's manless harp-strung castle.

Souls and bladders tested, we now sprawled uneasily on her front lawn. "Oh I tell you," said Juicer. He groaned; I sighed. He whispered to me of his love for Lucille. This frequent irrigationist talked fast, telling me the secrets he had told me the night before, and the night before that. I listened in suspense, like the child who can correct his mother if she leaves out one word of a story, but says, "Go on! more!"

"You already told me," I murmured sympathetically.

"And the time she was walking with Pattie Donahue, and I was crossing the street with an after-dinner cigar, four for a dime in my pocket, and she said Hiya, Ronald, and I just said, Hiya. I lit up with my Dad's lighter, I just happened to have it in my pocket. I showed her I didn't care—how much I cared."

"Jeez, that's tough, Juicer."

"She could of called me Juicer, everybody does. She think she's the principal or somebody? I showed her. Hiya, I just said."

"Good. That's great." I was proud of being the accomplice of a man capable of such disdain. Like all true lovers, we had made friends with monotony. We rehearsed Lucille's name, her face, her ways. "That's really great, Juicer. You already told me."

"And the time she went out for the play, the one about the people locked in an elevator, and I could have had a part, the elevator was stuck between the floors, and—"

"O yes, O yes, O yes." Fervently I joined him in this scratching toward a sense of history. Each evening we studied the workings of power in our chronicle; we lay on the grass while Juicer talked. We gloried in our emancipation from fear of earthworms. Once I squeezed a bug between two fingers, but let it go without busting it.

"And the time she was playing tennis on the court next to ours, you remember the time at the park—"

Pluckety-pluck-pluck said Debussy on the only harp of our suburb. A screen door slammed. Lucille-like arms were put akimbo on Lucille's front porch while Lucille went on weaving ambitiously at her musical loom. "You boys!" cried Mrs. Lake, Lucille's mother, a divorcee with plump arms going to waste. "Lying on the grass like that! Mooning away a spring evening like this! You come right in and have a plate of ice cream with us. . . . Lucille, you have visitors."

Lucille, wet at the brow from repeating her nocturne, touched at herself with a small lace handkerchief. I forget whether I dragged Juicer by his high-top shoes or whether he lifted me fainting from the ground to lug me in for a plate of banana ice cream with Hershey's on top.

"We were just passing by," I weakly told Lucille.

"We were just on our way somewheres," Juicer adroitly added.

"Someplace," I collaborated mysteriously.

"Mooning on the grass, just mooning," clucked Mrs. Lake. "A cookie with?"

"No thank you, Mrs. Lake," I said. "The banana ice cream Hershey's chocolate sauce will be fine. Thank you very much."

"Oh I don't want a napkin," Juicer added. "We were just passing past on our way somewheres."

Lucille, her face gleaming with faint musical sweat, had so far said nothing. She looked at us with her head to one side. She let us watch her spread the green harp-shaped cover over the gold harp-shaped harp. "You were just passing by?" she asked gravely at last.

"Oh yes," said Juicer. I admired his wit. Amorous mind like a steel trap! "Going somewheres," he said.

We ate. We sucked the spoons and sipped the sweet cold meltings. We put our childish dreams of love, power, and death (our chocolate-and-banana adult premonitions) into talk of ice cream, its nourishment in calories, its refreshing chill, its subtle assimilations to nut or strawberry.

"Very good cream," I said. "Franklin's?"

"No, Dairy Dell," said Lucille.

"Tastes more like Franklin's," Juicer asserted.

"It's the kind in bulk, not the kind in packages," said Lucille.

"Forty cents a pint in bulk," I said. "Thirty cents already packaged."

"You get more," she said. "They pack it down. Besides,

it's better. Quality ice cream, with ingredients. See how you thought it was Franklin's?"

"Franklin's is fifty. Thirty-five for package"—a pyrotechnic display of erudition.

"Really great ice cream," Juicer said, that resonant bass stifled by love. "You're right about the ingredients. My father told me about cornstarch once, drugstore ice cream. Those who profiteer on our trusting nature—" He perished, his palate puckered by hopeless desire.

"You got to be careful of cornstarch in ice cream and drugstores, Mrs. Lake," I concluded for him.

Mrs. Lake stretched and took her book, smiling as she arose. "Well, I guess you young folks must have things to talk about. I'm going upstairs for a while."

"Oh but," I said desperately.

"No, oh don't go," Juicer appealed to her.

Mrs. Lake nodded to Lucille with the patrician approval that a doting Roman pet lover must have given his lion before offering it tender bundles of martyr meat. She gathered up her sewing and her book.

"Good night, Mrs. Lake." I valiantly stood up.

"Good night, Mrs. Lake." Juicer cravenly stood up.

We waited until her footsteps were gone from the stairs. We both turned, still standing, to the Lucille whom we had adored in silence for years. She watched us, smiling from Juicer to me, from me to Juicer. I remembered one of my poems to her:

> *You in the darkness of my heart*
> *All light, all beauty, truth thou art. . . .*

Or perhaps it was to Pattie Donahue?

"Cones are seven cents at Franklin's," I said at last. I didn't mean Dairy Dell. "They give you the same ice

cream they put in the bulk, but it doesn't have the vios-
terol irradiations added."

"We were just on our way somewheres," Juicer said.
"We were just going."

"Oh you're welcome," Lucille said in her low throaty
voice, in the rich growl of a woman who knows ev-ver-ry-
thing that Loo-cille likes. "Please stay."

"We must go"—pronounced mysteriously together, as
if we had business other than kidneys and kinship in the
night.

"Ah!" sighed Lucille with a moral understanding sufficient unto our physical oppression. She nodded and smiled
and even gave our right hands her musicianly grasp.

As we moved down the street an arpeggio of trilling
female laughter spilled through the summer screens of open
Lake windows. *Oh ha!* A duet of thrilling and trilling,
purling and swirling glee! *Oh hahaha!* The pursuing melody tickled us, taunted us, chased us in despair from
street lamp to street lamp. *Oh hahaha hahaha!* We bobbed
like moths in the night air, borne by distant breath toward
the light just before us.

Oh hahaha, Mother! Oh hahaha, Daughter!

Was it because I was Jewish, Juicer owlish? We both ate
too much banana ice cream?

Had they overheard us earlier in the yard, or even over-
smelled us?

Did they know that we were merely faint-hearted boys
and lovers?

Oh hahaha!

Juicer hissed at me: "Why didn't you say you liked
the harp? Why didn't you compliment her on the music?
That's what girls like, to be goddamn hell nice to them."

"I wasn't thinking about that," I answered miserably.
I forgot to ask him why *he* didn't. "Why didn't you think
of some conversation?" I accused him. "Why did you let

me do all the talking? I had to hold up my end of the conversation all by myself. Figuratively speaking, it's a good
thing I'm an expert on ice cream. Chuck Hastings would
have literally thought of something to say."

"I was thinking about something," he said. He had been
bluffing, like the grasshopper which makes an ominous
noise, bending its abdomen 'in a determined and threatening manner,' as if it were a stinger. "I don't know," he
said.

"I don't know either."

The laughter of Lucille and her mother sang us to the
corner, and as we paused in the evening, an evening full
of May, both spiced and mild, we thought that we heard
the harp like a bee thinly ticking away through the flowered
air. "Wait, take a breath, pal." Juicer rested his hand on
my shoulder a moment.

Then we moved on in silence, counting cracks in the
sidewalk (*Break your mother's back. . . .*) accompanied
by corduroy zip, pants against pants.

"I think she likes us," I said at last.

"Did you see how she looked at me?" Juicer demanded.
"Did you notice that look in her eye, Dan?"

Neither of us had seen anything of the sort until this
moment when our memories began the task of accommo-
dation. But now we both began to see.

"Yeah, what about that look?"

We stopped and examined each other with suspicion. I
had noticed that look for him and he had noticed that
look for me. Lucille's eyes were a busy mirror, light firing
across them. Pulling at the harp, she perhaps remembered
better than either of us, and noticed that look in her eyes
only for herself.

Juicer and I felt all the delicacy of departure, the sense
that something has not yet been finished. Everyone gazes
at his own eyes in a mirror, but we looked at Lucille's in

our memory, saying what is at age fifteen reserved for oneself: "How beautiful! how wonderful!" We did not see into
our eyes; it was enough to see out of them. We were abashed
before patient, amused Lucille. Now that we had left her,
we felt the thrill and flutter which is our reward for swimming over unfathomed depths rather than ten feet of
water—a purely moral increment of danger. Lucille grew
to be, therefore, bigger than an idea: love oh love oh here
comes love.

"It's sure hard to get to know her." Juicer produced this
datum of his deep study. "Notice how all she wanted to
talk about was ice cream?"

"Did I!" I cried. "I tried to change the subject—poetry,
Thomas Wolfe, music. . . . No go. You notice?"

"Sure, Dan, she has secrets, that one. We couldn't
change her in one night's talk. I wonder what she thinks
about—I mean *thinks* about."

"I know what you mean."

"I know what you mean too, Dan."

What we meant: acceptance of each other's lies was the
truth we needed to survive this evening.

"She's afraid to let herself go with us," I said.

"That's it. On her guard. You never know what a girl
like that thinks."

Or any girl, we both meant.

"She's a mystery," I said.

"We can figure her out?" Juicer said, making a question
despite himself. "I mean we can figure her out, can't we?"

Our fantasies bounced flimsily on this board, each statement flipping up drenched with interrogation.

"She's afraid of us."

"Yes, yes," said Juicer, "that's what I meant."

We were captured. We broadcast to each other that
we were hopelessly in love, our dreams of power lassoed
by a girl caught in the suspicion, self-doubt, and ambition

of her own grasping birth pangs. We were sure that what we wanted was unique, invented solely for us and undefined until we took it. The privacy of sleep taught us to doubt, with cause, the sharing of dreams. We knew the loneliness of the imagination in those days; we skittered before the need to make it less lonely, more free, and feared to admit that Lucille could have a will like ours.

We thought Lucille's laughter came from outside ourselves, for each of me, for each of him, and yet our blind, deaf, and dumb dreams loitered in crowds without knowing it. We shared! Strolling, Juicer and I jumped for a branch and each caught a leaf, our triumph for the evening. The face of Eva Masters flashed through my head as I dived upward into the tree. Juicer and I had proved that gravity could be defied. Someday we would surely sail like birds.

2. *Platonists from the Three-Eye League*

"I LIKE JOOZE," SAID TOM MOSS.

"Whose?"

"Jews. I don't think it's true those awful things, do you, Dan?"

"Probably not. I'm one."

Juicer elaborately hoped to credit my vaunt. "Show me," he said. "Unbutton. Does it mean you don't get infections? Can you pee round a corner, through a keyhole?"

"Has nothing to do with that," I answered with dignity. "Also we eat pork in my family—well, not pork, but bacon, it's good for growing children. Has to do with cleanliness, my dad says."

"Will it grow back?" insidious Tom insisted.

"Nobody needs it. It's like getting your appendicitis taken out."

Tom grinned happily. "I was awful weak after I had my appendicitis."

This proved nothing. Juicer was willing to drop a ticklish subject which inexperience and unconfidence made risky. "How else do you know you're a Jewish person?" he politely inquired.

"Dad speaks with an accent. Kids used to chase me. Mother told me. Tom asked me."

"How else?"

"I don't know yet. I'm going to find out."

"You're also," said Tom, "going to be a lawyer, a football player, a poet, you're going to kiss Pattie Donahue, now you're going to find out why your whole family is jooze. You got your work cut out for you, Dan."

"And you?" Juicer asked, defending me. "You, Tom, what are you going to do? What am I going to do? What is the whole wide world going to do about everything?"

Tom would take his time before answering that one.

In our youth, we nostalgically recalled at fifteen, serious questions had lain athwart our minds. Do babies come from a pill the father gives the mother or is it the doctor who gives her the pill? How can you get rich quicker, digging to China in the back yard or collecting stamps? What makes a fast runner, long legs or lots of milk? Why are germs everywhere and constipation deadly? "Mr. Sluggish Colon will get you if you don't watch out. . . ." Tom Moss, Nietzsche's false Christian in Lakewood, Ohio, believed in the devil—Mr. Sluggish Colon. He ate the bran that redeems, but for the laughter he owed us, he paid only, Hee hee hee, snickeree.

"Who is our real mother?"

Hee.

"Maybe your father was my father, Juicer. It's possible." Snickeree.

At last these questions, and others as pure, slipped away from us, and now the extremest demands haunted our flimsy idealistic heads: What could we move with our bare hands that would be worth the moving? Whom could we love that could ever love the likes of us?—the questions of power and desire in fifteen-year-old men having to learn again the existence of others who were neither playmates, rivals, nor the parents which existed for our pleasure be-

tween meals and naps. Freedom and isolation, love and
dependence, brutal egotism and fearful flight from the mysteries of self—these abiding issues came to camp forever
in our newly bearded skulls and prickly, pickle-laden loins.
Dwelling with our burden of pickle within the lonely suburbs of self-determination, brewed in vinegar, fifteen years
old and ready to go, we were asked to accept cheerfully what Lakewood chose to give us. *We said no* in our
various uncheerful ways, Juicer, Tom, and I. We tiptoed
toward being, constantly tripped up; but soon there would
be girls to teach us how to say no and yes and no and yes
again; and then work. "A man should begin his life in love,
end it with ambition."

To this too we said no.

A man should begin his life with love and ambition, end
it with ambition and love.

Yea.

By day we guffawed on lawns, stacked our hopes under
trees at evening, and all night long imagined revenge for
snub and triumph for those astonishing adroitnesses which
no one ever noticed. We abided our time and exchanged
the worthiest nightmares within our small committee, our
cenacle of three bemused boys. We rode bicycles no-
handed, translated from the Persian of O. K. Khayyam, answered appeals for theoretical help from Howard Scott,
founder of Technocracy. "I haven't decided yet whether
I'm in favor of a world run by engineers," said Tom.

"Well, make up your mind by tomorrow. We'll meet
you on the playground after lunch."

We were actionists out of boredom with childhood.
Juicer was afraid of the accumulation of dream which our
desperation imposed, I moral about it, Tom content to
observe our gifts of fever and nonsense. "I'm fifteen, jeez, I
still can't drive the car. What for all this waiting?" Juicer
asked.

"To grow up! A long childhood is *essential*. Animals don't go through the stage much of adolescence, and look how stupid they are."

"Who? Which animals?" Tom wanted to know.

"Monkeys! Chimps! Jackasses! Parrots! Hyenas! Ferrets! Eels, goddammit, Thomas!"

"I was only asking. You don't have to get mad, Dan."

"Okay then."

Slyly he watched me sink; dim wallowing away from adrenalin. Then: "But you know (snort), some chimps are pretty darn smart."

Cripes. No use making metaphysics with Tom. But resembling me anyway, he looked for have-no-more-hunger food, rubbed his juts and knots of flesh, said, "What?" and asked: "When?" We didn't know what or when. The knowledge that scientific, sarcastic Tom and fat, fragile, poetic Juicer felt as I did was sweet to me. We had all three begun to look at our feelings. We needed company. "So shut up, Tom. Always crabbing."

"That's all right," said Juicer, "Tom's all right. He's a crab, but his heart's in the right place, isn't it, pal?"

"Do crabs," Tom asked, "have a short childhood too?"

This time we were discussing animal life and us over after-school sustenance at Franklin's Ice Cream Parlor. There were chop suey sundaes and beefsteak sodas to give us strength to face dinner with our parents, and the price list went up to ninety-nine cents for a concoction of mahogany syrup, eddies of grainy whipped cream, salvos of bananas, six emplacements of ice cream, the whole fortification topped by a bulletproof row of rivets, puckered and falsely incarnadined cherries. We partook more sparsely by financial necessity. Also Tom had discovered wheat germ, soybean oil, and fasting, which increase life or perhaps only make it *seem* longer. He snacked modestly on ginger ale and vanilla wafers.

Juicer and I sucked at our spoons. We mashed the rich sugared syrup into a gravy. We munched at Lucille's body across the room with sharp eyes, all the dark desire of morning sleep altered to mooning and giggling. "Good ice cream—a fine flavor—very tasty," we had agreed.

Then we walked, dragging Tom.

"What do you suppose Lucille thinks about when she's alone?" Juicer asked, his fat behind as disconsolate as his face, his meaty lips pursing, his hot hungry nearsighted eyes repeating: What does anybody think about alone?

"I don't know. School. Her music lesson," I said, and thought: *me.*

"I don't know either. The news in the paper, the other girls," Juicer said, thinking: *me.*

Who?

There were two matters, we both felt certain, which never entered her mind: Juicer and Dan.

"She never even thinks about you two, I bet," commented Tom Moss, anchor, anchorite.

"Oh yeah?" we said. "What do you know?"

Maybe she thought about Chuck Hastings. Perhaps Mr. Finney the football coach. Better even Tom than nobody!

Juicer slapped his thighs (laughter, cynicism, despair). I climbed trees by the lake (Erie, there before I was born) and gazed owlishly down, abstractedly musing while birch-bark friction irritated my thighs. Tom Moss kept his hands in his pockets while he listened or talked and was warned by his mother that he was too old to wet the bed. "It isn't wet," he said (involuntary love).

We had given up wrestling and, but not quite, touch football in the streets. We had passed unsatisfied the stage of writing letters to the editor. ("Dear Editor, Allow me as a faithful reader of your paper to tell you how I think The Cleveland *News* could be improved and made more interesting. I am twelve years old. Now first, the columns,

which although appealing perhaps to the intellectually im-
mature. . . .") In our recent maturity we found letters-to-
the-editor a less satisfying medium of expression than heaving rocks up onto Pattie Donahue's porch; critical journalism was not love and required nasty pale thoughts like
peachworms rather than lusty gang yells and a wiry personal throwing arm. But still Pattie failed to make an ap-
pearance to peek and count her admirers from behind her
mother's chambray curtains, her spirit absent on a date
with Lewis Snyder—body also.

We dreamed bad dreams and lived like good boys,
pleased proprietors of the reputation of terrible ones.
Juicer considered himself a terror; I was an assistant terror.
We talked out unasked in class, for example. We wrote
rhymes—composed by ourselves, not copied from adult
walls—above the toilet paper dispensers in the high school
latrines. Juicer, taller than me, could reach higher while
still sitting down; I, more scholarly, could attain to deeper
academic allusions with encyclopedias or the *Rubaiyat* to
coach a memory all tremulous with effort. Once I fell off
the seat, everything but my skinny behind secured by inspiration. Our spirits, full of themselves, had no inclina-
tion for anything but the soul of what we read: *Soul:* however, the gross matter of things noticed Juicer and me, if
not Tom. We quoted ourselves, calling it Thomas Wolfe,
Omar Khayyam, or James Branch Cabell. Tom, not a
scholar or an artist like us, a mere gentleman, was reduced
to drawing dirty pictures while we made classical refer-
ences.

"I drew a map of Madagascar," he giggled. "You know
what it looks like? Boy!" Snickeree.

"Looks more like geography," Juicer said.

Our friend Tom had long teeth like all his bones and
risked them in cracking nuts, thus earning our reluctant

esteem and chipping the edges. He nursed a sponge ball in his pockets to develop his biceps, swam in the YMCA pool which smelled like a baby's diaper, and wondered what girls really looked like; he was a fine upstanding lad. He had a dimple on his chin where his criticisms had popped up and swiped him across the face. Unaware of possibility as a principle of action, he waited in doubt as in a vestibule for the discoveries of Juicer and me. Already he had learned from us to believe in something we called "liking a girl" (from the Old English, hopeless adoration). His good sense helped him to sustain his reservations while preserving the forms of romance and our friendship. "Here I sit, broken-hearted—" he recited.

I was the first to discover Cabell.

Juicer was the first to discover Wolfe.

Nourished by ice cream and dreams, we shared these secret founts of knowledge with Tom—our link with the wide world—but kept them secret from parents and other spies. Juicer, however, could whisper the passwords—"Time, the River"—and I solemnly winked back at this communication across enormous vistas while our stunned and stupid classmates went on gossiping of scandal in dress and word, Miss Graves' cigarette-stained fingers, or what Lewis Snyder was reputed to have done to a girl named Black Lil (at least he copped a feel.) Or I could murmur the code word *Jurgen*—all wit, all beauty, truth— and only Tom's conspiratorial snicker would give away the knowledge ciphered in Juicer's bulging eyes under his great dark forehead, above the breakfast soft-boiled eggs in the corners of his mouth.

"You fellows live for culture, I mean Thomas Wolfe, don't you? Well, that's easy. I see what you got to do to be it, cultured I mean."

"No! no! not at all!" I groaned.

"It's for something else," Juicer explained. "We live for

love and anybody knows what we mean. We're looking for what we need to make ourselves—make ourselves—"

"Into," I suggested.

"Into," he agreed. "But listen, Tom, we're busy, aren't we, Dan?"

"Busy," I intoned.

"Making yourself into something"—and Tom snorted. "Mind if I ob-serve you for the sake of science?"

Corduroy was our chosen uniform, desperate and poetic, beer our ritual potion, sipped like sherry—"sherry wine, that is"—which we had never tasted. We labored to prefer the bitter of beer to the sweet nourishment of ice cream with its ribald flavors. Juicer's Square Deal sweater with its YMCA stamp was called his Shirt of Nessus, our Hellenistic scholarship straight from James Branch Cabell, who had replaced Edward G. Robinson as the prince of sophistication. Eclectics, we hissed *Jurgen's* rose-colored phrases through toothpicks in the gangster corners of our mouths. Practicing discriminations, we judged prize-winning legs from Atlantic City in the rotogravure, love crime in *True Detective,* the week's conscriptees for immortality in the *Saturday Review*. On Saturday afternoon we walked the railroad trestles and talked in verse for hours, in rhyme if not in meter, with only Tom to admire us, and we weren't sure that he did. Our regret even then settled upon the lack of a scribe to record our wit and the first flow of geniality. "That means genius and happy, a good combination," I said genially. Our laughter rolled us about on the lawn; we slapped our sides, we held our mouths and choked as Mrs. Kennedy the Widow Lady went by. Privately we judged Tom for being too lazy to write it all down.

"He doesn't want to be immortal," we complained. "Boswell is just as famous as Olsen and Johnson."

Even that late flowering of childhood, the anonymous letter to Pattie Donahue, was fallen into disuse. I had written: "Leave a message for me by the maple tree on the corner (there will be a stone to put it under) and I will communicate facts that will be sure to interest you. . . ." Now I wondered if I would ever dare to write to Eva Masters or Lucille Lake; I wanted to sign my name in great executive letters; I practiced signatures. Juicer and I had broken with Penmanship. I made a European "d," curly and lyric, and Juicer crushed his "t" under a magnificent Napoleonic hat. Tom's handwriting, on the other hand, remained provincially legible.

"Tom's handsome," Juicer said, "and anyone can read his writing, but I'm ugly."

"I'm ugly too."

"Not as ugly as I am. I'm a monster."

"Yes," I admitted, "you're a monster, but I'm just as bad."

We studied ourselves in the mirror and, out of fear and love, made pious mysteries of our doubts. "We're the two ugliest men in the world," Juicer said, "me worst."

The important word here, not lost on either of us, was *men*.

Juicer said: "I have a face like a frog."

"No," I decided, "like a hippopotamus. Fat mouth, lumpy skin. You yawn like a hippo I saw once."

"You think so?" Juicer asked eagerly. "As bad as that? . . . You're a buddy, Dan, we understand each other. You're pretty horrible, too. What zoo was that hippo you saw, lumps on the skin?"

The sin of hybris, comparing ourselves with the gods and the hippos, we cheerfully committed. We had no masters but ourselves: yet we recognized that, like the Greek gods, we were powerless to command love. "Love me!" we prayed to the world. "Give us strength!"

"You guys," snorted our friend Tom Moss the Philistine.

We had looked up the word Philistine and found it good.

We practiced the power of hate, when love seemed un-
attainable, by saying as children do the most ungrateful
words for our parents. I went further: I spent these things
openly on my mother and father, at first expecting the
words to kill them, then learning an important lesson from
the ease with which they grew accustomed to my wish for
their death. It was as if they expected it. It was as if they
had been children themselves once.

"You're stupid," I told my mother.

"You're an ungrateful son, spitework."

That was enough until next time. These conversations
took place in the kitchen near the sink or with a glass of
milk at the enameled table.

"You don't love me, your mother. That's what a son's
for, at least a girl helps in the house. Drink your milk."

"How can I? You go looking in my desk drawer when I
tell you not to." I had surprised her with her hair in a rag,
a dust cloth in her hand, and glasses on her nose as she
leaned into the debris of papers and articles whose use had
vanished but whose value remained—broken miscroscopes,
old valentines (they loved me once), rocks and sea shells,
pirate scraps of treasure.

"Secrets from me? A boy fourteen years old, a kit yet,
secrets?"

"Fifteen. Anyway, that's my business if I want to have
secrets."

"Secrets! Anyway it's my drawer; who paid for it? You
wouldn't have any drawers if it wasn't for me. I'm your
mother."

"I can't help that. You should stay away from what's
mine."

"Manners manners," she said. "When you want something you don't stay away from it's-mine."

"What do you want in my drawer?"

"Why should I want?"

"Then, *please,* Ma—"

"But what secrets altogether? I don't believe. If I need
to clean up, in your drawer, you're not allowed to keep
things from me, a minor, fourteen years old. Ever hear of
the juvenile court from human relations?" she asked. "I'm
your mother."

"I'll hate you then," I stated equably. "Is it worth prying
in my papers? Fifteen, going on sixteen."

"What secrets?"

"I told you that's my business."

"You keep a diary?"

It was called a *journal,* a more esthetic name. "What if
I do? You have no right to pry."

Finally she heard an echo of what I had said and
wailed, *"Hate* me he says! Listen to the kit. . . ." Abstractedly, as if suddenly remembering, she added her excuse:
"Anyway, I only wanted to straighten up a little. It's a
pick-pen. Why don't you keep clean? What if Aunt Sarah
comes and opens your drawer, she's looking for a delible
pencil? She's looking maybe for a box of something? I
don't care about your papers, Aunt Sarah would tell the
whole family about the pick-pen, we hide it in a drawer."

I left her talking and went out to call for Juicer.

"Wait! You want some cherry Jell-O I got left over?"

My back, leaving her, repeated what I had grown skilled
at saying and what she, with a peculiar tenacity, never
grew tired of eliciting from her son: "You don't know how
I despise you . . . how I want to love you and how I hate
you. . . ."

Later, when I heard that it was bad for the teeth to hate
—and besides, hate satisfies only briefly, demanding to be
renewed and increased, like morphine—I discovered the
trick of Tom Moss's moral acrobatics. I balanced as neatly
as Humpty-Dumpty on his wall. I learned that, by relating
to my busy mother the trivia of my movements, I could

soothe her concern with what she called my *secrets*. She
wanted to know of triumph and check in high school, sick
stomach and insult, broken shoelace, broken heart, broken
resolution—mere satistics. My obstinate silence, going off
to eat cookies alone with Tom and Juicer, had driven her
frantic to puzzle over the poor butts of paper in the drawer.
"Jean Thompson told Rosalie Fallon that she liked me," I
said. "Tom told me."—And thus my mother no longer
looked for a diary. All was in order: Daniel confided in
her these social questions of love and official affection. She
was grateful for release from her maternal responsibility
to study in cunning, a dust cloth in one hand, the signs in
my notebook: high school metaphysics and the record of
temptation, daydreams, poetry, books to be read, Earl
Averill's lifetime record at bat, other omens.

"My Daniel, he's a good boy, almost. He tells me everything, sometimes it takes him a nour. The girls are going
crazy about him, he should only pick a good one, a good
family, well off, he's old enough to think about it. *Think*
about it, I said. Knock on wood."

"How's his left eye?" Aunt Sarah would ask. (Aunt
Sarah had a son who was not good in school, sometimes
molested small animals, but had a perfect left eye.)

"A little nearsighted only. I don't care, he'll be a good
boy yet. The doctor says it's not really nearsighted, only
a little my-opicka."

She gradually forgot about the diary and only on occa-
sion, out of loyalty to habit, put her head into my drawer.
I always knew by the disturbance of the seismographic
hairs across my papers, but I no longer made a fuss. I
suffered her intrusions with a constantly increasing vocabu-
lary, which she also suffered, her mind lulled by the fact of
my presence.

Sometimes, finding this maternal glaze fallen across her
eyes, I asked: "Are you listening to me?"

She answered: "Naturally! But what were you saying?"
—thinking about my future with the big office and my
name on the glass door, her son the doctor. The drone of
voice signified that I was keeping out of trouble. *He con-
fides,* she would tell Aunt Sarah. "And how's school?" she
asked, since I had paused.

If she had understood my exasperation at her lack of
attention, she could have forgiven my reluctance to admit
that it was the fact of talking, not the words themselves,
which was important to her. She comforted me with some
lurid morsel of family gossip, knowing it had the soothing
effect of *The American Weekly* with its earth-destroying
predictions by high school physics teachers, its horrible
revelations by genuine Hungarian countesses, and its re-
liable reports of man-eating sea monsters. Careless of
causes but fertile in explanation, she never hid a family
disgrace. She said of Cousin Willy, in an asylum for fifteen
years: "His health isn't good. He had such peculiar ideas
it drove him crazy."

"Oh, psychopathia," I murmured. "Sounds like a bad
case of split personality. Did he see a doctor?"

"That's what *I* say, you should be a doctor," she sighed,
nodding moodily. "There's always sick people, a steady
thing. Knock wood, we should all stay well."

"Cousin Willy needs a doctor of psychology, a psychopathia. I can tell from the case."

She would hurry to tell Aunt Sarah, "He uses such big
words sometimes I don't even know what he means. Such
a good boy, and *smart?* Good in school!"

"His eye looks kind of red to me," commented Aunt
Sarah. "My son has twenty-twenty."

Sweating in the morning, shivering at night, good in
school, Juicer and I found no peace in nature either those
days. Birds were killing each other, stealing from nests,
and making love. The tumbling speed of spring, high nim-

bus, white sky, gave me no hope for peace, but encouraged me that I might survive. Also I admired the quick looks, spitting of seeds, and swooping descents of birds, and how feathers ruffled when red-eyed male found female. "Peep!" they roared.

Pattie Donahue, Lucille Lake, Rosalie Fallon.

We searched power in love and love in power. Girls are always older than boys; dread and desire will never grow weightier than they were in that fifteenth year. "Aah," Juicer said, "we'll learn how to dance. We'll be smooth like Lewis Snyder in social dancing."

"What if you don't want to?" Tom asked. "What about Chuck Hastings?"

Love me quick, someone! we prayed. Give me strength! Give me reason! Give me purpose!

Love!

Strength!

Sweet Ugliness, make us real under these Lakewood skies of pale perfect blue! (R.S.V.P.)

What we needed, *at once, right now,* was love, was power. Failing these, I could at least die a beautiful death, mourned by parents, friends, and the world at large, with my picture in the paper to replace the same old people who were usually dying. Juicer would be happy to write my funeral oration. "This brave heart that beats no more," Juicer would say. "What he might have been only I can tell. . . ." And then he would tell it.

"That's beautiful," I would weep from my plain pine box (shimmering jeweled casket on which bawling Pattie Donahue—Lucille Lake, Rosalie Fallon?—Eva Masters? —had poignantly thrown herself).

"I feel the way you do," Juicer said.

"I know just how you feel," I told Juicer.

"Me too," Tom Moss insisted. "Fellas, I'm going through the same period in my life."

"What's the matter, you crazy?" I demanded. "You think everyone feels things like Thomas Wolfe and us?"

"Some people got it easy. Look at Lewis Snyder. Look at Chuck Hastings. Do you think they're a virgin? Look at Dan's cousin Bernie," Juicer said. "They go out with girls already. They have all the money to spend. Do you think they have a soul? How could they? They don't even know the meaning of the word."

Juicer grunted like one who knew the meaning of the word. Tom grunted like one who did not know the meaning of the word. I permitted myself to judge the grunts, and also grunted myself. Only a chosen few, Mr. Wolfe from Asheville, Mr. Cabell from Richmond, Mr. Edward G. Robinson from Chicago, Juicer Montague and Dan Berman of the suburbs of Cleveland, could define *soul* to our perfect satisfaction. It required suffering and deprivation (Edward G. suffered at the hands of George Raft, Paul Muni, and the Law).

"My cousin Bernie drives his father's car already," I added to reinforce Juicer's argument. "What need hath he for poetry? Gets money for gas."

Juicer scanned Tom with the look of one who, having traveled widely, triumphantly visits an old stay-at-home rival. "Listen!" he said. "I asked Lewis Snyder. . . ." He paused for the effect of this revelation to strike us full: "And *he never heard of Thomas Wolfe.*"

I staggered ritually to communicate my emotion. Tom blinked his two small gray eyes. He blinked them again.

"Thought he was a center fielder just up from the Three-Eye League," Juicer went on. "The man who told us to look homeward, angels. The man who knew just how we feel."

"Poor Lewis Snyder."

"He's happy that way, I guess."

Tom considered a moment, scratching and scratching

the pimple behind his ear. "I think there's a center fielder
name of Wolfe up from the Three-Eye League, though.
Spells his name without the e. Biggest Runs Batted In in the
League last year."

Juicer and I accepted our duty to the world from which
we drew forth the things of the spirit. Our duty plain was
to make Tom Moss suffer as much as we did.

"O Time, flowing eternally, eternally god damn flowing.
O river," Juicer said. "Isn't that beautiful?"

"Beautiful," Tom submitted.

"What about the loneliness?" I demanded. "The loneliness, how Lost Helen of his Youth and everybody turned
against him."

"Beautiful," said Tom.

"There's a Runs Batted In for you," Juicer vindictively
muttered. "There's a Texas in the Three-Eye League."

"How about the way he walked alone in the streets?"
Tom asked eagerly. "All alone with the moon, if there was
a moon. Those goat cries—I wonder if any goats ever answered. . . ."

If the test of friendship is to be willing to give up what
is most precious, then goat-worried Tom Moss was a good
friend to us. He tried to give up his good sense for two
adolescents who flapped like scarecrows down the street,
chanted the nostalgia of olden times (last summer),
modeled their speech and their thoughts on books, looked
for ruin in beer, music, and love, since religion, politics,
and stranger vices were not yet handy, and groped for the
paraphernalia of age.

Tom was protected from foolishness by his lack of energy. We were naked mostly because we had torn off our
clothes, and the garments for which we first reached were
odd ones, Time, the River, and such emperor's castoffs.

"I give you credit," Tom said to both of us, who had
stayed up talking all night before a history test and had not

even opened our James Truslow Adams. In emulation of
our particularities he invented a gesture—he wanted one
also. First he frowned a line between his eyes, then
shrugged bitterly, then chuckled softly. If the watcher
asked what he was thinking about, he mysteriously intimated, "Oh, nothing."

Juicer invited us to watch him conduct Stokowski in
Tchaikowsky's *Third Symphony*. He beat time on the natural pine cabinet. There was pride. There was misery. There
were nicks on the radio. There was also suffering in this,
spelled with bitten cuticles and sudden bellyaches, un-
digested ambition wallowing in the bile of first love. We
tripped at the sight of the girls. Love, like epilepsy, was the
falling sickness. We did not know what we wanted, but we
wanted it bad.

"It's important to have a face," Tom informed us. "You
got to look like what you are."

Juicer and I were struck. "Then how should we look?"
we asked him.

"Not like a open can of tuna fish. Have character. Smile.
Puzzle. Practice. Think of something to have a face."

And in the meantime, while we learned to have faces,
we were hearing in civics class about Poland and Hitler,
Spain and Hitler, Mussolini and Hitler. On a test we were
asked to list five differences between democracy and Naz-
ism, and were given extra credit for additional, optional
reasons, such as, In a democracy all men respect each
other (Juicer thought of this), or, Nazzi-ism was invented
in Munich, Germany, whereas democracy came to light in
Athens, Greece (Tom's extra credit), or, Jewish opera
singers can no longer sing in Germany and also Albert
Einstein discoverer of relativity had to flee (me).

All this had no certain connection with our lives in
Lakewood, Ohio, but Juicer and I took silent counsel from
the bronze Civil War figures stolidly going green and

pigeon-bombed on the Public Square. Would we someday also be brave, wear puttees, look like Lew Ayres in that movie about a different war? We would. Would we careen about the sky in Spads and go to the rescue of Finlandia as sung by Sibelius? We would. We would also read *Ken,* which told about the War Lords, and we would send our dollars to World Peaceways.

One day an old Peerless containing a friendly young man who sucked his teeth lay parked near the entrance of Lakewood High School. "I'm Allen Turner," he said, "and here's something to think about." The young man left a bundle of newspapers to be distributed by volunteers among us; he said he was a Silver Shirt and gave out a telephone number to be called in case we needed a Silver Shirt. We spread out our copies of the paper on a lawn and, sprawling at our ease, studied Mr. William Dudley Pelley. "IS ROOSEVELT'S REAL NAME ROSENFELD?" he inquired, though he knew the answer. (This is a rhetorical device of tested power.) Another item announced: "BARUCH BERNARD A PROVEN ELDER!!!"

"If there are any questions, fellas, just ask," said Allen. "I'm having a little discussion club at my place on Sunday afternoon."

I ran home to present this newspaper to my father. These were civic events which I still hoped parents could reckon with. Dad stared. He went for a walk with me, but said little. He put the paper down a sewer. I had questions for him: When would I be elder enough to learn to drive? Well, then what's *Mrs.* Roosevelt's real name? Will Alf Landon ever have another chance, and what's *his* real name?

Just as there was trouble finding the real names, there was trouble finding the real questions.

My father sighed and asked if I would like to go to Sunday school. "There are clubs," he said hesitantly. "So you could join a club. You're supposed to know."

"It's on the other side of town. I have my friends here. Besides, I don't believe in Hebrew stuff."

Dad pondered. "Well, I never believed either," he said finally, "so I ran away from the stetl—" *What's the stetl's real name, Dad?* "But it's hard sometimes to figure out what to do. You're supposed to know. I got the business, I got things on my mind. . . . You want to try it? They got the Temple Branch of the Boy Scouts, Dan?"

No. I was hurrying toward another path. So we let it drop. As T. Wolfe and E. Hemingway were putting it down so succinctly, so contradictorily, you can't go home again to that main illusion where no man is an islande entire of theirself.

Amen.

Please bless Mommy and Daddy and foolishness and cliché and pretense. Bless our truth-mongers. Bless our wounded rhetoricians.

Good night, sweet principles.

But use the language, be healthy, tell the truth.

Amen.

Amen.

3.   The discovery of flesh in ideal form

ME, NOT EXACTLY GREAT YET,
I cut a fashionable figure in the historic halls of old Lakewood High. "Hi, Dan," cried my dozen intimates; the
others limited themselves to more decorous salutations:
"What you say, Daniel?" or "How's the boy?" I replied
with the noble lift of the head in recognition or, to closer
friends whose names I remembered, with a *hmmm* full of
quiet dignity. My costume, eked out from the clothes my
mother brought home from Bailey's, the clothes inherited
from Cousin Irwin, and the clothes I had begun to buy
myself, expressed my status: white tieless shirt with the
collar negligently turned over a green corduroy jacket, blue
covert pants polished in the seat after years of Friday night
and Sunday dress-up, woolen skating socks yellow at the
heel, tan moccasins. I had learned the importance of un-
washed hair; dirt and oil served better than brushing and
stocking caps to raise about my head a romantic aura, the
dandruff visible only to eyes more critical than mine and
certainly not to those which sparkled humidly in the heads
of cub reporters. On my forehead a dark forked tongue of
cowlick warned of poetry; the primavera fuzz of beard
lent me the authority of my glands; pimples and white-
heads indicated a participation in the sufferings of my

44

fellows while, in special cases like mine, they also spoke for black designs, sufferings, and insomniac broodings. Sometimes I wore a thick gray sweater rolled at the bottom for athleticism's sake, and to hide my knobby wrists. Once, in an access of fury after a night of words, I bought a pair of yellow suede shoes with crepe soles with the prize I won in an English contest, letting my mouth grow sardonic; I never wore the shoes, however, gaining sight of dignity in the scale of human values, ranking it above suede, and I finally filled the shoes with dirt, propped them in my window, and celebrated my new knowledge by planting watermelon seeds as memorial to abandoned vanity. The seeds never grew; the eyelets rusted; the laces drooped in the autumn rains like two disconsolate mustaches.

Why such shenanigans? (You must make an effort to fit these mustaches over those sardonic lips—now you see the Big Picture before it fades—now it's gone.) I was the prodigious editor, me, of the *Lakewood High Times*, a newspaper appearing every week during the school year, devoted to news, happenings, and pictures of interest to students of Lakewood High School, its alumni, and their well-wishers, judged one of the finest examples of secondary school journalism in Greater Cleveland, Ohio. While still a cub reporter, thus at an early age, I had filled with éclat the responsibility of interviewing Bobby Breen, the Nationally Known Boy Soprano, a discovery of Eddie Cantor. ("Although heard on the radio coast-to-coast every Sunday evening at nine o'clock, he is still as friendly, as unaffected, as modest. . . .") Later I composed an Armistice Day editorial which brought tears to the eyes of my typing teacher, described the installation of a new public address system with the aid of adjectives from Roget's Thesaurus, performed variations on the appeal to put candy wrappers in the baskets provided for that purpose, passed an examination in the differences of meaning among alumnus, alumna, alumnae, and alumni (graduates all), and thus, old before my time, an eleventh grader with the intelligence and richness of experience of a senior, was elevated to the position of Editor-in-Chief. I wore Gymknits shorts and a Skolastick T-shirt to my inauguration ceremony; underclothes make the inner man. Mr. Hodges, our faculty adviser, formally introduced me to the staff. I delivered a short oration beginning with a joke and ending with an exhortation to get behind the paper and write *write* WRITE until the National Scholastic Press Association passed us the palm, the grail, the olive wreath, first place in their annual competition. My staff gathered in the *Times* Room to do homage, pour Coca-Cola, and eat jelly doughnuts. Unreachable girls like Eva Masters suddenly seemed reachable.

During the first week, myself as impressed by this triumph as if it had been that of another, I dealt with family and colleagues with the cool impartiality of a hereditary executive. "You're a fine apple of my eye," my mother said, "hm hm, now you change to vinegar, you squirt, you lummox."

"Cider first! Cider first!"

For one week I enjoyed my dehydrated ambitions—just add flattery and serve.

But reality presses hard.

Blasé by the second week, a non-executive ectomorph, I discovered that I was essentially as before, my becoming not yet my being and achievement not the inevitable way to ease. I worked at my editorial desk with hardly a thought to my rolled-up sleeves and brow, drafting a renewed appeal to those subjects of Lakewood High who flipped candy wrappers behind radiators and/or stuck their chewing gum onto the walls of Comfort Rooms. In non-editorial moments I was myself guilty of both crimes of lèse-janitor.

By the third week I was neither exalted nor blasé. The

school hive deserted by its scholarly ants, radiators clicking
in the void of late afternoon, the roar of mechanical eraser-
cleaners stilled at last, the classroom clocks morosely wasting time, the smell of galoshes and chalk subsiding in the
chill, the extinguished sky casting its late afternoon shadow
into the *Times* Room, I composed my articles with the
stern but benevolent face which I had invented before a
mirror to serve as example to such admiring young journal-
ists as Marguerite Nedgely. Unconscious of the void, profligate with pretense, I squandered a face already becoming
as habitual as my signature. I served—I tried things out—I
just kidded around.

Sometimes, even among these public satisfactions of a
distinguished new critic of poetry and sanitary habits, I
paused to think of Lucille Lake, whom I adored for her
busy diamond-eyed beauty.

Sometimes I longed for a honey graham cracker with
marmalade and a glass of milk.

Sometimes I wondered if the tendency of Marguerite
Nedgely to offer herself up for kissing purposes in the ex-
hilarating proximity of the Assistant Principal's office
might compensate me for the terrifying virtues of Lucille
Lake and Patricia Donahue.

Once—putting graham crackers behind me this day—I
considered silent and watchful Eva Masters. Dangerous,
don't touch, I warned myself.

After these efforts of indecision, Juicer Montague, Tom
Moss, and I held a convention during which we decided
that we would remain aloof from temptation for the sake
of some vague future purpose (tennis? monogamy? College Board exams?). Juicer swore that he hated all women,
Lucille Lake first. Tom swore that he despised all females,
especially Rosalie Fallon. I argued the unworthiness of
girls for our attention, especially in view of my arduous
duties guiding the *Lakewood High Times* and Juicer's

promising future as editor of the Lakewood High School Yearbook, the *Vu-Point,* pronounced: vyoop-oint. We knew the joys of random oath-makers—firmness of character and devotion to the horde. Tom too might attain to some high power as treasurer of his home room or chairman of the Safety Council.

"No more women, only literature and touch football," Juicer proclaimed. We swore with him.

The next week I fell in love with Eva Masters. She was a small pale dark-headed creature with eyes like inkwells, smudged with brooding, a mouth plump as a baby's, and a precocious little body upon which she put College Miss clothes instead of the usual schoolgirl skirts and sweaters. She wrote a column for the *Times.* I smelled Blue Grass cologne when she brought me her copy, composed in green ink on letter paper with the *i*'s circled. She designed her gaze in a frame of black, matted by eyeball white about the iris of purest blue; there, in that eye, an ambiguous intention swelled and spread awash about me in the shadow of her observant tilted head. She parted her lips and flicked me up with a curly pink tip of a tongue. She merely looked at me. I spun crazy as a barberpole inside. I violated my pledge to Juicer and Tom. "What's the meaning of this?" Juicer demanded.

"She's a poet," I apologized. "She told me she writes poetry."

"Poems in prose or poems in poetry?"

"What about Lucille Lake and Pattie Donahue, not to speak of Marguerite Nedgely?" Tom asked. "I'd just as soon leave Rosalie Fallon out of this."

"I don't know, she won't show me yet. The poems," I said.

"Tom's right," Juicer said. "It's not profound to be fickle. Look at Galahad—"

"Look at Poe with Annabel Lee and the lost Lenore."

Juicer attempted to make up in deep feeling what he lacked in rhetoric. He stubbornly shook his head. "No."

I pursued my advantage. "Girls," I argued, "they're just girls, but she hopes to be a poet. That's a fact. I know she's telling the truth because I saw her looking up in Clement Wood's *Rhyming Dictionary* when I was at the library using *Roget's Thesaurus of Synonyms and Antonyms*. She told me she knows most of the *Rubaiyat* by heart."

"A poetess," articulated Tom. He claimed our attention. "Does she know about the underlying meanings of Khayyam's *Rubaiyat?*"

"Sure, all of them."

My friends studied me with dismay gradually moving toward textual analysis. At last Juicer, the more magnanimous of the two, extended his hand in friendship and offered an opportunity for pardon. He craftily demanded: "What does she think of Thomas Wolfe, that Eva Masters?"

I had been transported. I had forgotten to ask her. "Great," I lied. "That's all we ever talk about," I double-lied. "I think she likes him," I said.

"Her father had to sell one of his cars last year," Tom informed me. "He's not a big success in business. Rosalie Fallon told me, she's my source."

"I don't care."

"That big house of theirs by the lake—" Tom closed his mouth crisply, "—is only a front." He had warned me, thus performing the duties of friendship.

"I don't care," I said, "if he sells the other car. I love her for her own sake. It's a Buick convertible."

My abrupt flight of passion toward Miss Eva Masters moved both Tom and Juicer. Never having studied her, therefore confronted by pure potentiality, their most profound demands were satisfied by Eva. I could love her, they decided, and retain my crown in that little tribe with

three kings. They admired the high romantic cunning of
her swipe at my chastity; they envied me the wallop I had
suffered. It happened like this:

At about five o'clock one afternoon while I sat in the
deserted *Times* Room at my editorial altar, licking phrases
from a pencil to describe the senior class play ("One of the
most superlative in recent years") amid academic air exhausted by children and spinsters, I glanced up for a moment to press my fingers to the bridge of my nose in a
gesture of fatigue validated by more films than I can mention. I admired my executive devotion to duty, gazed
through the soapy sheen of glass at the window, and let my
eyes discover the familiar scholarly litter which is the re-
sult of eight hours of effort toward order—paper, Kleenex,
eraser lint, gum wrappings, all the sheddings of schoolchild
suffering. Encased in a gray sleeveless knit sweater with a
V-neck—thus to my mind the nasal, vested, ulcered journalist of the movie city rooms—I glanced up past my
jacket (*op. cit.*, green corduroy) which was suspended by
a nail over the desk.

Rustle and sigh from behind the files. Rustle-rustle, sigh.
Sigh. Eva Masters arched her back, stretched her soft arms,
rustled, sighed, shook her small scented head: Eva Masters
stood up. "Hello," said Eva Masters.

I ducked my neck for one last despairing glimpse at the
receding dream entitled, "Daniel Berman, City Editor."

"I bet you didn't know I was there," she said. "I will
bet you."

We were alone. The fatal sequel to this insight—my mind
worked fast in those days—was that I loved her. Forever!
We were alone. Now and ever, forever! The disease of
premature imagination.

"I would be very surprised indeed if you knew I was
here at all. Were," she said.

"Yes, I didn't," I said. "I mean no, I didn't." I realized that this response failed to display my native trigger wit, but did Romeo say anything that we remember as clearly as what he did? (Yes, alas. 'See! how she leans her cheek upon her hand: O that I were a glove upon that hand. . . .')

"What are you doing?" I improvised.

"Nothing. Sitting. Writing a poem." Demurely with eyes and nose she indicated her notebook. Was it about life, deep feeling, a jug of wine and thou jugging beside me? If there were any doubt, it was dispelled by the tilt of nose and dilation of eye.

"Ah," I said. ('That I might touch that cheek. . . .')

"You didn't hear me?"

"Not a drop." I found an even more appropriate metaphor: "You were quiet as a—"

"I was quiet as a mouse," she sang sweetly, "and twice as busy. I was just curled up there snug as you please so's no one could see me."

Narrow-eyed and ungenerous, I wondered if she could somehow have prepared this speech in advance. I asked evasively: "What kind of a poem?"

"Free verse."

"Ah!" I could no longer conceal my admiration, my self-respect supported only by the muscles under the editorial pencil behind my ear. The pencil began to leave me but, paralyzed, I could no longer move. The pencil accelerated. Cold as the finger of fate, it nipped my collar and slid down my back. I shivered as it lodged near my spine. In the meantime I was gazing tenderly at Eva Masters. "I wisht—" I said. I had met my match at repartee. I was downed by art and mystery. There was nothing left but to adore her, and sweet love suffused me while the pencil traced a mark on my back. Inwardly I met the challenge of experience, but my new feelings poisoned my ability to act. "I wisht, I wisht. . . ." Still sitting behind the desk, shielded by it, I followed her moving and her breathing. That girls differed from me was a fact only recently made clear and bitterly nice: I studied the differences as indicated by what her body did. She wore a red blouse tucked with disturbing folds into a navy blue skirt. The cloth formed little pockets about her breasts, little nips pointing down her legs. It was the pleats, the creases, the swellings, and the slippings which vaguely disturbed and excited me. The true meaning of tailoring in love gradually acted on me, not to mention the desire to be hurt. "A poem," I breathed, and wishting: "I wisht."

"What are you looking at?" she stated, having been created one million years ago with the knowledge of what I would look at.

"The sunset out the window," I said. "Look the colors."

"Very lovely,"—without looking. She smiled and touched her own hands. Signs of control, signs of confusion. Eva, all confused, learning to be different, was starting that long climb which changes a tomboy into a girl and sometimes into a woman.

"Would you like, Eva, would you like an assignment next week, a feature story? I'll give you a by-line."

She gazed at me with pity, with laughter. Her way of leaning tried to tell me that her fantasies of power were the issue of antique desires which could not be satisfied by journalistic triumphs even on a high school newspaper which had won a gold cup in the Inter-scholastic Competition. She wet her lips. "I'm cold," she said.

"Well, they turn off the heat at four o'clock. It's not winter yet. It's natural. Do you know Chuck Hastings?"

"Yes, a little."

"Ah! a little!"—already stupified by jealousy of this rival genius.

"I'm cold," she said, looking at my jacket on the nail above my desk.

"Usually it stays warm enough until five-thirty," I said, "but sometimes when it snows or rains outside." She bent over my desk. "But sometimes when it snows or rains outside," I said.

"How much do you weigh?"

"A hundred forty-five, why?"

"I only weigh a hundred," she said. "My brother James says I'm too delicate because I lack a protecting layer of feminine metabolism."

"Oh"—I gave my hands a brisk rub—"is that very grave?"

"No, it just means I have to be kept warm. I have a tendency." She leaned and smiled.

"What are you looking at?"

"Your pencil."

"Indelible. I never erase."

"Ah!" she said in her turn.

I blushed and lowered my eyes: "But sometimes I cross out."

We then communed in memories of Greta Garbo in the snow, coughing magnificently while THE END hove up on little wires, a prop man's apocalypse and time for tears and crackerjack. Her great pale eyes, black within blue within white, bulged like stewed onions toward the future suspended over my head. My corduroy jacket had elbows reinforced with leather. Destiny moved cleverly and sullenly across the face of an ancient and lovely child. She frowned.

"I'm cold," she said.

"Are you still cold?"

She removed my jacket from the nail, murmured, "Do you mind?" and slipped her arms through the sleeves. She walked a few steps with it, trying it on, putting her hands in the pockets, making herself small and defenceless in my jacket. She hooked her hands in the pockets with tinted thumbs protruding. She looked at me and looked away.

"I'm not cold," I said in admiration.

She turned, head cocked like a bird meditating the open door of its cage, the notebook for free verse under her arm, considering herself in the window glass. Her small white hand brushed against my lapels and I telepathically shivered although the lapels were resting on her breast (*chest,* I carefully thought). "Is that all right?" she asked. "The buttons buttoned like this? I know you only button the middle button." She made a great deal of talk of buttons. She had other notions in her head. "I notice the way boys button buttons."

"I'm not cold," I repeated.

She lightly whirled, smiling and murmuring toward me past a wrinkled nose, "I'm quite warm now too, Dan." I might have vanished altogether into the realms of pure ecstasy if I hadn't stiffened my mind with effort to recall the movie in which the star had wrinkled her nose like this. As forfeit against unsuccess I chewed my tongue before asking if I could walk (*accompany*) her on her way home. However, I remained seated—never lived there an editor so vertiginous as I. I was knocked for a loop.

> *O Eva Masters, who wore my coat,*
> *You made an editor a goat.*
> *You swung your hips of small dimension,*
> *Medium mobility, and vast intention.*
>
> *Recall that day amid steam heat*
> *When blood spoke blood,—and what a feat*
> *In city children, bred to wish,*
> *To gulp down love like feeding fish!*

4. The genius, the honorary genius, and the merely superior

MR. WELCH, A MAN MOST
notable for manipulative skill with a toothpick while talking, professed history in our high school. Once a Teachers
College athlete, now going to flesh in a sedentary occupation, he betrayed his suppressed ambitions with a fierce
quiver of hair in his ears and nose. He had a hairy face
despite the patented Little Dandy devices with which, clip
and snip, he barbered his mustache, his nose, and his ears;
it was a rough face with crevices where bad meat odors
lurked, and when he leaned forward they surged toward
us from their hiding places. "A face like an armpit," Juicer said. It was true that his hair seemed distantly nourished
through the coils and oils of more private places.

An informer had reported Juicer's playground confession about drinking beer regularly. I had murmured a
nasty word upon entering Miss Poster's English class while
everyone, plus Eva, admired my recklessness and Miss
Poster wrestled in full gripe with an unsuccessful pretense
at not hearing me (she diagrammed a sentence). With
suburban delicacy—to us it seemed hypocrisy—Mr. Welch
had not mentioned these and other provocatory incidents
which motivated his summoning us to a confidential cor-

ner of the Male Teachers' Rest Room. Instead he alluded
mournfully to our "class work," our "attitude," "citizen-
ship," and "the future."

"Of course it's a stage in your life, boys. Do you have
trouble sleeping? Night sweats? I mean tossing and turning. Bad dreams? Horrible thoughts? I only mean your
own good," he said, "I don't mean to be curious. You fellows," he had added to ingratiate himself.

Juicer and I, leaning at our ease, knew that we out-
numbered him despite the rustle and sip of his colleagues
in the confessional. We remained silent. Fattish Mr. Welch
was married, but we could not see the profit of it in his case.
He did not seem to be a lover; we could not imagine him;
most likely he too had horrible thoughts. He recognized a
certain reserve in our attitude. He turned first to Juicer
and addressed him in a tone of respect, rubbing one hairy
hand against the other: "As you may already know, Ronald
—Juicer, I believe you are called—you have the highest
I.Q. rating in the school according to the Stanford-Binet.
An intelligence of 162. Let me congratulate you, Juicer,
if you will permit me. A very fine performance indeed.
That makes you a genius by twelve points, I believe. We
expect great things of you, Ronald—Juicer—at least an A
in History and not so much talking in class. I hope you
don't mind my speaking out so frankly. . . . And you," he
turned to me with interest, "your intelligence is only
slightly less. One forty-nine. One fifty would be genius. I
believe you two boys are friends. Fine. Excellent. Very
nice. That is as it should be, but you should try to influence each other for the good. Will you now? Say you will?
Learn from the good and fight the good fight against the
bad? Fellows?"

Gravely Juicer arose to the responsibilities of his championship in the Stanford-Binet League. "Yup."

"I will ever strive to influence Ronald for the good," I

swore, moving my hand toward my heart, "to the best of my abilities."

"Ronald," Mr. Welch said, deeply moved, "do you have any further questions?" Juicer thought a moment, searching for a response that might adequately express his validated statistical profundity. At last he leaned forward, tapped Mr. Welch on the stomach, and asked:

"What's Lucille Lake's Intelligence Quotient?"

"Yes," I said, "what's Lucille Lake's? I mean Stanford-Binet. I mean Pattie Donahue."

Mr. Welch leered; his tongue murkily tickled the secret. Did he know that when I said Pattie Donahue, I meant Eva Masters? Did he suspect how I loved her and thus did not dare pronounce her name? When it snowed, we would walk; did old Wobbleface Welch know it? He turned up the corners of his mouth so that I saw a wink of the eye of the anchovy that swam in his breath.

"That's their business now, isn't it?" he demanded. "Isn't it now, theirs and mine?" he asked us to admit. "However —" and he dimpled with the amorous ease of one in the know—"however, Lucille Lake is a very very bright girl. Talented."

"Gifted?" said Juicer.

"Gifted," Mr. Welch agreed. "In the upper three percentile or better."

"What about Pattie Donahue? Say, what percentage is she in?" I owlishly inquired, thinking about her pink cashmere sweater and the glimpse of her rounded upper arms. "Is she talented, gifted, in the upper three per cent?"

"Never mind those thoughts. I know," he said, wagging a finger which seemed to hang from at least six loose joints, "I know what terrible thoughts are entering your mind. I have to cope with reality all the time in my job, but ignore it and it'll go away. It's your age. But remember, Daniel, you are the People of the Book."

"Who, me?" I felt more like the People of Pattie Dona-hue, the Person of Eva Masters.

He solemnly nodded. "Out of the mountaintops on high in Galilee you brought down the Law, given by the Almighty for our guidance on earth as we learn by doing. The Ten Commandments."

"Who, him?" asked upstaged Juicer Montague. "And who amended them, tell me that. Who amended the Ten Commandments and brought down music, painting, stained glass windows?"

Mr. Welch was surrounded. "Whoa," he said. "This is not our purpose today. Christianity contributed even more than the Semitic peoples, Phoenicians who gave us our alphabet, Syrians, Egyptians, Algerians, Hamites, and er uh gosh—Eddie Cantor Haym Salomon Bernard Baruch Hedy Lamar—our many somewhat swarthy American brothers—JEWS!—excuse me—such as those specifically Christian great world ideas like—Rousseau, Beethoven, the concept of loving kindness—but that's not the question, Juicer. Everything is one great continuum, experience teaches that. Someday you too will study sociology, the science of human communications. All men are interrelated, boys."

It would be a long session. The great truths out of Mount Morningside were passing in review. I felt myself developing a slight case of palsy, ingrown giggles disrupting the flow of saliva to my sense of reality—Juicer had St. Vitus Dance, mildly, suffering because of the nails protruding from the flung timber in the air—God it was hard to listen! Our thoughts met in midair, embracing to vow: Welch must die in a just cause, that of silence and verity and blessed silence. Die, die!

But he lived on, alas.

He died imperceptibly, as do we all, every instant of blessed time; and he killed an afternoon for us. We had planned to join some jocks in a softball game.

Mr. Welch was opening his arms to the spirit of universal love. We should appreciate the extra increment of human interrelations provided us by zoning policy, Lakewood's progressive school system, and the cosmopolitan balance of a person of the Book (my father had a grocery store) with a people of the Law (Juicer's father, once in Dartmouth, now dirtied his collars in federal litigation). "This is a settled, cultured neighborhood, good education, solid homes, gas heating with thermostats in many of them. Almost everyone is above the normal. But you, Ronald Montague, and you, Daniel Berman, I pronounce you not merely first rate, not merely outstanding, not merely unique. . . ."

Static. Slobber. Coughing. All sentences must be humanly interrelated, even completed if possible. Coughcough. Charrrrop. He left it in his throat for another opportunity. He broke off the toothpick. Charrrr-ropp! That time he got it. Into the handkerchief with it. As he was saying?

Juicer murmured thoughtfully, "You were saying how we are not merely first rate, outstanding, and unique—"

"Oh that's enough for me!" I said modestly, hypocritically.

"First rate, outstanding, and unique," said Juicer.

Mr. Welch sprayed him with triumph, with muzzy breath: "Yes! Interrupted by internal affairs! But you two are actually ver-ry ex-ceptional, even where many children have all the advantages also. There! You fortunate young men and women! It's not everyone I could say this to. Why, if you make good use of the advantages at your disposal" —Mr. Welch was rather wound up that day—"fine homelifes, good libraries, French lessons according to the conversational method, I can almost promise you happy and successful in the deepest sense of the word lives, and you can mark my—"

"Words," Juicer finished for him in a whisper. One of

the distinguishing qualities of intellect is the ability to anticipate from evidence.

Mr. Welch opened his arms to us, showed his grayish gums in a smile, and nodded in dismissal at last. "Go and realize your potentialities," he said. He fluttered his eyelashes. "I think I drank too much coffee. Nerves, enthusiasm. Forgive me, fellas. Farewell."

"I'm a genius like Thomas Wolfe!" Juicer whooped when we were safely out of the school building. "Let's get a beer down at Mick's."

"You think so?" I asked, brooding. I wanted to hurry directly home and write a great poem before dinner in order to assure myself of my merit despite a score of only 149, one point short of genius. "I had a stomach ache that day, the day of the Stanford-Binet test. My scalp itched from washing with Fels Naptha. I was looking at Pattie Donahue." (I told Juicer everything, but I could not tell him more about Eva, not yet. We had to consummate our love; we had to walk in the snow. I bore my secret as I bore my I.Q.—noisily.) "Listen, Juicer, you try guessing how many blocks when you're crazy in love. My underwear was all wrinkled. I could have gotten a better intelligence."

"That's okay," Juicer assured me. "You're almost a genius. I'll help you in any way I can. I give you every confidence. I'm sure that Thomas Wolfe would too."

"I didn't sleep good the night before the test," I said. "My pencil broke twice. I kept looking at Pattie Donahue. I may have looked at Eva Masters, too." Then, despising myself for these cowardly excuses: "But I don't believe in it anyway. Never catch Edgar Allan Poe—Thomas Wolfe —James Branch Cabell—no, never catch a real genius with a Stanford-Binet. They got more important things to do, that kind of geniuses. What about Chuck Hastings?"

Ferreting out my discomfort with the intuition of a

genuine genius and twelve points to spare, Juicer said: "This morning I measured myself, it was six inches even. I borrowed my mother's tape measure. How long's yours?"

"Never measured," I said, smarting, generalizing my dislike toward all statistics. "Anyway, it's quality that counts, Juicer. You could be a genius by Stanford-Binet and never write a allegory. You could have a pee-boner ten inches, and still be virgin. You only need a few lines for a poem—who cares how many inches in a dong? Quality, that's the answer."

Juicer blushed. It was not his fault that geniuses are sensitive. Momentarily, I forgot that, although already the author of an allegory, I too remained a virgin. Then, with the rapid world-historical emotional perceptions of a man with but one point missing, I said, "We can fix that up too, Juicer. I know a place, pal—I heard Lewis Snyder talking about it—"

We still expected enormous victories with each new day. We awakened to imminent mastery; we scrambled fat or leanly out of bed into a possible world funneling open toward probable us; the world? Our gift from ourselves, an abstract domain for invention. I kept a pad and pencil by my bed to be ready for that middle of the night when I would awaken out of fructifying sleep in order to break the sacred bank of inspiration and scrawl the greatest poem ever written on any subject: *Greatest* was a material form. (Coldfooting around for scribbler's tools, I didn't want to awaken the folks. "It's only me, Ma, writing 'Paradise Regained'. . . ." "Well, make sure you close the Frigidaire.")

Juicer would have strangled anyone (or threatened it) who suggested that he was not the world's most outstanding genius; he needed no achievement but his own assurance, although, when I disputed his position, he pointed out: "I got an intelligence of 162, and 150 is enough. I sure give them something to think about when I almost flunk French 3. One sixty-two! Jeez! And I'm ruining myself drinking beer at the West Side Lounge with the Fenn College men!"

This argument had an effect on me, brought up, as I have said, with respect for bank accounts, special license plates, class queens by election, and other numbers, but I affected contempt. "Tests! Stanford-Binet!" I said. "Counting blocks I suppose." I snorted like Tom Moss. "It's imagination that counts—Thomas Wolfe didn't need a Stanford-Binet to write *Look Homeward, Angel*. He just needed passion and a lot a diaries. That's what it needs. Journals."

Quick in his satisfaction as in his sympathies, Juicer consoled me. "It's all right, a 149 is only one point missing. You can make up for it by *hard work*."

"Don't believe in Stanford-Binet"—made an iconoclast by one point.

"But it's all there in black and white," Tom Moss interjected. "What do you mean, don't believe?"

"Yeah, what do you mean?" Juicer demanded. "They got me right, didn't they? They got it all figured out—idiot, imbecile, subnormal, normal, above normal, intelligent, superior, genius. That's me, the last one. That's us if you could just pick up another point someplace, pal."

"I'm just superior," Tom admitted, "but if I work hard I'll get far."

"Sure you will," we assured him.

"Mr. Welch told me. He told me him, he's not even superior, but look where he got. One of the best line coaches in the area."

"Sure. That's all right, Tom," I said. Although accepted by Juicer into the magic circle of an Honorary Genius, I could not forget my past. I remembered what it had been like to be merely superior—the dullness, the mediocrity, the hopeless ambition. It was the glimpse of the banquet from the window. Tom's narrow nose with its blunt tip

lent itself to the image of being pressed against some invisible glass while he grieved outside in the snow. We ate
truffles, roast duck, sweet potatoes, and strawberry ice
cream inside. Afterwards we had more ice cream and sent
the remains of the duck out to Tom instead of throwing
them to the panting great Danes who crouched by the fireplace. There's plenty of good left in the bones if you have
patience to crunch.

"Say," Tom inquired one day, "is that a *revised* Stanford-
Binet or only an Army Alpha?"

"What do you mean, Army Alpha? It's an I.Q.," Juicer
said.

"Oh, an Intelligence Quotion," Tom said solemnly. "I
was just asking."

"I'm an unsanitary genius," Juicer declared expansively.

"That's the only genuine kind, the genuine article," Tom
said. "I've been making inquiries. Geniuses are known for
being dirty. Never heard of one he wore a tie, only necker-
chiefs."

"Wha? I wouldn't wear a neckerchief, you think I'm
queer?" Juicer said with contempt.

"Got to," Tom snapped out. He went through his ape
maneuvers of snort, scowl, shrug, and chuckle, but he
betrayed his envy. "Who knows if maybe it's not best to
be superior, better than genius? Why should I take Mr.
Stanford-Binet's word for it?" Despite his muttering and
cynicism, he had a way of gaping silently that said: "What
are you two about? What have you got for me to figure
out?"—a conviction that Juicer and I possessed the key to
some puzzle, when in fact the only way he could get what
we had was by ceasing to figure. "Oh yeah?" he might
mutter while this gaping question fell like a loose sack
over his thin skull; but only for a moment, for then he became the great dog philosopher once more. "You think
you know, but *I* don't know." He ducked his head in small

cynical nods to prove that we were deluding ourselves; not deluded for a moment, he doubted all but his own doubt.

"That's all right," Juicer said, brimming with excess: "You're still our buddy, Tom. You are. It's the Three Musketeers—though don't think I still like that book," he hastened to assure us.

"Yes, *The Three Musketeers*," I said, "but of course that's old stuff. It can't touch life, real life."

"They made a good movie version," Tom said.

In the honesty and brutality peculiar to youth and genius, we could not in clear conscience admit Tom to equal status although he remained our friend. He was a trusted ambassador from the world with which we deigned to ally ourselves, not a citizen of that other fair world over which we actually presided. Elected by acclamation (our own), Juicer and I felt that Tom's nosebleeds were not sufficient to qualify him as a passionate lover. He claimed it was only sinus; we needed it to be Saint-Saëns. He was too clearheaded; that is, he made nothing but confusion of his confusion. He was cynical. He disliked rhymes only slightly less than free verse. He had not yet read *Of Time and the River,* by Thomas Wolfe.

Mr. Welch, we suspected, back in Metempsychosis from whence he came, must have been something better—a barn owl thoughtfully hanging, a quick black otter—before he became a hairy, chuckling, optimistic hyena. Everyone seemed to run animal risks in consenting to grow up. Tom was a lamb who should beware of growing sheepish.

5. We were all the great

JUICER, TOM MOSS, AND I HAD
never yet gotten drunk like great men. Flamboyant Juicer
could get served in bars, but pimply Tom and skinny Dan,
we only got the horselaugh from those wise ones who
served P.M. at twenty cents a shot in the Bar & Grill
near the Railway Express. We were at considerable dis-
advantage. How could we drown our sorrows in drink, as
so many famous men have done, if the suburban ordinances
continued to frighten the bartenders away from our three-
times twenty cents? "My mother lets me have a sip when
company comes," Tom argued.

"So does mine," I lied.

It wasn't the same thing anyway. Tom and I looked to
Juicer for analysis of the experience of drinking in The
Hot Shot Bar & Grill. He just slapped down a twenty-cent
piece, we imagined, and said commandingly, "Here!" We
had never even seen a twenty-cent piece—sheltered awful
bourgeois lives we led. But Juicer also looked to us for
the fine sympathy of our heart's unease, which lived on
milk. "He's all right," Juicer said of Tom, "just dead."
During that summer's leisure, we discovered that all three
of us, despite variations in accord with differences of character, got carsick fom streetcars and were helplessly in love

65

with women who spurned us. Juicer wept over busy, economical, harp-playing Lucille; Tom told us of teasing, economical, and frivolous Rosalie Fallon. Publicly I vacillated
between a comradely sharing of Juicer's passion for Lucille and a throwback junior high school lust for Pattie
Donahue. *Pubicly,* secretly, there was Eva Masters, with
whom I had an understanding. We hardly spoke, but we
waited. We circled each other in the halls at school in
order to prevent explosions and unnecessary loss of life.

In other words, I was totally scared and fleeing back to
the boys, as we flee homeward in a dream, our shoes dragging glue. Eva and I had said that we liked to walk in the
snow, and we each knew that we were now irrevocably committed. I promised myself the gift of life and love, if it
would only snow; if only it would not snow, Juicer and
Tom and I could stay as we were, with the girls out there,
beyond, in cashmere, safely roped off.

The autumn was moving into the last late Indian summer, leaves burning but the screens still up. Eva too, my
distant meteorologist, sniffed the air. When that snowfall
would come, and we were ignited into keeping our promises to each other, it would not be our fault; it would be
fate, the turn of the seasons; but the seasons always turn
and we knew it. Hoping for a reprieve, I told Tom and Juicer that my parents admired Lucille. "Peppy," my mother
had said when she saw her in the class play. "Frisky," my
father had said. "Very lively," they decided together. But
neither Lucille Lake nor my parents nor my nightmare
wager on love could slow the season's turning.

"Who do you really love, whom?" asked shrewd, wicked,
and grammatical Tom.

Juicer groaned. He was on my side, but hell, I was a
pain sometimes.

"You're flighty," Tom assured me, "not true, not loyal.
Sir Galahad died for his beloved, I think."

"What if, just suppose, just supposing for supposers, what if Sir Galahad had Eva Masters for a beloved? Do you suppose he could make out, or just die?"

"Dan's a Don-wan," Juicer loyally defended me, "he likes to make out."

"A Casanova," I modestly argued. "I don't think Sir Galahad died, he only wasted away. Anyway, Sir Humphrey Bogart wouldn't croak for a damsel."

Tom replied carelessly to all these compliments: "I don't care." Tom saved pennies in a piggy bank, liked the smell of gasoline, and had pimples. "Constipation runs in my family," he explained.

"Runs?"—a primitive snicker from Juicer and me.

"That's a pun," he stated, nothing put over on him. "It's from good living in the sedentary life. The lower intestine gets lazy. Kellogg's All Bran will give it a pickup." He made a small double chin, pure skin and contentment, as he expertly blew his nose and softly held his achievement between his fingers in the handkerchief. Everything in Tom bespoke this consideration, this hoarding of himself. No coarsely moral All Bran could purge him of private contentment. His eyes, never unveiled of his prenatal inner sufficiency, looked out through some cool smoke distilled over their ironic gray surfaces; his nose, sharp and thin as his mother's blue-tipped one, cut down straight to the middle of his mouth, bleeding it thin. Be just to him; he was our friend; therefore even his nose was redeemed by the dimple in cartilege at its end.

However, his movements, his arising from a chair or his moving across a room, had none of a boy's spendthrift energy. As economical of himself as a skeleton in a dream, I sometimes saw him as the medical student's joy, clicking, ambulatory through nightmares, alive only by the gift of another's fantasy. He took something from Juicer and me; he joined us in our jump without conception into life, to

be on the safe side, while he saved himself for an idea of
what he wanted. I loved Juicer because he was frightened
in his bowels and kidneys; I might have worshiped Tom
Moss, that lamb, the suburban-model calf of gold, because
he had no body to be frightened in. He thought and then
saved; he got what he wanted because he never wanted
enough. On his cowl was written in irridescent spangles of
dandruff, visible only in the dark of my furious imagination:
DON'T RUSH ME. . . . DO I HAVE MY RETURN TICKET?

Visited by hay fever, one nostril sealed off tight by a
passionate, dilatory sinus, Tom snorted at unsuspected moments: "I have (snort) more customers on my (snort)
paper route than anyone on the West Side—" Growing
more economical with age, he built an ironic attitude
toward life upon a foundation of these exclamations.
Mucus conditioned wit; life depended from sinus and slippery handkerchief. "You know what kind of a girl she is?"
—he was the first of my friends to learn to speak in in-
sinuations. He indicated Pattie Donahue.

"What? what kind?" I asked.

He snorted but did not answer, looking sideways from
his smoky bean-gray eyes with their sad red allergic rims.

"Then what kind is Eva Masters?" I demanded.

No answer.

"So what kind are Lucille Lake?"

His eyes, squeezing, said *Heh;* and nothing further till
he chose.

Athletic: a fast runner also when he chose. This saved
him for sports, a speed to win prizes, unlike my speed
squandered on slow events while fast ones were greeted
by the movement of the stalk's turning to the sun. Kind:
this out of Protestant teaching in his home, lacking the
energy of cruelty. Abnormality—acts made public in a
darkened hallway—found him neither informer nor par-
ticipant. He stepped slowly, softly, and judged. Femurs

clicked, eye sockets observed, ligaments adjusted the lean
skeleton to an almost adequate tailoring. Why did he like
me? There was one excellent reason: I liked him. I needed
him, just his evenness and sparseness; I took his self-
sufficiency for strength, not knowing how he needed me.
He followed me like the medical student's obsession. The
skeleton has no motion, no life, but thanks to the breath
with which the student animates his dream, the skeleton
wiggles. Tom enjoyed this wiggling, too. Patiently he
breathed what he wanted. Juicer and I gladly gave him the
loose feathers of our words on the night air; he was mildly
tickled when we discussed *Life* on stoops or lawns, our
heads propped on copies of *Spicy Detective* (15¢) and the
Rubaiyat (49¢ with overprinted drawings for underprinted
adults). The ambiguous blue of evening shadows on a
wall became blue and ambiguous for him because we
said so.

"Blue?" he demanded. "Looks more like black to me.
Shadows are *black*. Ambiguous? Make up your mind,
wyncha."

"But it is a wall, Tom," said Juicer. "Walls everywhere,
separating souls. Souls don't need walls."

"But apartments do. What else you put a door or
windows through?"

"That's deep, Juicer." I nudged him with my toe. "You
hear what Tom said? He made poetry, a symbol."

"All right, but I'm pooped now. I didn't get my nine
hours last night. See you tomorrow, fellas."

Don't you move! Juicer and I for some reason said. We
needed Tom as a ship needs ballast. We needed Tom as a
wall needs doors and windows through. He sighed and
loyally stayed, valuable, spreadeagled on the lawn in the
missionary position.

Tom Moss was profoundly modest, wanting power but
not the trap and wrap of power, the use of knowledge but

not the display of it. If later he did exercises in his room, chinning himself on a bar, standing on his head, push-ups, it was for a sense of control and understanding of his limits, not for the consequent display of muscles on a beach while the girls said "Ah!" and inclined one knee before the other (for indeed they had two) in case a Hollywood scout lay concealed in the sand with camera and contract. The rare brown blood which filtered through his drip-grind brains arose to the cheeks when Juicer discovered his weight-lifting equipment and satin shorts in a carton under his bed.

"Hell, I sent away for them to Johnson-Smith."

"You can say that again," said Juicer, his fat flabbers deeply gasted.

"Hell, I sent away for them to the *Johnson-Smith Company,* Juicer!"

We had no idea that Tom could imagine his own improvement.

Smoky, beany, water-colored eyes; the paradox of liquid and bones into flesh. Watery mouth, watery nose, bleak liquid face with sharp ripples. A cloudy day at sea: your lungs filled just to look at him, but it was all right—you grew gill slits. He drowned slowly in his own ambitions; that is, he succeeded. He had a smile the color of a fish's belly. The bubbles frightened him when he passed gas in a bathtub, not knowing himself and the rich explosiveness of possibility below even his Calvinist soul. His sphincters clicked tremulously after drinking spoiled milk, dreading his proven capabilities. Juicer and I loved him and feared him as old cons love and fear a prison. His existence put the extremest question concerning larceny in the heart. We, gamblers in love, loved to see how much Tom could get away without.

Later—it only shows—he became an aesthete, wearing pajamas all day one summer. He had already read a theory of art in one of his older brother's books, a psychological, in which he found the explanation for most things: "It's because we had an unhappy childhood," he reasoned. "Look at Shakespeare. Look at Tchaikowsky. Put them on the scales. Look at me."

"So birds sing because they're neurotic?" I demanded.

"As neurotic as birds can be," Juicer assured us.

"You don't take it seriously," Tom said, meaning that we didn't take him seriously. He was right, but we liked him. We only took ourselves seriously, but we could take seriously those elements in him which reflected the serious in us. Such serious young men! And what a coincidence to be all three unhappily in love!

"How well do you know Rosalie Fallon?" Tom asked Juicer.

"A little."

"Oh! a little!" Tom said. He turned to me.

"Intimately," I said.

We all sighed. "My brother the newspaper reporter he's not a virgin," Tom said.

Juicer and I elaborately did not reply, but we respected him for having a non-virgin in the family.

"What kind of girls does your brother think is best?" I asked at last.

"Red-headed," Tom sinisterly replied.

"I heard peroxide," Juicer suggested, trying to regain his dominance. He was a little wild that day. There was talk of a new manager for the Indians, too.

"I think Pattie Donahue," I said, "is best."

"I think Lucille Lake," Juicer said.

"I think Rosalie Fallon," said Tom. "Didn't you really think Eva Masters, Dan?"

To get drunk seemed the logical solution to all our problems. What an original idea! Hot burns, cold freezes,

and drunk consoles. Goaded by ambition to jump crashing
through our growing panes, we mistook puns for philosophy,
rhymes for poetry, and hot whispers for everlasting goals.

> *Be Tender, Be bold*
> (*We Wanted to Be*)
> *Be Human at Least*
> *And Possibly Free*

We employed three milk bottles to abet us in our undoing.
We each took one and bled off a fraction of an inch from
our family bottles. My father had five, two liquor and three
wine. One afternoon I unlocked his cabinet with the key
hidden from the maid, under the rug where she swept over
it every day, and felt myself slip away into ruin among the
money-like labels. Cynical, fifteen, I recalled my youth,
when I thought that imperfectly canned cherries, rotting in
swollen tin, could produce a brandy to be drunk only by
connoisseurs, a class of men who wore bow ties and onyx
rings. Financial and crafty in those days, with cartilaginous skull and vertiginous spirit, I dreamed of making my
fortune quicker than Dick Whittington by cornering the
gassy-cherrycan market before Ferdinand Klabber could
discover my secret.

Now tycoonery, wealth, and my picture in National
Magazines had given way as ideals before the love of Eva
Masters (or was it Lucille Lake?), and I would have sur-
rendered my career as a great criminal lawyer for a moment of bliss with soft music in the background with Pattie
Donahue (but it was Eva Masters). I coveted poetically
now. I too left hairs in the bathtub.

The house was deserted, my conscience crowded. Specks
of dust fumed in the air; no fly buzzed, but I could hear
the moths chomp-chomping in my mother's rug with healthy
teeth that never touched chocolate. A ray of sunlight came

searching for a prism to inform, a slipcover to fade, a guilt to illuminate. It found the dust in the air and me on my knees. A metal music the alcohol made as it diversely trickled into the bottle. My illicit heart rapped. I replaced a dirty bottle cap, Fairmont Dairies, Vitamin-Rich, Thursday, with its lifted lip and its smell of a baby's mouth; then I sneaked. I was wearing, I recall, brown corduroy pants which squealed one leg against the other as I went to hide the bottle in the garage.

During this time, Tom, cool as the racing driver in a cigarette advertisement, confiscated drop-by-droplets of his paternal Christmas Cheer, which made no difference to the Mosses at Christmastime and endured throughout the year. In the parlor never used, from the bottles rarely uncorked, he followed me astray. He too hid his drainings—a mixture of port, Dubonnet, and Scotch—in the garage among the old newspapers which his mother bundled for twenty cents a stack from the paper-rags man.

Juicer—we could count on both his sweaty boldness and his cold fear—sloshed the stuff on the rug near his father's pipestand. He got down on his knees to towel it up, astonished by its magical insubstantiality, and he left a track of pink lint on the floor.

We told our parents that we planned a camping trip in Rocky River, a state park nearby.

"You will catch your death a cold," my mother said.

"We'll take along something to keep us warm," I said. "Anyway, it's Indian summer. It's supposed to be hot, the almanac says."

"Blankets," said Tom, jabbing me with his bony elbow.

"All right, take along," my mother said. "Maybe in America they do this."

Juicer growled and gnashed his teeth mysteriously: it was a habit which he practiced now that he had lost another habit—cracking his knuckles—because of something Lucille Lake said to Jack Mamble about Lewis Snyder. ("Cracking his knuckles is not very nice, is it?" Or so I had reported. Actually, it was Pattie Donahue who had said it to Rosalie Fallon about Ray Russell.) He was great for distinctive gestures, Juicer was. (Be Possibly Free. . . .)

Mother remarked ignorantly: "I'll pack up some sandwiches and a thermos bottle of hot milk."

"And what's the matter with coffee?" I demanded.

"Coffee! A bunch of kits coffee! You want to catch nerves?"

Juicer gnashed, Tom winked, I squirmed between shame and knowledge of secret depravity. "So maybe they mean Sanka," my father suggested soothingly.

"Postum I'll give them maybe, nice hot Postum to have a good time in the thermos." Our bottles lay tilted in ambush outside; tame Postum masked our plot, and trivially smelled good. "Watch out for Mister Coffee-Nerfs the kits your age fourteen years old still growing boys. . . ."

"Fifteen," I said.

We comrades boarded a streetcar toward our night in camp, groaning over rails between brick, carrying eggs, bacon, and vice in a milk bottle, each thinking of his uncle the drunkard. I had no uncle the drunkard, but I borrowed Juicer's—he was always generous with me. And when the weather broke, Eva would be waiting.

At the last streetcar stop on the line we dragged out blankets, baskets, and gear; our brave eight-eyed band (counting my four) moved into the woods of the reservation. This Birdseye, canned, pickled nature, established by happy decree at the edge of the growing city, turned us back to paleolithic challenges. Need I say the park smelled? It smelled like desire and passing summer. Crickets skittered into silence about us. A rabbit stared and fled, its tail lifted, immoral. There was a clotted woods with beer bottles, then a clump with ejected items of contraception, and then the trackless forest; beyond lay savage wilderness, the tumbling ends of the earth, and Columbus, Ohio. A mist lay lightly upon a future in which no headlights could be found advancing. We sniffed turf and found it good.

"Daniel Boone," Tom muttered, rehearsing his mutter (a man's best friend) while Juicer learned to gnash. Tom had discovered that a word muttered might pass for an excruciating joke; a clean articulation would mysteriously fail—he studied at fifteen the use of ambiguity in art. "Lewis and Clark," he said.

"Doctor Livingstone and I. Prezoom."

We no longer doubled up with the small boy's ritual exhibition of laughter. Valorously we left civilization behind us, men of serious purpose, explorers of distinction making their way in the bitter struggle of Man against Nature although this particular sample of Nature voiced no reciprocal animus. Half a mile from the trolley we found an open space. "A clearing," I noted. "Hunters maybe. Maybe *outlaws*."

"Who knows?" gnashed Juicer.

At the edge of a cliff we looked down upon the skinny stream which had eaten away this valley during a ten-thousand-years' nibbling. This too had been made a useful analogy by grade school teachers. "A little bit every week into great oaks doth grow, if you are patient and good children," Miss Aspeyer had reported.

"Ah!" said Juicer, forgetting to gnash in the emotion of expectation. "Now for that stuff."

"Maybe we should wait awhile"—Tom futilely regretful, looking back to his imaginary innocence.

"Look at him the sissy," I said.

Juicer looked at him and gnashed contemplatively.

Tom swaggered, knees knocking. "Boy am I thirsty," he muttered hollowly, mournfully. In a moribund voice he said, "I—can—hardly—*wait*."

We sat among fallen, shrunken leaves, gossiping insects, and rolled blankets. We built a fire with *Plain Dealers* and charcoal carried in Mrs. Montague's shopping bag. Night had come, time only for the first show at Loew's Granada, A Bit of Old Spain on the West Side, but late in our destiny with this woods unmeasured by clocks. The *Plain Dealer* which I shredded said that Roosevelt was leading the nation toward bankruptcy by trying to replace perfectly good battleships with new ones; Hitler had died and an impostor was wearing his mustache and persecuting the Jews; soon there would be a revolution in Russia. But that was last week's newspaper and history had already revised it. It was now by means of airplane construction that Roosevelt was trying to bankrupt our children's children; Hitler had resumed his own work; the revolution in Russia would be led by visionary international powers centered in Mexico City. A beacon from the airport swept the sky. Just like explorers we sat and pondered and congratulated ourselves.

Juicer rubbed his hand, producing a theatrical proof of anticipation. "Should we begin, men?"

"Wet our whistles."

"Have a little one, eh?"

"Try it on for size."

"Down the hatch, what-do-you-say?" Juicer demanded.

"Shall we?" said Tom. "Yeah." He answered the question after searching in vain for more urbane declaration.

We stared at each other in silence. Finally I said: "My father he drinks a lot a helluvalot with his brother Doctor Berman. The dentist," I said. "My uncle."

"Swell." Juicer, who ran to meet his fate, sniffed, frowned, and uncovered the three milk bottles. We prepared our rite to a suburban Dionysus, terrorized revelers, cross-legged martyrs, Greeks and well-behaved lambs. Sheep Tom Moss broke a holy moment with his profane bleat, "Aw! We're wasting time." He fell upon this moment in which we played for the ruin of age, and jealous of the greater good which Juicer and I drew from it, he destroyed it with a contemptuous reminder of our status as neophytes. As larvae. As apprentice self-sorcerers. "Aw, quit stalling," he said. *Tilt!* something willed within him.

"Listen to the wind in the trees," I was saying.

"Hear the whistle, the train whistle," Juicer breathed.

"It makes you think," I said.

"Time, the river, a train whistle," said Juicer.

Tom Moss clacked his tongue. "You guys are stalling," he muttered. *Tilt.* He broke by abrupt movements of disdain our moment made sacred for the invention of literature and the presentation of important silhouettes to the moon. "Stalling, you heard me."

This sounds as if Tom Moss were always sly and sullen and sarcastic, but that isn't true. It only seemed so. Actually he was like Juicer and me, sarcastic, sullen, and sly. We had a hard fifteen-year-old time of it that year. We hurried to what we hoped was our fate; I put the rest of the *Plain Dealer* on the fire. ADMIRAL HORTHY SAYS HUNGA. . . . Then the flame took it.

6. The yea-sayer, the yes-sayer, and the nay-sayer saying: "No."

I REMEMBER THAT WE FELT very large. We felt great, I remember, with great arms like those of fathers and thighs like trees. In a forest without mirrors we peeked into each other's eyes and found our own splendors reflected back; the eyes seen alone in any face are magnificent. Juicer's actorish orbs, surrounded by troubled flesh, made their appeal to me. I passed him the milk bottle; he licked the glassy lips and passed it back. We quoted the *Rubaiyat* without blushing, but held in secret what we learned from gazing into our own eyes. I clicked my tongue against my teeth; I licked my lips; I leaned my elbow into pine needles. I was studying to lean and fall easy into earth—a hard study for Americans and not yet learned by me.

"Jeez!" said Juicer. "*Of many a wise man I did frequent,* daDadada Dadada DadaDa, and so forth—*the same door that in I went.* Jeez!" He pawed the air, tremendous, physical, hapless, like a circus strong man dumped into water but unable to swim. "Jeez, you get that? Cynical, eh? Poetry!"

"And philosophy," Tom mournfully agreed. "What a man."

"Who, me?" Juicer demanded.

"No, O-mar Khay-yam," Tom said. No one would ever catch him admiring anyone alive. "Whom do you think you are? You think (snort) you could rhyme *frequent* (snort) with *in-I-went?* You think you know that much?" He snorted and left the question open on the laden night air to confound us.

A mediator, I changed the subject by a quick shift to the timeless topic of fathers and what men are sometimes known to do. While Tom and Juicer took consolation from a dairy deposit bottle, I said: "Before my mother made him stop, my father used to walk around the house in his bare feet eating onions."

"Raw?"—Tom.

"How many?"—Juicer.

"He liked them better barefoot," I said, "the onions. My mother told me."

We passed the bottle, drawing up our knees to consider the barefooted onions and the oddness of parents, our legs singed by the fire in which coals snapped and green pine needles sizzled. I felt, Juicer and Tom rushing to contradict each other, that animosities parallel to our friendship might be washed loose. This knowledge held me from a free drunk—Juicer and Tom uptilted the bottle. We examined ourselves through the solemn commentary of alcohol. Juicer, a saint, a flagellator, twisted from the hips with embarrassment and observed: "My belches used to taste like sulphur, but now they taste like marble, chocolate and vanilla."

"Mine taste just plain," Tom said.

"Plain what?"

"Plain belch. Belch-taste, that kind of a taste."

Juicer and I gazed at each other: Tom had no poetry in his soul. We expected very little from the Rubaiyat of Tom Moss.

"The moon's got into our brains," Juicer sighed.

"And made us belch," said Tom. "Don't fritter."

Juicer winked with one awful eye to remind me that some men grow obstinate and stupid with drunkenness. A disappointment if our friend Tom were one of these. I felt the responsibility of having introduced a poor relation to friends when Juicer pulled the left corner of his mouth into a dangerous dimple. "What's that, fritter?" he asked. (*Wink*.)

"Fritting."

"What do you mean? (*Wink!*) That's nothing at all, that—not even frittering."

"Fritting,"— Tom stubborn with idea. He shook his head in a way that would have disturbed the jowls if he had had sufficient flesh. Only the wax vibrated, hanging by golden threads in his ears. "Fritting," he said. He snorted while Juicer took an exasperated pull at the second bottle, one that Tom had brought. "So don't do it anyway," Tom mysteriously pronounced. "Bad for the frit."

A master-of-ceremonies, a moral chaperone, I called out with false jollity: "How do you spell that?" Juicer glared at Tom across the fire. He turned to me, and in rapid succession—*wink-wink-wink!* Tom pressed his thin mouth into a noose and sucked his teeth. "I saw you winking at Dan. I don't care. We should have a chaser for this stuff." I made small-talk, sacrificing my grand designs to peace in the family. Juicer didn't mean anything by winking, I assured Tom. His ideals clogged the tear ducts. Okay, said Tom, use Murine. From the gulley a mile away a train whistle guided the night toward a melody for fifteen-year-olds who had read Thomas Wolfe. We sighed and poked at the fire. Tom squinted into the coals, thinking Deep Thoughts and gathering umbrage about his thin shoulders. Juicer groaned, took what he considered to be a *swig* at the bottle, and pounded his thigh. I made signs in the dirt with a twig and modestly covered them over, these immortal drawings lost to the eyes of my fritting, winking friends.

Eva Masters, Lucille Lake, Rosalie Fallon, we thought, in reverse order.

"Oh," said Tom, the shrewd one.

"Ah!" cried Juicer, the psalmist.

"Hm," I brooded, philosopher, criminal lawyer, coach of Ohio State, secret lover, me.

"The train going somewheres, away, away," said Juicer.

"Carrying their destiny they know not where," I sighed.

"To Pittsburgh, I think," Tom said. "It's the Scranton-Pittsburgh mail train, B. & O."

Juicer wondered how to write the sound of a train whistle, and in capitals or not. "HOOOEEEE," I suggested.

"That's a lot of hooey"—Tom.

"Haven't you got a soul?"—Juicer.

"What's the matter, you crazy?"—me.

"No soul at all," Juicer complained.

"You *know* what we mean, Tom," I said.

Juicer, a sleek saint, a fat believer, turned and implored him: "Tom, no kidding now. This is *serious*."

"SEERiyoos," said Tom.

Juicer had a soul, of this no doubt, if a soul marks the limits of character. On one side he collapsed under a word and harbored the rancor of a cool glance for months; he went to sweat with wounded pride in his father's garage, breathing the comforting fumes of gasoline and imagining himself poisoned. He could be a bear, muzzle horrible with bristles, because no one had warned him about the porcupine of ill-will. But, drinking, he swelled with good-nature, loudly joking, oily, jostling us, lolling at his ease on his great flank, extravagant, contempuous and full of love, sometimes winking, frequently breeding schemes, suddenly weeping for Lucille, smacking his lips over my mother's heavy wet rye bread, declaiming the *Rubaiyat* or Thomas Wolfe with his actor's precocious bass, roaring with laughter for the exercise of shaking his belly with its hairy folds of purple flesh, dozing with snores on his back while he said: "I'm not asleep! I never sleep! I only need two minutes of sleep a day!"—at last finding the sleep of the just while, still sweating, he dreamed of abrupt female capitulations.

Juicer's social gesture of solemnity (a parody of it) had always been to stroke an imaginary mustache. Now, capable of growing one, he came to a decision. "When?" I asked.

"The next time I'm marooned on a desert island." Afraid of this commitment, which was one in fact and not pure vaunt, he dodged the question like a practicing idealist by a joke and by moral short cuts akin to his manipulation of his father's collars in their bluing solution.

"Bet you wouldn't do it if Lucille Lake didn't like it, it tickled," Tom observed cannily, this prodding his great exercise of the imagination, equaled only by his preoccupation with abrupt reminders of mortality. He could say with no provocation: "Choked on a poppy seed, had the mumps and died."

"Who?"

"Fellow I heard about. Read in the paper. Man had the hiccups, then died. Fellow perished, his rowboat sprung a leak. Don't know how there'll be room in the world for anything but cemeteries"—this was a genuine concern. Death bothered Tom, crowded him. "Fellow swallowed a nail, later died, almost thirty years. . . ."

On this warm autumn evening, pine-shadowed, illicit, we were engaged in construction of a great castle of drunkenness about a small gray shed of loneliness because Pattie Donahue, Lucille Lake, and Rosalie Fallon were absent and so was Eva Masters and we did not yet know what to do about it. Locked in the habits of children, we were being attacked by desires beyond the childish and did not know how to strike back. We had not yet learned to take what we wanted—nor yet to give it properly. Our imagination of love was either all rape or all mystic union, a heroic dragging off or a soft coming to. I slapped at a bug and my ear rang. The mosquitoes disputed the tender skin behind our haircuts; we scratched and made poetry. Juicer loved Negroes because I was Jewish; perversely sane, stout fellow Tom took for granted what appeared before his eyes. All three of us found the suburb incomplete, and searched an audience for the first stammering prayers of love and ambition. Around us whirled those strange suburban days in which Shirley Temple was the most passionate partisan of the Spanish loyalists, Neville Chamberlain believed in the infinite perfectability of Adolf Hitler, and the nationl debt seemed high; in the suburbs of Cleveland, the suburbs of adult life, the suburbs of a terrible war, we felt obscurely diddled by experience and struck back with deep thoughts. "Life," even Tom sighed. Our mood had touched him with its humid breath.

Juicer said: "Ah!"

I quoted the poem about fog and catfeet (it comes on with little), learned in the 9-A and put in storage for occasions of communion.

"O the River," said Juicer. "Time, O."

"I know what you mean-o," I assured him. "I feel the same way myself."

Juicer's stoop and lurch expressed clumsy thoughts but ardent ones; he loved what he loved, with appetite, and wrestled to understand the rest, things that could neither be eaten nor drunk. Not really dreading it, he talked precociously about Evil as he might have spoken of ptomaine; it did not exist for him. His strict parents had punished him enough so that his conscience remained free: this is a great gift. But, with an abstract play of intelligence, like a pro-

fessional chef at the Cordon Bleu school, he baked the
notion of evil in his head. "I'm going to be a Catholic, I
think," he had said one week. "They understand evil, the
devil, all that stuff. Look at Dante. Look at Tchaikowsky."

"Tchaikowsky wasn't a Catholic, he was a Russian."

Acceding to my superior information, he had decided
against the Church. The next day, constantly fleeing himself, he decided to be a novelist like Thomas Wolfe. "I
can eat as much as he did. Once I ate a dozen eggs,
scrambled with milk." He roared and clapped his flanks
with appreciation of this feat. "My mother never knew
where they all went."

"Thomas Wolfe would tell his mother," I objected. "She
would read it next day in his journal."

We both secretly knew that we could write as well as
this great author (this famous man), but expressed a
sacrilege justified only in our dreams by displaying our
ability to eat. (By lying: a storyteller is a furious liar.)

"I ate four steaks, not minute ones," I said.

"Cube steaks?"

"I said steaks, real steaks."

"I ate a whole apple pie."

"Crust or just the innards, the apples?"

"Crust and everything, and a slice of Velveeta cheese
too."

"I ate four baked potatoes."

"Once I had dinner and then I forgot all about it and
had another. Chicken pot pie."

Now I paused to think. Tom watched us with the open
disgust of the pedestrian for motorists murderously racing.
"I drank a bottle of milk of magnesia," he said. His skeleton clanked with tight jealous giggles. "You guys really
talk a big meal. . . ." He did not understand that the
stretching of morals (our stomachs at fifteen) prepared us
for the heroic life, our two heroic lives, counting Juicer's.

Our careers so far had been overfull of banal hope and too empty of years, but remembering mirror views with the bathroom light tastefully behind us, we bided our time in hunger and admiration.

Our foreheads grew hot against the radiance of our fire. Silent over snapping coals while Tom tended the woodpile, we then dreamed of tragic death, cut short in our primes, Juicer and me, respectively, with newspaper articles in black borders and our parents sorry for all their injustices to us as they peered despondently into our coffins.

"O the River," sighed Juicer the Genius, "O Time."

"You'll choke on it yet," Tom muttered. "You'll die of poetry, that kind. It doesn't even rhyme."

It became certain this evening that Juicer would knock off Tom's block or its equivalent—pretty soon, before Tom's block had a chance to fall off of its own free will.

I whispered to Tom, "You *know* what he means"—the insistent moral pressure of the artist who works with allusion and obliquity to produce delicate effects of discovery, inviting his audience to join in the party which makes an artifact, just as the colonists joined in the wedding celebration by putting up a log cabin for the happy couple. It was a plea, a social requirement, and an invitation: "You understand him, don't you?"

"No," said Tom.

Tom Moss was going to catch it from Juicer. We all knew that.

7. *Men of Indecision*

STARLIGHT, PINE NEEDLES, LEGS stretched out, campfire, cigarettes, late hour, no apologies to parents or watches, Rocky River Reservation. Terrible imaginary lust, terrible gossiping metaphysics, terrible actual responsibilities to ourselves. We had each drained off into milk bottles a sample of alcohol from our parents' closets in order to ease the way toward immortal truth and beauty. We took it straight in burning gulps, bourbon and Scotch and vermouth and various subordinate blends all impulsively married together.

It began to thunder, and there were bluish white flashes in the sky; the trees moved sullenly; we felt unsafe, childish; but heat, not rain. We had advantages. Summer, Indian summer, and strong digestion, stoic Indian enzymes, were on our side. We had hope. We had time. We had a sloping bottle left. So: "What's a man?" Juicer wailed. "I want to know." Although we had almost emptied the second bottle, we still had not discovered what it is to be a man and the Great Books had not yet come to tell us.

"Let's have a seminar, like in college," Tom suggested. Juicer looked at him with the expression of a deep thinker who has had the toilet door pushed in on him. Tom's instinct to try us had led him too far, even by his own sense

86

of such things, so that now he attempted reconciliation in his dry skinny voice: "A dis-cus-sion," he said with a sincerity that seemed to startle him; he hiccuped. "I am too serious."

I thought. I figured and worried. I wanted to make a joke, which would mean a pun. I wanted to answer the question, which meant my future. I said gloomily at last, "Men drink and make love."

"My father belongs to the Temperance Union," said Tom.

"I'm an only son," Juicer said.

"Course he still takes a nip once in a while," Tom said, waiting for Juicer.

"It's still true. Tell you what—" But I told them nothing. "You know what I mean. . . ." The poor little truth we hold in common: We were not men.

"Love," Juicer sighed.

"Love," said Tom.

"We all drink and are willing," I concluded, "but that's the problem. It takes two."

"Aye, there's the rub," Tom classically alluded.

"It has to do with Lucille Lake," Juicer said.

"It con-cerns Rosalie Fallon," deliberated Tom.

"It's a question of girls," I generalized, thinking: Patricia Donahue or Lucille Lake? I thought: Eva.

We brooded, we sipped, we ruminated; that is, in the primitive sense of the word, we chewed our cud.

I asked at last: "What's a woman?"—this meaning, How can we make Rosalie Fallon, Lucille Lake, and Pattie Donahue love us passionately—desperately—wildly—maybe even neck with us? (With me. Eva.)

"We haven't even decided what a man is, our seminar, a fine seminar this is turning out to be," Tom complained.

"First," Juicer shouted, "what's a woman? Tell me that!"

Tom subsided, muttering, "What's a woman?"

"What's the matter, you crazy?"—this my father's objection, spoken in the friendly inquisitive tone which I have taken from him. Behold the complication, belligerent words to the most ingratiating music, spoken by the man who wants his independence and also wants to be *liked*.

"We'll have to change all that," Juicer suggested.

"What?" asked Tom.

"The WORLD."

"Oh, *that*." Tom's lips said *Pouf, only that;* he blew air into piny air.

"Yeah, reform," I said.

Tom glared at us out of his pink carroty face, judging and bored, a flicker of doubt in the sad fanatic eyes, red-rimmed from lack of belief or Vitamin A, grieving for what they would miss of love. He nodded and prodded at the fire and took the bottle without waiting for us. The embers flared; he huffed and put the cork back. He remembered (I think) being led to the toilet, squeezing the light from his eyes, full of sleep in his mouth and grudge against his parents. Milk and this was his waking life, dream and this his sleeping. How can we ever overcome the hungers our parents held us to, though we were eventually fed? Our love for the food is another thing from the despair and mistrust of repeated hungers. "Reform," he said, "cure cancer with Feenamint. I don't believe in it."

"I—don't—like—cynics," Juicer said ominously. His thick spleeny face brooded over Tom, the face of a poet with cheeks, chin, and nose bulging, surrounded by bad shaving and spoiled dreams. "You're a cynic."

"Maybe he's right," I suggested with a fine diplomatic idiocy, listening to nothing but the war in their blood, sunk to the role of the statesman who serves merely to reduce the pleasure of the inevitable battle.

"What's he got to be so right about?"

"Right?" Tom asked.

"So goddamn right."

"What?"

"Goddamned!" cried Juicer.

Swear words such as "toothpicks! . . . shyster! . . . am-scray! . . . macaroni! . . ." had already given way to approximate scatologies. "Bushwah!" Tom yelled.

"Drink!" Juicer commanded.

"Drink!" we agreed.

We drank and then discussed questions. We listened within ourselves for the jargon of courage, mystery, love, and evil, and heard the schoolboy slang of animus and puppy mewling. Abracadabrists, submissive to poetry, we thought of women as queens. Like royal persons they had to make the first gestures toward us.

Without quite deciding what a man is, in great haste to know everything, we pronounced our sympathetic magic about women.

"Lucille is musical," Juicer said.

"Pattie is beautiful," I said.

"Lucille is intelligent," Juicer said.

"Pattie is lovely," I said.

"Lucille is proud and deep."

"Pattie is the girl I've always liked. Naturally I also know Eva Masters."

Jealous and lonely, Tom said: "Me, I can have Rosalie Fallon any time I say boo."

"Then why don't you say boo then, you?" I inquired.

"Who *wants* Rosalie Fallon? Just try saying boo to Lucille Lake."

Sneered Tom: "Maybe I will. Remember when I went to Clayton's birthday party with her? Course"—a justice lover—"that was five years ago and I never went anyplace with her since. . . ."

"I remember now. I mean I forgot," Juicer said.

"The same thing," said Tom.

"What do you mean, did you kiss her?" Juicer suddenly demanded.

"What's the matter, you crazy?" I said to the night and the fire. "Tom was ten years old then, it was Clayton's tenth birthday. We played pin-the-tail and Lewis Snyder threw up from too much cake."

"I didn't live in the neighborhood," Juicer morosely recalled. "That was in another time, and besides, the wench was prepubescent."

"It was from too much pop, that's why Lewis Snyder threw up all over Rosalie," Tom corrected me.

"I lived on the East Side. In an apartment house with a self-service elevator. Clayton never even thought of inviting me." Mourning this snub, Juicer drank, three slivers of beard slipping on his Adam's apple like minnows in the firelight. He signaled to us to share the bottle. We drank, anesthetized to the harsh metal taste by recollections of birthday parties past and by sympathy for Juicer's hopeless love. Others knew Lucille before him. We were drunk. We were elevated amid the rustlings and chirpings of the park. While our insides smoldered and nature showed its powers in the grass and nighttime trees, Juicer studied Tom with a diver's deliberation from ten thousand leagues below the sun. Subtle as a blow from his hairy hands, he turned and asked: "Are you in love with Lucille Lake?"

"Nope," said Tom.

"I knew it," Juicer bellowed, his worst suspicions confirmed. "You're in love with Lucille."

"Nope," said Tom with a calm that argued innocence to me, guilt to Juicer.

"You want to take her away from me!" he cried.

"I do not," Tom patiently explained. "I'm passionately involved with Rosalie Fallon, in fact I worship the very ground she walks on."

"Who?" Juicer panted.

"Me."

"What?"

"Whose ground she walks on?" I interpreted.

"I mean Rosalie Fallon's very ground she walks on," Tom said, "that's what I worship. Her sweet smile, her tender glance, you know what I mean. Fellows, she's my ideal of feminine attractiveness."

"Hah!" Juicer roared, unable to imagine anyone not in love with Lucille Lake, "you lie!" Drunk as he was, he yet managed to reply to Tom's dignity and eloquence with a fine literary exclamation. "You lie," he wailed, "and then you add insult to injuriousness." Squint-eyed, he blinked up and down the blanket spread before the fire. When I looked at his pupils I realized that our fathers' whisky had displaced most of the blood in his head. He reached for an unsheathed boy-scout knife, missed it with his first lunge, then successfully fumbled toward it. Tom yawned and crawled to his feet. Juicer followed with the knife. "You're trying to take Lucille away from me," he said.

"I am not," Tom argued as he ran away. He stopped behind a tree. "If you hurt me with the knife you'll be sorry," he said, smothering another yawn. "My mother will call your mother up on the telephone."

"Don't kill him with the knife," I said, a peacemaker. "Come and sit down by the fire, it's getting chilly."

"I'm going to *get* you, see?" Juicer cried. He regarded the knife in his hand with surprise. Perhaps we had suggested the idea. "I'll teach you to take Lucille Lake in vain. Arrh," he growled, shivering slightly.

I respected such passion. All passion is dignified because it means that the gods have possessed us, we know not what we do, and in the movies they played the loudest music at these moments. Juicer and I, if not Tom, could be as lonely, desperate, and wild as any actor we knew personally. I listened for a chorus of six hundred massed harps

stirring in the reservation. I heard crickets; I heard reluctant night birds raiding the icebox, nibbling crickets at
snacktime. I moved the lunch baskets out of danger from
the fire and stood up. "Don't kill Tom with the knife," I
repeated, "it's dangerous. He didn't finish the eleventh
grade yet. That knife is too sharp, you could hurt yourself,
get a thrombosis."

Juicer swayed but refuted me with an immense swooping and cutting of the forest night: "What does that I wonder have to do with it? Honor is at stake, my future. Can't
you see I love her? I've always loved Lucille ever since last
summer."

The pertinence of joining such logic with such passion
sapped my mediating energies. I was tipsy and all for
letting fate have its grand way. "Don't," I said, *distrait,*
"just don't. Why don't you sing *A Night on Bald Mountain*
by Mussorgsky instead? Think of his family, think of how
he's been our friend so long"—myself dismayed by the
weakness of my argument. "In the orchestral version by
Leopold Stokowsky, the great conductor. . . ." Lit by fire,
incited by the vast vague of the nighttime park, rendered
single-minded by our fathers' liquor, something like this
duel seemed inevitable. The accusation that Tom loved
Lucille made him a criminal, unfaithful to friendship with
Juicer, although the complex strategies of our association
rendered it acceptable that all the world knew I adored
Lucille except on the days when I adored Pattie. The world
had not yet fully grasped the truth about Eve and me.
Dizzy from a Chesterfield, I followed as Juicer began his
careen after Tom. "Why fight?" I asked. "What's the use?"
—a reasoner! a feeble wheedler! a stale philosopher! "Who
knows," I mediated as we crunched over the twig-fallen,
leaf-strewn trail in angry Indian file, "if maybe Lucille
doesn't love Lewis Snyder? He sure thinks he's a sheik, that
Snyder."

Tom plunged into the dark, still uncontrollably yawning; Juicer lumbered after him; I pursued dutifully with switches of branches swiping me across the face. Juicer invented groans of rage, jealousy, and the lust for revenge. "Arrh," he said. He huffed. I followed. The woods thickened; we could barely see as we crashed through the brush. "I'm going to get you," Juicer called ahead to Tom, gargling passionately.

"I'm getting tired," Tom complained. He exaggerated his gasping. "My mother got me up before seven this morning. I had to go to the corner. Look here, Juicer, I'm your friend, I wouldn't—"

"Arrh," said Juicer, lumbering ahead.

At that moment there was a cry, a slipping, a rustling, and Tom abruptly vanished in the darkness. He was gone. Juicer stopped as I collided with his panting bulk. "See how I scared him?" he asked me with some perplexity.

"Careful that knife," I said. "Where's Tom?"

"He must have fainted. I don't know where he went."

"He was here just a second ago."

A stir and whimper which came from almost directly below informed us of Tom's domicile at this juncture in history midway between the NRA and Pearl Harbor. He had fallen into a pit dug across the path and he refused to climb out. "Are you all right?" Juicer shouted solicitously into the darkness.

"I think I broke my arm or my head," Tom returned with a quaver. *"Now* do you believe me when I say I wouldn't steal the woman you fellows love?"

"I didn't say you would, Tom," I said.

"Why don't you climb out of there?" Juicer asked.

"It's nice and soft down here. I'm tired of all this running and arguing anyway, that's all. You can go back to the nice warm fire, you guys. Just leave me here. I don't care. I'll be all right. Tell my mother I got lost in the forest.

Don't worry about me, don't even give me a thought. You
can eat my breakfast, the eggs, the bacon, and the marmalade sandwich. Why don't you just go back and discuss
Thomas Wolfe or Lucille Lake or something?"

There was no doubt about it. Tom was crying.

Juicer turned to me in the darkness, his great head in-
credulously a-shake. "Do you think maybe I hurt his feelings?" he asked me.

"Naw," I said. I didn't want two weepers on my hands.
"We better persuade him to come back to the fire. It's
probably damp in that hole. One two, let's persuade together."

We crouched by the pit and called out our arguments,
our assurances of undying friendship, our exhortations to
rise and shine. Juicer's tears plunked down but we heard
no echo in the dense brush. He put away his knife before
he began to cry. "Please, Tom, please, old pal. . . ." Juicer
and I were bawling and thinking of how this dramatic
moment could best be expressed in our journals. Finally
we turned from immortal prose to practical maneuvers and
extended our arms to rescue him. Tom stood up and
walked out of the pit. What we had thought of, in the darkness and the drama, as a bottomless pit, at least for the
purposes of literature, had been a shallow trench in which
Tom had rested at his ease, prudently muffling his voice
with his hands to encourage our will to see him in mortal
danger and dire distress.

"Okay," he said, "let's go back to the fire. You want
me to have my sinus attack again?" We started back along
the trail. "Don't forget the knife," he reminded Juicer, who
groped on the ground where he had dropped it.

We were all sobered by this experience, purged of pity
and terror and slightly bled by burrs. Tom bore Juicer no
grudge, proud and flattered by the attention—could Paris
resent being made the subject of an attack by Homer, a

poem by Menelaus? Tom and Juicer were depleted by emotion, however, and submissive to me. Leading them back, I felt that elevated joy which follows a gratuitous good deed, that kindliness toward the object as the most imposing witness of one's virtue. These two witnesses stumbled along, breathing noisily, half-asleep, their swollen eyes slipped shut in the expression of cunning that a child assumes after weeping. In the firelight Tom examined and squeezed his scratches from which a pale liquid oozed. "Capillaries," he said, remembering his general science.

"If you rub dirt in them they'll leave scars," Juicer suggested. "That's what they all do." It was the stylish thing after duels, we had read.

"You want me to get (yawn) infection?" Tom demanded. "I don't suppose (yawn) you brought along any hydrogen peroxide. I got a slight trauma, I think . . . angina . . . (yawn)."

They sat blinking and cross-legged at the fire while I arranged the blankets. Exhausted, obedient, they lay down and I tucked them each in. "Are you relaxed?" Juicer asked.

"Am I relaxed?" I replied.

"Are you?" he asked Tom.

Tom murmured sleepily, "I'm so relaxed my teeth are falling out."

"Not me," Juicer said. "Another night far from Lucille Lake." He began to whimper again. "Goat cries," he sobbed. "These aren't even goat cries like in Thomas Wolfe when he was in love. I'm just frittering like a baby."

Wrapped in my own blanket, I tried to comfort him: "They're just like in Thomas Wolfe."

"No they're not, they're *not*."

"Yes they are, Juicer, just like. Of course"—pedantically—"more like Eugene Gant than George What's-his-name."

"Webber," said Juicer, subsiding into sleep.

"Goo (yawn) night," from Tom. They snored on their backs. I sat up to make certain once more that we would not burn our feet in the fire. Since we had feet of clay, perhaps they would merely have baked. A deer mouse shook its horny head and scampered off into the void.

"Lucille," I murmured into the dying embers, feeling old, world-weary, and dissolute amid the alcoholic breath of my friends and the symbolic black of the night. The poison ivy I would soon notice signified the power of evil in the world; calamine lotion stood for man's helpless reply to the rending fates; tragedy imposed itself while I lay awake by a fire, scratching and thinking, at one with the universe, seeking remedies and rhymes. The extinguished coals also provided material for symbolism. In fact, everything symbolized; only girls had the prosaic but tormenting obstinacy to mean themselves so specifically. I stared into the woods after the mouse, sniffed at the damp earth, dozed, murmured: "Lucille, Lucille." Perhaps I also tried Pattie, Pattie, Pattie.

But I knew the truth beyond words. When the weather broke, Eva would be waiting.

8.   *The literary lover's burden*

We walked a promenade in
the first snow, Eva Masters and I. We had said we would.
We had exchanged allusions to this effect. It was not exactly snow—a ropy November drizzle—but to us it seemed
the very original crystal flakes invented on the Seventh
Day by God. I mean the snow in well-known paintings,
novels, and the tone poem by Sibelius. A mediocre Cleveland snowfall brings beauties beyond anything known by
the musical towers of wintertime Manhattan or the gleaming tiled roofs of Paris. Why? Once I walked with Eva
Masters, our hands touched. Our elbows touched. Our
souls peeped forth in their leatherette bindings like the
children set out in suburban yards with straps to keep them
from wandering into the traffic. Gloveless, her fingers
gripped mine. My blood quickened toward the tender skin
of poetic meditation (her brother's) and of cold cream by
Pond's (her mother's). I did not dare shiver for fear she
might think me subject to vulgar chill. Chapped knuckles
never entered our reveries.

"Eva?" I asked.

"Daniel Berman," she answered me.

Those snowflakes, they were bits of lace showered upon
us that evening in our City of Homes. It was rice, those

97

snowflakes, polished seeds of the future which melted as
they touched our touching arms and puddled as they
slipped to our paddling feet above the water mains, the gas
mains, and the unspeakable sewers of a prosperous suburb:
lace from the gown in which Mrs. Mayerling would have
been married, if she had been married, if she hadn't signed
a suicide pact, if that was her name. The streetcar on the
boulevard intoned the march from *Lohengrin* against
gravel and rails. We breathed the special quick sad breath
of silent lovers; our eyes streamed in the cold. Woosh
went the clouds across the moon: they wooshed and we
wished.

"What?" I asked.

"I wish," she said, "I wish that this night would never
end."

Her eyes narrowed from watchful ignorance toward the
cunning slits of the expectation of the body. In the next
moment Miss Eva Masters was capable of a renewed widening of the eyes in the unfolding of desire and the body's
knowledge, that humid suburban flesh melting like fine
soap in the bath of its native oils. In the next moment,
myrrh and frankincense, wet fatness and wet sleekness:
her nose ran with rut.

In the next moment we discussed high school social history. Do you like Miss Farrell?—No, but I like Miss Sar-
ling.—Is she the new French teacher? —"Yes, still young,
she just got her certificate, and she'd really be quite attractive if she didn't have such, oh you know, piano legs. . . ."
She touched the tiny up-pointed tip of her nose with a
handkerchief bearing her father's monogram.

"The snow is good, the way it makes things new, very
good," I said, meaning to praise nature.

"I love the snow. Oh Daniel Berman how I love the
snow. Do you remember how it was when a child you
woke up in the morning, and it snowed last night, and you

looked out your window all fresh and dewy-eyed from
sleep, pure I mean, innocent I mean, and—?"

That this night would never end. . . . Both my end and
her night wished this.

"I wish," she said, "that a night like this could go on
and on."

We walked on and on, our eyes submerged in the approval of wet snow. What about Mr. Oliver, Chemistry and
Biology? (I asked.) —Handsome, very. —Yes, that's what
the girls think, but he's got a broom up his back. Juicer
Montague says he saw him put it there. —At least he's not
round-shouldered like some men I could name. I don't
mean you, Daniel, you're just distingay. I'd rather just not
talk about it, those round-shouldered sheiks, oh dear. (A
stiff stare, the dramatic glaze and parted lips of a girl admiring her sorrow in the mirror.)

"What's the matter, Eva?"

"Nothing. I do not choose to speak of it any furthermore."

"Which?"

"The round-shoulders. I believe you know of whom I
am speaking of. I do not wish to mention his name, the
round-shoulders. I choose the path of silence."

I could not understand the bitterness of these remarks.
That is, I understood them too well; my spleen and my
liver turned over to make room for the gland of jealousy.
I staggered faintly, I morally lurched. Heartburn fumed
within me; my knees grew heavy; translation of these
symptoms into French helped a little: *Ah! Misère!* I took
a bilingual gulp of air and breathed aloud, "Ah-h." Jealousy coated my tongue with passions no milk of magnesia
in the little easy-to-take pills could ever scrub away.

She had been in love before. She came to me impure.
Black Jack Mamble, the round-shouldered and leering
vice-president of the Student Council, had ridden in the

night to swipe her virtue. Now I remembered the story of
Ferdinand Klabber's party, when someone had unscrewed
the fuses. Girls lay in hellish abandon over boys' laps.
Hands found flesh to pluck, lip to lip. In the squealing
dark Jack Mamble had copped a feel. Wench! *Fille legère!*
Low type! Double-crossing skirt!—I suffered in all my
dialects. (Inconstant creature of ruse and female of the
species!) My outrage skidded past last week's avidity for
Lucille Lake and/or Pattie Donahue. I, I a man, was
corrupt and fallen in principle. We expect it; we blame it
on Adam, Original Sin, and Superior Opportunity. Is it
not written that we shall bring forth our rhymes in pain?
But, despite the duty to be pure, Eva had perhaps already
been taught the first hard lesson of love, where to put the
nose while kissing. I studied her face in the lamplight as
the ropy snow slithered beside us. Had he touched her
above or beneath her cashmere, the politician, the snake?
Had he stroked her hair? Then no amount of washing in
Lux could cleanse this stain, false steady date! "What do
you mean, round-shouldered?" I inquired. "Not Chuck
Hastings, I suppose?"

"Oh," she breathed, "let us nevermore stir up the embers of the past."

"Embers?"

"The dead embers," she smiled wanly, "the whetted
ashes. Anyway, *Chuck,* he's got cunning shoulders."

I assented in an impetuous moment of charity and devotion. *Caritas:* I would knock Jack Mamble's block off
if she said the word. The word: Knock-his-block-off. But—
and women know this—a new source of love spilled from
her confession and repentance. I could forgive her. After
all, many fallen women are later stamped okay in literature. Why should I throw stones? Another had thrown his
first.

"Look at the moon," I said, wondering if this excerpt

from dialogue could bear the weight of my feeling. To pep
it up I added casually, "The moon is a great silver gong
against which night beats itself." I picked up a rock and
lobbed it toward the moon. Falling short, it returned to the
wet asphalt with a click and a skid.

"Oh!"—a movement either the flutter of passion for
having so inspired me or the impulse to reach in her pocket
for a pencil. "Did you just make that up compose it yourself, Dan?"

"About the moon?"

"Yes, the moon, the silver gong, the night?"

I plucked the lint like petals from my pants pockets. In
the majesty of my devotion I confessed. "No, Juicer Montague made it up. I mean he read it in Thomas Wolfe.
He's my best friend, Juicer Montague. . . ."

"I heard he drinks whisky, they smell it on his breath. I
would like to know your friends, Dan. He's going to have
a beer belly if he doesn't watch out."

"Or maybe he read that one in the Ben Hecht. For sure
it wasn't the *Ruby-Yat*."

"You express it so well, too. You mean of Omar Khayyam, don't you? Who's Ben Hecht?"

"Oh, he's just a great poet we discovered one Saturday
afternoon when we were taking a walk in some part of the
great, teeming, mysterious city or other. No one ever heard
of him, but he's really great. He's really a quaint and
curious volume of forgotten lore. The moon is a great
silver gong against which, see?"

"Beautiful. Really lovely," she murmured. "A nice
thought. I liked the one you had in your editorial last week
too, about how an active student body is like the citizens
of a great nation, and—"

That this night would never end, I more or less thought.

"The way you say things it's wonderful, so moving, so
posilutely poyn-yunt, if you know what I mean," she con-

fided. "It must be very helpful for a writer and editor to have profound thoughts like that all the time. I'd like to sit in your head awhile. . . . I'm glad you're not laughing at me, Daniel, because I really mean it. . . . I mean just sit and look. I mean read. I only have profound thoughts once in a while, and then I have to write them down quick to save them for my poems, so what good do they do me?"

"That's all right," I reasoned sympathetically, "as long as your poetry is really great."

We walked down through the Lakewood Country Club toward the deserted winter beach. "My father is a member of the Club," said Miss Eva Masters. "I can get you in a member's guest privilege, it applies also to daughters too according to the Constitution of the Lakewood River Country Club and the Bill of Rights as previously amended. I would really love it."

Impressed by this offer, I nevertheless felt a certain bitterness that she was already neglecting her ambition to sit in my head and watch me crank out profound thoughts like Vienna sausage between my ears. Now she would rather sit in the beach house, sipping Coke. These creatures in dirndl skirts and pink angora sweaters might enjoy Immortal Truth for a short while, but then they would want something real, like a formal dance and an orchid. Was Eva the transmigrated soul of various lady poets or was she merely herself? Did the true flame burn in her or did she only smoke? The country club girls were well-known for their smoking.

"Look the beach," I said. "The waves, time, infinity, the silver sand in the moonlight. Eternity. It's late, I bet you. The moonlight is like a. The moonlight is like a—"

She eyed me critically, her pupils two astronomical points of doubt, black with meteorology. "The moon is behind the clouds," she forecasted, "and so is the moonlight."

"Yes, but—oh yes, but—" She had definitively withdrawn from her seat in my head. "Yes but," I said.

"Oh I know what you mean, Dan, I was just saying. I know what you mean. You mean the stones so sad and cold, the foam on the waves, the beating beating always beating."

"That's right," I said. A difficulty in such intimacy—she took the anthologized words right out of my mouth. Edna St. Barrett Poe never swiped a line from the well-known author of "Ulalume," or The Lost Lenore Unbounded. "Have you ever read the works of Thomas Wolfe?" I asked.

"The night like a black blanket over all," she said. "The lonely rocks covered with somber black water and the angry teeth of foam. Listen the gulls, how somber they are. They swoop and sadly mourn—"

"The *Rubaiyat?*" I inquired. "T. S. Eliot the modern poet? Edna St. Vincent Millay?"

"The angry teeth of foam, you mean?"

"Yes, I was just wondering, that's all."

"That part, the angry part, or the other part, the part about the gulls how somber?"

"The angry part. That was a good part."

"Oh, just that part. . . . Made it up myself, composed it one evening at dusk when the lights were hanging low. Looks as if they're biting, see—they chew on the rocks— they nibble—"

"Oh I see it. I saw it," I assured her, not to be outdone in textual criticism. "Just like you said, nibbling. That's a really great picture-word, Eva. Really somber."

She moved closer to me by accident and stayed there by design. Eva had compostulated a heap of improbagullities and I, oh I, Dan Bertrand, would reap the lovewind, panting. Intimacy breeds confession; confession breeds literary principles. Her breath frosted my glasses. She said: "I love adjectives, Dan." We walked on in silence for a moment after this avowal of simple faith. "Look the beach," she murmured at last. "The awful waves, the silver sand in the moonlight."

"The poor fish," I said. "Is that how you pronounce somber—sombruh?"

"French," she snapped. "Flowbert, Racing, Corneal, my brother James read them all.

Jealous of her brother the college man, I looked far-off, my home-tested method of producing a far-off look in the eyes. We moved along the beach and she lay on my arm (I adored her) with the rich weight of winter underwear when I carried it down from the attic. She smelled of her mother's cologne and the damp night, not moth balls and my mother's belligerent fly-toxing. "Tell me about your parents," I said, "I want to know."

"Will you tell me about yours?"

"Yes."

"Well," she began, "my father hates Roosevelt."

"He must be a reactionary. My father—well, *he* says about Roosevelt—"

"My father just *hates* him, period. I think he's a reactionary all right."

"Personally, Eva, I think his real name—Roosevelt's I mean—is just Franklin Delano Roosevelt. I really believe that."

"Oh so do I, Dan. That's immaterial, I always say. You could change your name to something nice—oh, like Daniel Bertrand—and you'd still be *you*. Immaterial."

"Thank you, Eva."

"Oh you're *worthy*, Dan. Do you have a middle initial? No? That's perfectly all right."

Liberalism reigned, Berman persisted, Eva sighed. We touched hands in silence. Hands spoke as suburban politics could not; Roosevelt kept his name (far from our suburb the thousand-year-Reich was already bringing eternal peace to millions); there was snow and secrecy and desire which equals hope. True love troubled itself forward in the night of Lakewood, yielding nothing to the streetcar in clumsy pell-mell clattering. On that beach in Lakewood, lacking even a middle initial to clothe my nakedness, I said finally, "Yes, our parents, who are they, what are they like, why. Their customs and habits. We are our parents' children." She struggled to rise to the sonority of my oratory on the beach. A Demosthenes with pebbles under the tongues of his shoes, jealous of Jack Mamble, Eva's brother James, and the pronunciation of sombruh, I roared into the wind off Lake Erie: "I must know, Eva, as my quest is knowledge."

She deliberated. My declaration plashed warmly in her plump poetic little heart and sent ripples of luminous study scooting across her brow. "Yes!" steamed her breath. What responded to my challenge sang fine and clear in that stormy soirée by the lake which will remain in the heart of man as long as the heart of man remains in me. (*Nota bene:* At best we all ripen, grow old, wither, and die.) Said Miss Eva Masters in a voice terrible with self-knowledge and the tragedy of the race: "My father, born in a small frame house with running water however in Indianapolis, Indiana, in 1886, is a Wharton School of Business and Commerce graduate. He majored in Personal Management and so learned how to deal with people in this four-year course concluding in the Bachelor of Business degree, in a firm but friendly fashion, always be cheerful, see the other fellow's point of view, and fair, and put square dealing above profits always. It pays in the end."

"My father knows the value of a dollar too," I said.

"He has since worked for many firms, and always he departed with the highest recommendation and best wishes for the future, having given full satisfaction and no hard feelings." She paused and then cried out: "I shall speak to you of my father! Sometimes he goes back to Indianapolis to look at the little house in which he was born and where his mother passed away, it still stands, when he has a fight with my mother. She doesn't understand him at all, he's very sensitive."

"My father's sensitive too, even though he never went to Wharton. He never even went to Baldwin-Wallace or Ohio State and he's not reactionary."

Eva's face darkly turned to me as I perceived a wet droplet, a mist-carried child of sorrow, glistening as of tears on her cheek. I would revolve toward her in my turn when our inner weather granted me a dispensation for deep feelings. She suffered pain and sorrow, Eva did; she was mortal albeit corny and sometimes ricky-tick.

"My mother on the other hand," she continued, "only attended one year at Oberlin, majoring in music and dramatics. A lot of good it did her. She has revolting taste in music, not sublime at all, all she likes is scales. That's what she wants me to play all the time, scales scales scales, good for the discipline—"

"They think discipline is a muscle, parents—"

"Czerny and scales," she insisted, "when I can play a theme from Tchaikowsky's *Fifth* after I heard it only once, the lovers' theme, you know it I'm sure, with two hands—"

"Don't you mean the Romeo and Juliet tone poem in I forget the key?" (The advantages of thus casually introducing my insight into the necessity of key overweighed the paltry handicap of not recalling which one.)

"No, the *Fifth*. Both hands. The symphony not the overture. You're thinking of *Finlandia*. The one that goes—" And her round thirsty little mouth, lipsticked, chapped, and ardent, opened with song on the beach as we strolled, the waves striking their lucid bass against the breakwater, her soprano nudging the cartilage of my ear. Without interrupting her song, I led her around the whitening belly of a fish, the fish gawky with death, me with desire. I wondered if I dared to kiss her at last. It would be a shame (I minced with chivalry and scuffled with stones) to waste such background music. We halted. I listened to the winds from Canada and my heart. She hummed low, regarded me under brooding lids, shivered in her teddy-bear fur coat.

I held her shoulders. I looked deep into her eyes. I took aim. I felt the blood pulsing in my pulses. Boomalay, boomalay, boomalay, boom—no, that was Vachel Lindsay. I was a Congo of passion, a jungle of literary precedent. What would Eugene Gant or George Webber do in such a case? Surrender to the blind forces of the desire to neck? Look up the remedy in *My First Two Thousand Years?* Eclectic, fancy, the angry hairs of my neck prickling all the same, I loved in furious intervals, like an anthology. At last, having fumbled in a false past, I gripped her to me, muttering, "Now my father and mother. Now you take my mother and father, for instance, they're altogether different. My father he's self-educated, a self-made man. He got what he got without a college diploma, just plain hard work and application. Everyone says he got what it takes—I say it takes what he got, a little saying I made up. Oh, I don't mean he's an ignoramus, he read everything. Not Thomas Wolfe of course, he's too old from another generation, but Shakespeare, Tolstoy, people like that, Sholem Aleichem—"

"Shawn O'who?"

"Aleichem. The Russian Mark Twain."—Shalom! peace! "Now my mother she doesn't read much. She cooks, takes care of the house, things like that. I guess you know my father has a store? She helps out in the store Saturdays. He lets her drive the Peerless. It's an old model car but a good one, even more modern than the latest models, really lovely, an eye-knocker, looks like a bug, the only thing is the noise—we want a Pontiac if business is good next year. Everyone says the Pontiac is a cheap machine, but I say it's the best in the low-priced field. Now my mother, she waits on trade. That's what you call it in retail business.

Sholem Aleichem is very well-known among the people who like him," I concluded abstractly, my stomach aching after this ersatz of lies, evasions, implied apologies, and fears.

"Do *you*," delicately inquired Miss Eva Masters as we did our little dance on the beach of her father's country club, "ever work in the store? Wait on trade?"

"Sholem Aleichem," I said, and imagine St. George turning the sword in his hand, figuring out which end is which—"is the Mark Twain of the American citizens of the Mosaic persuasion"—O tempest toss'd!—"I mean Mark Twain among the Hebrew people, I mean the Yiddish Mark Twain. He's very good if you get to know him, if you like that sort of thing."

Vas sagt der Teufel?

She lippily breathed fumes of tact. It was her turn. "Dan," she said, "my father always brought me up to forgive my neighbor's trespassing as I would want him to forgive mine when I walk through his yard on the way to school, and that's the credo we live by even though I have a fight with my mother every Saturday morning, and anyway I'm a freethinker now, no more Christian Science for me, I didn't go to Sunday school since Daddy sold the other car. He doesn't go either. The big Oldsmobile."

She forgave me my striving. She loved me for what I wasn't as much as for what I was.

"Some people say," I said, *"some* people think—"

"Dan." She touched my arm. "It's stopped snowing." (She meant that the rain had stopped.) "Daniel Berman, do you like me?"

"Eva. Eva."—"Dan."—"Eva."—"Dan."—It went on like this with approximately two Evas to one Dan, but she made more of it than I ever could. She sighed, stretched, yawned, leaned, her face a puddle of event in the unraveling lamplit out-of-doors; she sniffled twice and clenched

her teeth, saying, "Oh—the snow—will fall—will fall."
Ainsi parla la sorcière. I glanced sideways to see if she were
working from notes. I hugged her closer to admire her
iambs. Her head flopped back. I saw the dark side of teeth
below me. We embraced, we nuzzled, we growled together,
swaying on pebbles while the moon resounded above us
and our blood swam like up-ended, sucking fish among the
seed of desire in our veins. I mean we smacked lips. O Eva!
What a falling to was there!

Iambic Eva, suburban daughter,
Kissed and kissed me by the water.

I touched her cheek, I touched her nose,
She touched my heart and brought forth prose.

Then kissed her I, and kissed me she,
Promoting verse to poetry.

—Thus rain is snow while snow insists
That love must reign. The rain persists.

I felt it on the back of my neck again, first passion,
then precipitation. She moaned. *Goodness.* . . . And that
groan of love served as the revelation of the year for me, as
was my sigh to her. "Aye-oh," she said. I spoke along the
same general lines.

It would take a heap of explaining to bring it within
the ken of Juicer Montague, who really understood me. We
walked on back. A drop of rain jiggled like a lost and
lonely raindrop against my spine. Prose is a difficult
medium for a man of feeling, and even harder for a couple.

"My mother waits up for me," Eva whispered at last.

"She's a very superficial woman. With all my heart, it's better to be a reactionary like my father than superficial like my mother."

"Mine puts the key in the milk box," I said. "She gets sleepy. Under the cream bottle."

Words alone could not speak for us. We needed whole stanzas. We clambered back up the sod of the park toward the street. "Oh my it's late," said Eva the Iamb-Maker as the convent clock struck metaphor. We walked. There was straight street again, street lamp, street simplicity and responsibility. The MacDonalds' yellow-eyed tomcat crouched watching for sewer rats, his chin sneaky with greed, adaptable to simile. I held her hand (Eva's) over the slippery curb. "Sometime I went to tell you about my big brother James in college," she said. "My brother James the neurotic, remind me, won't you? Please do. He's a poet, you know."

"I *know* what neurotic means."

"So do I, my brother James told me. D'you have any neurotics in your family, Daniel?"

I examined the rosters. "No-o, I don't think so"—made relatively fearless and a lover of truth by venereal triumph. A disappointed frown tightened over her nose. "Unless me," I said in conciliation, "I don't know yet, I'm not old enough."

"You're not nervous enough, either," she complained. "My brother James has a twitch he calls his tic, he doesn't eat, he drinks black coffee."

"I don't like coffee that way."

"He's cynical, too. Not even with sugar."

"Like Humphrey Bogart?"

I realized immediately that I had committed a faux pas. For this junior miss a brother of Bogart would not be real high-type neurotic thing. "No," she articulated loftily, "like an artist, like a man who suffers, like the late Lord Alfred

Byron and Sir Peter Ilyitch Tchaikowsky the celebrated
Russian composer and genius for music, dead these many
years but nonetheless still immortal. Do you know the Con-
certo, not the first movement—*everyone* knows that—but
the second movement? Sometimes I think I inherited poetry
from my brother. Like a neurotic, I mean. I'm talking
about James. Someday he'll be famous and people will
whisper as he walks by, There goes Eva Masters' brother
James, she died, he's still alive though unhappy and rather
introverted, they say."

After a respectful silence in the presence of the dear departed, I said, "I know what you mean, Eva. But you're
really pretty healthy, you, and you ought to live for my
sake. And you could finish those poems you started. Just
drink lots of milk and keep regular and I don't think you
have anything to hope for. Fear for." At the stony mum-
ming that adequately gave me what-for, I strove to make
up for my shallow and selfish plaint by invoking friendship, the sublime and the unknowable, in which Socrates,
Aristotle, Juicer, and I, as is well known, have always been
so interested. "Oh Eva, if you would only get to understand Juicer Montague!" I cried. "He's a great guy, my best
friend. So profound, and he's got a wonderful memory, too.
All he has to do is read a thing twice. I think he might
grow up to be a genius, or maybe even a neurotic. . . ."

A wan smile of forgiveness. A tic in the corner like
that of brother James.

"I can't say the same for Tom Moss, my second-best
friend," I admitted for the sake of justice. (I had won her
back!) "Sometimes I think he *lacks something*. One thing
you can be sure of, *he has no soul,* or very little at the
most."

And we walked in mystery like the night, accoutered in
clouds, borne by love, burdened by poetry and the desire
to pee. "Oh there are sad tragic things in life," said Eva.

"Oh sadder than anyone knows," I responded, flexing my abdomen for mercy.

"Except?" she breathed softly.

"Except you and me," I said.

No relief nor surcease of our bladders' sorrow. The tides pulsed on the enuretic shore of our souls, almost drowning us, I say. Have I remembered to describe her face?—pale and soft and damp as a fine linen napkin after a banquet, her eyes rich as the embroidered escutcheon of the Cunard Line. Her mouth like a delicate pudding, wet with sweet juice and articulated by clever baking, steamed in the evening air. Even in memory of that hour my fantasy turns to aqueous baroque. The cry of kidney met the fatty suburban adenoids of inhibition—irresistible forces, immovable objects. Furtively, in longing and desire, I regarded each alley and wall. She seemed suddenly pigeon-toed.

"I'll never forget you," I said.

"Our conversation. The current of understanding mutually. This walk in the snow and the wet and the lake and the water," she panted as she desperately hopped and jiggled. "Everything, I mean how we have so much in common—"

"Yess."

Oh, we communed together, Eva Masters the Submerged Poetess and I, *will this night ever end?*

9. *"He who eats fire trails sparks"*

IT SEEMED THAT MR. AND MRS. Masters found gall in the association of Eva and me to discuss poetry, life, and the Town Meeting of the Air. "You stay away from that Daniel Berman," they said. "He's a bad influence, the kind that sullies. He's silly, too."

"Everyone," argued Eva, "says he's very sensitive. How can you expect a sensitive boy like him to wear clean collars? And with all his duties as editor-in-chief of the *Lakewood High Times*. Of course, he's a *little* bit silly."

"Never you mind," said Mr. Masters, mindful of ambition, "eh? Next year? What about next year? There won't be another editor next year?"

Aware of the growth of desire, Eva cried out: "But I won't care about such things next year! I'll be a freshwoman at Bennington with primary questions on my mind."

"I thought you said Smith," her mother said.

"I want to go to Bennington. They understand."

"What do you mean," demanded an exasperated Mr. Masters, "they understand more at Bennington than Smith, not to speak of Mount Holyoke? If you go and turn wild now with all the good upbringing we gave you, can't you just stay in Cleveland and attend Flora Stone Mather? Fine scholastic standards? eh? Perfectly. You can read poetry there just as easy as for four thousand dollars a school year, not counting vacations and trips to Yale. You think I didn't read poetry? Want to hear me recite some Middle English?"

Eva prudently guarded a terrified but grudging silence, complaining only, "Who wants Yale? They probably never even heard of Thomas Wolfe, Ben Hecht, and James Branch Cabell's *Jurgen,* whereas people like Juicer Montague and others I could name can quote by heart."

Euclid Masters turned to his wife, Deborah, with controlled exasperation. "What on earth's the matter with you, Deb? Every time I try to settle the question of this Berman boy we begin discussing girls' schools. For once and for all. Why don't you go read the *Post,* they finished the serial story in this issue, go ahead now, *go.* Here, tell me how it comes out. They win the contest? Marry after all?"

Mrs. Masters, who had already discovered the futility of finishing the serial story (one immediately began another), realized that Eva's father might exercise his influence more powerfully alone with Eva, if not heart to heart at least head to head. She sat by the fireside in the parlor under the Harvard Classics and the bound copies of the *Wharton Business Review* to read the *Saturday Evening Post.* "Dear me," she sighed, hating to be so profound, "it takes a father to speak with a daughter."

Thought Euclid Masters: That how you talk to a wife? Josh her? Jokes? Don't let her know it? All right. Now, how do you talk to a daughter? Perfectly—all his faith in the weight of the fear and pity of others. Like Chuck Hastings an atheist toward himself, convinced of his possible presence only by the twinges of hypochondria, he celebrated but one holiday, Specimen Day, when he carried his urine to the laboratory in a ketchup bottle. "Ingredients: Sugar, salt, cloves, garlic, malt, fine sun-ripened tomatoes. . . ."

"Now Eva, tell me what about it?" Mr. Masters asked heartily, having spent a career working men and machine tools, having forgotten to look,* giving his daughter's head the paternal tousle that gratified so many instincts and came out so well in home movies.

"That's what I want to know," Eva said coolly.

"I mean that Berman boy, don't you think you've had enough? No matter how secure my reputation is, it won't protect you if people start throwing dirt. Reputation, eh? Don't they love dirt? I don't want you to rely on me blindly, Eva, although of course I wish to assure you that I will never desert you in your time of difficulties. Not rely blindly, eh? Perfectly. Would you like to go up to Maine for the Christmas vacation? Of course I planned it as a business trip and just take a few days, but nothing's too good for my favorite only daughter, eh? Yes? Yes?"

Ardent Eva said, "Daniel Berman fascinates me, Father, I must admit it. Perhaps he is evil as you say, but I can't help it. I am carried away. Of course, I always remember to remember that I am a good girl, Father—"

Gravely: "I expect to hear that of a daughter of mine, Eva, it goes without saying—"

"But in a platonic way he has hypnotized me. He's a genius, I really mean it, I do. He looks at me and I want to collapse on a Persian carpet at his feet like the one in Somerset Maugham's book *Of Human Bondage,* in a platonic sort of way, of course." Carried by the tides of feeling, she allowed her daddy to know more than the truth: "Father! I feel myself humanly bonded to him!"

"Daughter! Oh, my poor little Eva." She ran across the room to be welcomed into his arms. She laid her head against his shoulders, father and daughter united in dread of me, her swollen eyes squeezed back into her head.

*I like him little. I begin with a bare minimum of sympathy for Euclid Masters.

"Ouch, careful of my operation," he said. "Yes? Now, what has he done to you?"

There was silence for a moment, their breathing intermingled while she tried to remember what I had done to her. This is a difficult moment for any father to girls. Her eyes blossomed open with wonder. "I don't know, I don't know," she panted.

"What! Eva!"

"Everything," she said, "in a strictly platonic way. Nothing."

Euclid Masters, exercised on the Bible and the *Wall Street Journal,* regarded his daughter with fearful piety. Platonic does not protect absolutely. He recalled that among Daniel Berman's element the possibility of an immaculate conception is not to be sold short.

The Masters home was a house of crabs. They obscurely swarmed; they moved sideways over each other, claws everywhere. Even the youngest, Red Masters, with his motor bike and his tinker box full of hard candy, his skinny and freckled athletic lunge and his world-munching smile, returned home after school to swim in an overheated colonial-style aquarium. "Cripes," he once told me he said over and over to himself in bed, "cripes, cripes"—a prayer for this house in which his mother fell asleep alone in her room, dance music from the ballroom of the Hotel Cleveland soaking through the wall near her ivory bedside radio. It murmured and squeaked all night while in his own sleep Red said Cripes with the sadness of pleasure mysteriously forfeited. They all waved their claws, destined for ice, in a dense element. His mother's mouth opened in sleep while it was argued that there would be bluebirds over (the white cliffs of Dover), and the aerial of her radio trembled against the breeze outside her window in that suburb.

A *pretty little woman* was Mrs. Masters, with features

paper-pale, like fish food, a body dieted and tended for perhaps her radio's pleasure, a woman who rode a horse sidesaddle Saturday mornings at Miss Patterson's Ranch. Some years ago she had learned French and how to play the piano; now her soft lips were pressed shut against dust and in judgment. In unwatched moments the eyes of Eva's mother narrowed and darkened with incomprehension, disturbed sleep, the underwater mystery of an aquarium. To the question, "What's the matter?" she replied: "Darling!" She telephoned the society editors of all the newspapers to inform them of important birthdays. In the family she was favorably compared with Billie Burke, that perfect love of an American mother. She fluttered like a bird among the other girls in their new spring collars. Slowly age was opening her up with an odd thickening at the lower part of her face in the expression of birth and death, the long large mouth and the low jaw of a woman's body in pain. "Really darling, no!" she would cry. She hated to see, admit, or know anything.

Euclid Masters, on the other hand, a clever man, human by virtue of a dehumanizing operation, dressed himself like an umbrella in expensive dark cloth over the infolding mechanism. He recognized grace in a high wind of feeling and struggled against it, a genteel knob like a handle in his back just below his shoulders, a deformed hump caused by nothing more brutal than self-denial and by bending over to eat his pudding with a fork. His mouth also reflected at its wrenched corners the clumsiness and stiffness of the cripple. An investment engineer, a personnel manager, he paid off his life without meeting it. He owned a black continental overcoat, nipped at the waist, a modest strip of black fur at the collar—this a debt to old-time daring; he carried a carved cane he had bought in Italy, an eagle's head for handle; thin tufts of gray hair glistened like slivers over his ears, on the lobes, in his nostrils, against the dry folds of skin crumpled along his jaw, over his full mouth pressed shut with a false dark line showing dried saliva. It must once have been a violent and sensual mouth. Bankrupt of desire, it was now a mouth wholly occupied in forgetting its debts.

Tall and bent, possessor of hair of a distinguished gray, combed with the hypochondriac's care, the yellow ailing scalp showing only when he lowered his head in the pain and piety of wishing someone well, he was still an impressive man despite his stoop and his talk in anxious ritual questions: "Going to school? Studying hard? Latin? Greek? Don't study Greek these days? More practical education? Perfectly. Yes. Yes-yes." In the full dignity of money and intellect in that parlor lined with great books on built-in shelves, he would lean forward from holding his stomach and suddenly raise for emphasis skinny pink furry little hands like a monkey's:

"Perfectly perfectly," he explained to his younger son, Red. "Why business? a sure thing, eh? the spirit of our times? you understand that? The Lord moves in strange ways. Salvation imperfect at best? you never know? conceived in sin? Perfect filth. The age of doubt, eh? Went through it myself. Perfectly. Deep truth, isn't it, that Ford and John D. are saved? John D. a Cleveland man himself. Calvin might have been. They know it, don't they? The sign of the good will of the Lord. You don't feel that yet. Make a dollar first, a blessing from God. I understand. A clean conscience. Can't make an omelet without breaking eggs—one of the new Germans said that. The good fight? Yes, son, I'm sure of it." His hoarse speech finished, his hands fell back into his lap, filling with arthritic veins and the abstract groping of a crab in the butcher's ice.

There is, I believe, an abyss in each of us. We hop like goats among the debris of our innocence and the great spaces of our passions. This gives room for sport and knowledge when we pause to polish our horns against rock or browse and lick with our fellows at the salt. "There is no crime of which I am not capable. . . ." We live among the echoes of this abyss, and lonely as we are, we know at our best that there is space for others within the dangers we run.

Euclid Masters knew nothing of the sort. He had worked like a hero, carting, washing, judging, and forgetting, until his abyss was clean of the shale, fungus, flowers, eels, and currents of the past; and like all vacuums, it longed to snap shut. He had eaten the fire of fear in judgment, self-denial in self-aggrandizement, power in ambition, so that his innards were consumed. He had never danced with a witch, and the last gray mouse of hope had long since run out of his mouth. He digested poorly. Part of his lower intestine had been removed in an operation, so that he excreted through a rubber tube into a flask worn next to his spotted, veined, and shriveled belly. What he most disliked about this arrangement, a gift of science which saved his life, was his lack of control over a mechanism which did its stupid work at dinner, at love, and at play. When he lost at solitaire he felt a pain in the absent gut; the doctor warned him not to gamble; but are we permitted to deny a man his pleasure even when all that is left is the pain of it? "He likes to play solitary? So let him enjoy, he enjoys," as my mother would say.

Said Euclid Masters to my friend Red: "The basic fact of city life is the movement toward possession—the movement of it, which gives the wanderers a jump on us—not the possessing. We've got to beat the Bermans and their brethren, my son, at their own game. They know how to beat us already, eh?—with our own rules."

Of the abyss he was left with only a pitted face, gnawed from within by the fear of desire, an abstract consuming flame—this the nibble and kiss of the witch's departing mice.

"My family is difficult, very," announced Eva. "My mother, my father. You know about my brother James. Red is a good kid, though. I like my kid brother. Fond, I really am."

"So is mine," I said, "a family. My father brings home a crate of iceberg from the store and my mother says, What am I supposed to do with all this lettuce? and my father says, Do? It's California iceberg, you want me to let it go for restaurant trade? How do I know what you should do with it? . . . I suppose all families are difficult."

"Is iceberg what they call lettuce in retail trade?" This was the prim early part of our walk, when Eva, pouting and malicious, refused to hold hands as we scuffed through the December snow. Later she would grow cold and kissable for the sake of ethereal unities and bodily heat.

"I wisht my father had a good education," I said. Sighs, steaming breath, wisdom of stoic acceptance. My parents were really my parents. "He knows everything about vegetables, yes, but what does that have to do with life? Just making a living. My father."

"My brother James has a little saying," Eva said. "He says that whenever you leave home it's ten years too late. That's the neurotic way of looking at it, I suppose. Don't you think he's right?"

I tried to think if Juicer had a little saying. All he had was big sayings. I said:

"How would you make a living? Who would tell you to go to bed when you're sick? Who would pay your tuition in college? Of course, I plan to work anyway, me. It's good experience if you keep a journal."

"I write in my diary before I go to sleep. It's the very best time."

"Poets are supposed to keep journals, not diaries," I informed her with the critical fervor of a man who wished (wisht) he had the discipline to write in his every evening, journal, diary, or account book. "What could you say in a diary?"

"Oh yes?" argued Eva. "I'd like to know half of what James says in *his* diary."

Well-motivated, bewitched, even stirred despite our pretenses, we went on seeing each other despite her parents' disapproval. Disapproval was easy for them in judgment, difficult when it required the decisions of an active movement. Out of crustacean immobility and the privacy of their insulation in ice, each from each, they barely made me aware of their disapproval. I knocked softly at the. knocker on their door. "I'm calling for Eva," I would say to Mrs. Masters with a shyness of respect for the mother of the woman I loved and the emptiness of embarrassment in the seat of the pants. "That's a lovely fire you have there in the fireplace. A wood fire." Or to Mr. Masters, the clever one: "Good evening, Mr. Masters. Lovely evening outside. Yes, you can see the Big Dipper."

"What? Stars?"—affixing the cards to their solitaire places without looking up. "I've seen it already. The Big Dipper? That what you saw?"

"They also call it the Big Bear," I might learnedly add, my voice abruptly dying as Eva paused for my sake at the landing on her way down the stairs, descending step-and-dip in the majesty of her new navy blue skirt and the grace of her deportment. Her cheeks sagged briefly in solemn expectation. She was wearing her pearls.

"Stay home tonight," Mrs. Masters said to Eva. "It's too damp to go out. You'll catch a cold. You'll ruin your new shoes, your death of a, why get all dressed up just to go for a walk?"

Her pride's magic circle could admit my knowledge that in a poetic way she adored me, worshiped the candy bars I touched, and wanted to die neurotically in my arms, but she turned furious and flushing on her mother for betray-

ing that she cared enough to put on her new gray suede
sandals. "They're just comfortable, that's all. They're not
dressed up. They're not even smart or what they're wearing this year."

"Get me a clean deck," said Euclid Masters. Said Mrs.
Masters:

"Why don't you two children just stay home and talk
and sit by the fire? You can say whatever you want. I
won't even listen to you. I'll just make hot chocolate with
wafers for you"—now in memory my heart aches for this
woman who, unequipped, accepted a duty to hate me. She
admitted authority as authority was being admitted all over
the world. The dried tears etched a sharpness into her
voice, but she clung to suburban cookery and love for her
only daughter. Behind her glided the silence of her husband and his clicking cards as he cheated at solitaire.

And, like all lovers, I was cruel. "Thank you very much
for the kind offer of the chocolate," I said, giving Eva her
cue, "but—"

"But Mother, but we *want* to go for a walk. It's good for
you to walk when your homework is done. You sleep
better. It's a little tradition with us."

"What?" rose up the voice of her father. "Did anyone
see the nine of hearts? It's missing. You have traditions
now? What do you think that word means?"

"Euclid," said Mrs. Masters, "you must—" She appealed for aid, faltered, sat down.

"Can't a man have a quiet talk with himself in the evening? Comes home all tired out? Works all day?" Euclid
Masters looked at me. "Do you have many friends?"

"Ronald Montague, Tom Moss," I said complacently.
I was on to this line of cross-examination. Eva had warned
me. "I like games, too, and other forms of social inter-
course."

"Some people think he's surprisingly well-adjusted," Eva said for me. "Now we're going out."

We left—"Back in less than an hour, I promise"—without his approval but with the assent of his weariness. True romantics, scorched by the effort to show more than we felt, not yet seeing ourselves, we searched illumination in discontent and condemnation. We wanted to be tender. Eva needed even tenderness to come from the devil. I was an exotic in the suburb, a brooding fantast, a dark figure of the forbidden in corduroy pants and sleeveless sweater with a run in the knit. It was a run like lightning. My Thom McAn's shoe was cloven at the sole.

The fire of denial in her father put fire to Eva Masters: fire searching fire, and unless he fought her back soon—a problem for his clever defeated slothfulness—she might end as irretrievable by him as a lit match. By other matters he had been consumed in this way, and was now a waxy blackened stick.

"Dan."

"Eva."

We kissed on the walk and saw, through the blinds, the silhouette of Eva's mother watching over Euclid Masters' bent head as he won another game of solitaire. The winter air smelled of washed ashes and terrorized desire.

"Down to the lake?" I asked Eva. "To the park? See the Big Dipper, the Bear?"

10. *Human Nature and Conduct, by the well-known philosopher and thinker*

TOM'S DUTY, AT A SIGNAL FROM
Juicer upon discovery of that familiar calfish gaze awash
over my eyes, was to lean over and pinch me back into
the world. He performed this task crisply, with rectitude.
"Ouch! I was listening," I complained. "Who said I was
thinking about Eva?"

"Oh yeah? What were we saying?"

"It was about Thomas Wolfe, it was about Yin and
Yang." I comforted my martyred biceps. "Anyway, what
good is Yin and Yang if I'm black and blue? Why pinch?
I was just contemplating was all."

"Contemplation my eye, you were melting away," Juicer
said.

With the abstracted stupidity of a seminarian, Tom Moss
recited, "Contemplation his eye, you were thinking of girls,
namely Eva Masters."

"What about Lucille Lake, Pattie Donahue, and Rosalie
Fallon?" I defended myself. "I gave them a thought too."

"We were talking about Chuck Hastings, he's back in
Lakewood, haven't you heard?" Tom asked. "The coast is
clear from which he took it on the lam." We shared Tom's
jitters at the prospect of rivalry from the legend of Chuck

124

Hastings, the well-known genius, poet, philosopher, and juvenile delinquent.

"And what if I *was* thinking about Eva, so what about it?"—as embarrassed as if they had caught me making balsa-wood Spads and Fokkers. "There's no law says I *can't,* just that I *shouldn't.*"

Taken by a new mood, chagrined and retreating before my somersault into love, Juicer returned to his sales talk for mysticism. "Waste of time, individual girls," he said "They're all contained in Yin and Yang, the Eastern oriental philosophy. Even Chuck Hastings. There's this Yin, see, it yearns for this Yang—that's real contemplation for you. . . . Better than the Dance Micawber, better even than a genius like Thomas Wolfe or Chuck Hastings. Jean Thompson saw him on the streetcar. Goat cries was nothing compared to this. . . ." He glanced sharply at me and then looked away. Jealousy. Reproach. Despite all crispness of gab, Juicer lay in bogs of shame.

"What's the matter, Juicer?" Tom taunted him. "Scared of Chuck? Look like you choked on a pickle, had the mumps and died."

Tom Moss watched us from behind hard, humorous, salt-baked eyes, opaque even in drunkenness and the dark; the vitality we found in them was our own excitement reflected back; the judgments secretly motivating his downward gestures and sly quick thrusts of two pinching fingers or narrow pink sarcastic tongue were uncontained in the oracular glare. "What I notice is," said Tom, "Chuck's not thin he's emaciated." He felt the flesh of his own chin and regarded Juicer with pity. "Chuck must really suffer and know what vitamins to be deficient and not get sleepy or the beri-beri. Very skinny."

Juicer's eyes, frail above the early jowls and premature manliness of his beard, wigwagged helplessly out at me.

"Dan," he asked me, "what do you think about the Whole Truth?"

"Had the mumps and died," chanted Tom. "Jean Thompson says she's going to give a party, that's what she's gonna give for Chuck because he's a genius."

"From the standpoint of mature love?" I asked.

"Yes, you take the river and time, you take all those feelings, you take the world so much with us. . . ." Sometimes, after quoting from Thomas Wolfe, Juicer, who was corrupted by a strong grain of honesty, would gaze fixedly at me a moment, like a merchant who has just named a rube's price and wants to retreat if possible when the swindle is caught. No protest coming, he relaxed and believed the swindle the true price, a salesman who had sold himself. He had even overdrawn his account in nostalgia for the uncle barely remembered: if no loved one has died, we must invent death at that age. But for Juicer there was always a tax, an aftertaste: He was the man born to drink because his imagination and his honesty were an oil and water which would not mix.

Therefore, each for reasons of power within his own reasons, me for a Byzantine pleasure in patterned things, Tom for a critic's need for things to criticize, Juicer for a continuing thirst after some world-glue to piece himself together, we discovered Yin and Yang. We wondered if it were best to wish, to do, or to know, but decided for will, which implies all these in the becoming and consummation of action. But we did not know what to will.

"We want to be worthy of ourselves," Juicer cried.

"We really feel that way," Tom said.

"Yes, but why?"

Then we prayed for a dispensation to risk our lives, to find a cause, to sleep in the tent of a hashish-crazed Arab, to battle Indian war elephants, man-eating tigers, mustachioed varlets, and Chuck Hastings. (Hitler had marched several times already. The mobs had moved. But Europe is far from Lakewood, Ohio, insists Lakewood, Ohio.) We careened through suburban nights like the sharkfish fins of nine-month babies across their mothers' bellies, a great stir to ourselves, hardly a ripple in the City of Homes. We learned to smoke and, scholars, read paperbound brochures concerning "The French Kiss, or A Sure-Fire Continental Method to Make Love." The book preached at us like Dr. Martin, principal of the high school, giving us vocational guidance: "Read every word at least twice if you want to be a lover, otherwise you will only be mediocre." Nicotine slaves with fingers that would be yellow, we felt the call. The succubi appeared on schedule during sleep. Juicer whispered about Saint Theresa. Tom discovered the Rosicrucians in the back pages of *Spicy Detective*. I mooned after Miss Eva Masters and hinted darkly.

"Tell us! Tell us!" cried Juicer and Tom.

"Loyalty to the woman I love. Oaths, lockets, those nights together. Terrible, terrible responsibilities," I would have liked to mutter.

"Who?" hooted Tom.

"Remember what Khayyam and T. S. Eliot said," Juicer warned me. "We all grow old someday, but did you read in *The American Weekly* about Dr. Metchnikoff?"

"Bogomoletz," I snapped, largely recovered from my impromptu prose poem, a medium with pitfalls. "You're thinking of yoghurt and the well-known Bulgarian bacteria."

"They're spores, little mushrooms," Tom informed us primly. "You boil the milk, see, then you put in this Bulgarian mushroom—"

"A germ!" cried Juicer. "A germ to make you live a hundred and twenty! I read it in *Liberty*, that's the kind of germ for me. I don't care what he says, Chuck Hastings never hitchhiked there. Is it Bulgaria-on-the-Caspian?"

We were of the generation which changes our fathers'
money into talk by an alchemy employing—what a catalyst
was there!—only the magic pass of imagination. We needed
power without the tools our fathers used, demanding love
rather than commanding things, and before we could attain
to our dominion in the world we had to find it within ourselves. Discovery and mastery, these were the social equiva-
lents of sweet desire. Metaphysicians therefore, nervous
about Chuck, we looked for practice in love to make perfect. We suffered from delusions of perfectability.

A party!

Jean Thompson, the economist of geniuses and other
interesting people, planned a welcome-home-to-Chuck
party in her recreation room. It was a celebration for both
Christmas and the returned prodigal. By discussing philosophy, crime, travels, and the Town Meeting of the Air
over the basement ping-pong table with its ravelly sea-green
net sagging under the weight of our scrabbling fingers and
deep thoughts, like Pattie Donahue's brassière under the
pressure of tugging fingers and hormones, we would not
disturb Mrs. Thompson's Friday evening bridge club upstairs. They played contract, we challenged Chuck; the
same apple juice and Nut House Assorted Tasty Candy-
Covered Pecans could serve us both. We gobbled; they
nibbled; we all gabbled and sometimes secretly touched
knees in tribute to hard cider.

The difference in age, however, made a difference in
quality: their grown-up love, confirmed in pants and pan-
ties, only occasionally hauled their knees together by a
grave material affinity, while we flagrantly footsied and
flirted, the thick and thin of our voices claiming: *Love me!
Love me quick, somebody!* "Would you like to play table
tennis?" Jean asked.

"Ping-pong? No, let's talk."

"Table tennis, anybody? Chuck?"

We felt it our duty to worship Chuck. He assented. You might say that he conducted our choir of praise, humming the themes like some bedroom maestro with his radio turned up and his mirror illuminated for Chuck Toscanini the Terrific. Or like Chuck Akhnaton, the well-known Egyptian pharaoh, he nominated himself to uplift our souls from Juicer Montague's eclectic metaphysics and Jean Thompson's assorted nuts. In some respects he resembled a mummy—the shriveled yellow skin, the hands and head too large for a wasted body, the bottomless eye sockets of thought beyond the Nile. But his agile Adam's apple and point-making finger made him less the Styx-swimmer dog-paddling toward Coptic limbos than a high school intellectual intimidating the navel-eyed little girls. His regard a knot of fury and ambition for glory, claw-faced and scratch-mouthed, he said, "I've seen things would make your back crawl. . . . I've talked with men would cut your throat for a plugged dime. . . . I've read books you can only get in a certain little bookstore I know about in San Fran-cis-co, Frisco. . . ."

I listened to the avalanche of saliva rustling down Miss Eva Masters' lovely throat. I recognized danger in the fragile murmur of her lips, an alarum in the abstract flutter of her hand away from mine, unholding it. My nostrils, breathing fire, itched with a desire to sneeze as I mobilized myself for trouble and battle-doing.

"All right, Chuck, name one of those aforesaid books," I said.

"You were really in San Francisco, Chuck?" said Miss Eva Masters. "The Gold Coast? The cable cars?"

I sneezed. "Someone open the window," I said. "Quick, there's dust from the furnace."

"Got me a waiter-on-tables job on a gambling ship off the San Francisco coast," Chuck remarked in his new West-

ern accent, "Frisco. Used to watch the lights of the Golden
Gate Bridge and the Chinee junks coming over the Pacific,
that Southern ocean, from China and Tannu Tuva. Rented
me a tux with tails, that's the kind of job I had. Stood on
the deck like that. Sometimes used to stand and look and
think for hours on end without a stop—"

"I think you mean Timbuctoo," interrupted Tom Moss
the Pedant, "since Tannu Tuva has no sea coast according
to my stamp collection."

"Oh not nice to call a Chinese man Chinee," said Jean
Thompson, gazing significantly at me. "Chink neither,
don't you think?"

"Thinking about the uncharted islands and the monsters
of the deep, the treasures to be found in frigates of old. . . ."
He dreamed on a moment while we marveled at the uncharted treasure of smoke which fumed out from his nostrils. "Have you ever heard of John Dewey's *Human Nature and Conduct?*" he asked with shriveling forehead. "I
used to read it often."

Sang the words, went the music. . . .

"Sometimes thought," said Chuck, "I'd learn to be a
wino, Gallo wine, or a mystic, Eastern philosophy, instead
of just the universal man I am. No patience with sham, pretense, or immaturity."

"You've really lived," said Jean Thompson, "but still, a
Chinese person is a Chinese *person.*"

"More than that—explored life. Tested theories, both
empirical and mystical. And also" (sly obbligato by this
holy swimmer with an end in view) "I've associated with
lots of Dan's kind in my travels."

"Who?"

"Juice."

"*Who?*" I asked, feeling squeezed.

"Jewish folks," he said, "workers, peasants, merchants,
and intellectuals."

"Oh Chuck!" cried Jean. "You're so outspoken since you went on your universal travels."

"A dirty mouth," whispered Juicer sarcastically. "Wash it out with Gallo soap—*oo Chuckums!*"

Tom said, "Foo. But he's pretty smart."

He was pretty smart for us. Trouble always is. He didn't mean anything by it; he just wanted to remind us of larger issues so that he could concentrate on the smaller ones.

Jean Thompson, our hostess and the salon-keeper, wobbled on her heels as she offered us to eat, graciously putting to ours a face soft, smooth, and sleek as a half-licked ice cream cone, sodden with the tongue's soft preening, rich with the advertised quality of *healthy ingredients, pure shortening.* She made her investment in kindness, an economist too, a suburban coupon-clipper with her mother's mouth for boys and as much desire for them as a blunt scissors. Slack-eyed, syrup-lipped with hospitality, she encouraged us: "Perhaps a pecan? Oh do. No? A carry-mell? That one over there"—tipping the box. "You will always find a chart on the cover of a box of Nut House Tasty Delightfuls. It's invaluable, too." (Everyone love me, but not too much: give her a child to feed, not when she gets her certificate from Baldwin-Wallace, but *now.*)

Went the words and sang the music. . . .

Discussion ceased while we refreshed ourselves. Chuck waited with the tolerance of noble maturity for the body's petty itchings to be gratified. "No thank you, a vegetarian," he told the cubes of white bread slippery with Bred-Spred Patty (made from the finest-grade Spam livers, raised on Kellogg's Corn Flakes and ultraviolet light by white-coated attendants in pants coming neatly to a forty-five degree angle at the crotch). While upstairs the grownups dreamed of slams and discussed maids, and outside the wind whirled the fine December snow about the chinks of brick at the cornices, Chuck in the basement transcribed poems and paragraphs into a little notebook, dangerously flourishing his indelible pencil in an atmosphere redolent of ping-pong, coal dust, taste-delightfuls, and intellect. I watched Eva. Eva watched Chuck through brooding lids, the hussy, curled up against the fireplace painted on the wall. Tom looked at Rosalie Fallon with the expression of a man who walks around his parked car before going on a picnic, to see that all the tires are inflated. Juicer breathed hoarsely, stared at his hands, and longed to address a deep insight to Lucille Lake. Lewis Snyder, the sheik and cynic with Dr. Jerrico's Little Wonder Grip of Steel, grinned like Humphrey B. at Stanford Leary, the clown: "Why is the Blue Boar Cafeteria a place where midgets sleep? A rest-runt!" Stanford, the life of all parties, was a breezy individual, large empty spaces in his character, drafty with hooting winds.

The wind hooted outside ominously silent in the chimney painted behind Eva. I looked to see if she noticed my teeth's profligate gnash, a waste of new fillings; her large soft neck only piped thoughts of larcenous, literary Chuck down from her head past her narrow shoulders and into her organs. She dreamed of a conversation piece built for two. She stretched like a cat, her vertebrae clicking, as he went back to cross a "t." He devoured her over the ping-pong table and crossed it again. What could be more poignant, more significant of inner life than a double-crossed "t."

"A taste-delightful? A bred-spred? A paper cup of something? Ohio State cider, Dan?" Jean Thompson asked. "Please do, O! Imagine, the Golden Gate Bridge!"

Went and sang, sang and went. . . .

If Eva deserted me I might search immolation—a date with Tom's Rosalie, Juicer's Lucille, or herself's Pattie. Consolation is the apocalypse! I could defeat Chuck at ping-pong and argument, deep thinking and table tennis: but the question seemed to be love. (Love the question? Love the answer.)

Words, music. . . .

Rosalie Fallon, a compressed little creature, very small, with quick hard small gestures, a piggish little nose, and pierced ears with a pearl in each, had a body morally corseted so that it did not jiggle as its fresh weight and new flesh gave it the right to do. Tom referred to her as a *piece,* but she was a whole lump; she knew what she wanted, I believe—herself—and that is something little girls may possess only with considerable sacrifice, since before they can have any value to themselves they must be valued by others. What is mentioned as their cruelty is only the use of men as bookkeepers in the inventory.

Cute Pattie Donahue, on the other hand, possessed of a primary truth in her narrow practical brain, barbarously selected a father for her children: chose by soaring heavenwards as does the queen bee, until all drones but the strongest fall away, and then, when he finally attains her embrace, he disintegrates, dead in a spasm, while she returns dragging his ecstasy and his entrails as a plume behind her. What she wanted of him came afterwards in the hive's collective worship. Small-pawed, desiring everything, she could feel secure only in the death of all but what she created.

To Rosalie the others—having them, that is—provided the ends of her self's glory; to Pattie they were the means, her self-possession still the sole end. These two economists were friends (that is, allies). Rosalie had a talent for drawing pictures, especially of small plump girls. Bestial Pattie, capable of a larger arithmetic, had a talent for admiring.

Lucille Lake in all this seemed too busy to bother. Brisk, diamond-eyed, solitary but not lonely, incapable thus far of all satisfactions except the imagined ones of which she

was not yet capable, she too had drawn instincts of economy from the suburb-as-wet-nurse. Her palate remained
stiff against yea-saying, her fingers agile for harping. She
hedged without commitment, murmuring "Eyewash" to
Chuck. She said worse words to Juicer: "How are you,
Ronald? I'm glad to see you again. Hello." Her busyness
too, her abstracted fluttering in music, her long stride and
her tennis, had something to do with love, but she needed
a long time to imagine how. She could waste herself until
ready for devotion; Pattie and Rosalie felt the contempt
and fear of ants for the improvident grasshopper whose
needs are metaphysical. This polite harping cricket was a
grasshopper with a light, a firefly in fact.

"Congratulations on your editorship of the yearbook,
Ronald!"—love and power were still the music and the
words to a humming in secret behind Lucille's tawny head.
She turned a trick like that.

"Who," cried Jean Thompson, having proposed table
tennis and modified our digestion, "has something to say
about Norman Thomas on the recent Town Meeting of
the Air?"

"Me," volunteered King Chuck. "Socialists never do
anything constructive. Talk is all they ever do. What we
need"—ominously he lowered his voice and took a cookie
—"is a *revolution*. Or even extreme measures—a caucus.
There's a little group in Frisco—"

"Are you may I ask," boomed Juicer, sprouting a wing
collar with congressional hair on it, "a subversive communist? I'm just asking."

"That would be nice," said Jean Thompson. "Divide up
everything equal. My mother buys turkeys for the poor
people so they can have a nice little Christmas too, but the
trouble is they spend all their money on hard drink and
liquor. There you are. I don't know what to do."

"That's right, the poor people don't appreciate what you
do for them," Rosalie Fallon said. "My mother says."

"I hardly know what to think next either."—Jean Thompson.

"You can never tell, though. Some are really grateful." —small-pawed Pattie Donahue, a lover of paradox.

"This is a party, eat drink and be merry. Jingle all ye bells. Why talk about that stuff."—Stanford Leary the Master of Ceremonies.

"What we need is more secret agents. Wire-tapping, espionage, foreign powers," snarled Lewis Snyder the Private Eye. "We could push the table next to the furnace and dance. Kay Kayser's on."

"Personally I'm a communist myself," murmured Tom Moss, content with the way Rosalie had winked at him. "Juicer and Dan and I are also freethinkers and Rosicrucians, but we don't agree about communism. Dan's a socialist. There's a big difference, they say."

"When I was young I did frequent. . . . Ever read the *Rubaiyat?* Ever read anything by Leon Trotsky the well-known Russian revolutionist?" I challenged Chuck, willing to fight it out for Eva on the ground of politics if he refused the gamut of Khayyam.

For perhaps the first time in their lives, these two agreed on something: "I think we ought to let Chuck explain himself," said Lucille Lake for reasons of coolness and reasons of order. "I think Chuck should give us the story of his life and the fruit of his experience," said Eva Masters for reasons of heat and confusion to me.

By my side Juicer pummeled the flesh of his thigh for a moribund cause. "The works of Omar, of Leon, of Tom Wolfe the great dreamer and James Branch also?" he said.

"Shush now, you Ronald Montague."—Jean Thompson the hostess. "Stop your whispering to Dan, please. It's only courtesy to the other guests, don't you understand?"

"I heard of them too," said Tom, "in addition to my Rosicrucian library of free books and pamphlets."

"They found a man on the desert all dried up and dead"—Chuck Hastings silenced Tom. "They brought a man back to life, they rubdowned his heart"—Juicer and I listened. "He said it was all black on the Other Side. Spiritualism, that's what it was due to."

"Sounds more like massage to me," Tom said.

"Did they have faith in Henry Ford either? Said it would never work, that's the answer. Someday they'll have air-cooled engines—you remember I told you. And a couple of other things, too." The finger jabbed, the forehead unfolded, the words and music suffered from needle scratch. "Atheists are more honest than other people. What I tell you is God's honest truth sure as my name is Chuck Hastings. You don't have to believe me if you don't want to."

"Hiya, Harry Hastings," I whispered to Juicer.

"Shh! I'll make you sit separate."—Jean. "—ly."

"It is of little importance to me whether I am understood or not," Chuck commented. "I can wait. In San Francisco Frisco only morons don't believe in spiritualism these days. You will be sorry when the time comes." He folded his arms and bowed his head.

"Let him speak. Questions later."—Lucille.

"Tell us, Chuck."—Eva.

"Now everyone be quiet. It's Chuck's turn."—Jean Thompson. (Me green with my prop pipe, my arguments, and my jealousy.)

A minister's son, a scandal, a boy who was caught three times shoplifting and then used bad language in the juvenile court, Chuck Hastings gave us a sermon on his year of wrath, when he hitchhiked to San Francisco. Let his father worry: "I'm a nihilist too, I don't believe in graduation from high school." He denied all with the faith of an elderly clergyman, gulping like his father after a hard Sunday morning or like a fish. "I don't believe in anything. I'm sure of it," he said, his pink eyes fixing us with the blank

stare of easy domination, having the strength of a failure
of imagination in the exercise of mediocre energy. Those
rabbity eyes needed no respite from gazing: "This is how
I had my revelation that atheism is the great truth of our
time, maybe greater than spiritualism."

"Greater than air-cooled engines?" Juicer asked me.

"Shush!"

"It's all right, not everyone can understand," Chuck
said. Each of us separately felt that he was looking deep
within us (although without us) at that moment when he
attempted to support his faith in the Void by a misquotation
from Dr. Ratner's introduction to John Dewey's *Human
Nature and Conduct.*

"Nothing exists! Life is a fraud! I only imagine you
sitting there watching me, prove I'm wrong. You're just
figments."

"Figment Newtons?"—Stanford Leary.

"Don't sneer, I warned you. It's a discovery I made
on the gambling ship off the San Francisco skyline. I
worked in a circus, too, Mills Brothers. Nothing exists, I
tell you. I'm an absolute idealist and a complete nihilist."

"You're a regular dictionary," cooed Jean Thompson,
"Britannica cyclopedia."

"You ever see anyone like that for believing in nothing?"
Juicer whispered to me.

If there were a devil, I now like to think I thought, *it
would not be one who decided against God, but one who,
in eternity, came to no decision.*

Mephistophles Hastings waited for the murmur to
subside. Eva Masters sighed profoundly and hoped he
appreciated her sympathetic breathiness. How he had suffered! How well the smoke curled from his nostrils! "You
want to know about the little group in the back of a little
bookstore in Frisco where we drank red wine and"—he
paused to imply *plotted*—"planned? I mean I saw life. I
mean the terror that purifies. Can they hear us upstairs?"

"A revolution in a bookstore," I said crisply. "What you going to do if no one's interested? Where's your organization? You can't have a revolution if it's so secret no one ever heard of it. You might as well have a Yin and Yang, a Rosicrucian club. You might as well play softball for Rosenblum's Bloomer Girls or the City Ice and Fuel."

A long yellow finger jabbed at my skeptical face. "You may be clever the way you are, Dan Berman," the nasal voice pronounced, "but I'm *wise*. I've seen life in the raw, the way people are." He hunched sadly over the burden of his experience: "So to speak. No one really exists." Tall, stoop-shouldered, with yellow hair tightly curled over his skull, he wore this yellow-knit substance clipped short, as if a tight woolen cap had squeezed his brains into the crevices of his fish-bony nose, which jutted out full of mucus and menace. "Oh if you only knew," he murmured tolerantly, almost two years older than I, "wisdom doesn't just come from books."

"It doesn't come from talking, either. What do you think, Juicer?" I asked with eyes only for Eva. "But let's talk about your Frisco revolution, if it isn't too secret to be mentioned."

"Very curious," Juicer boomed. "Interesting proposition. I get you, Chuck. But is the time ripe?"—mooning over Lucille Lake, wanting to hold her in his arms and find enemies to protect her from. Look, Lucille, how rhythm is the rationality of music, but love the reason!

"Progress is always a revolution, my brother James says," Eva stretched and murmured. "Revolutionists sacrifice themselves for the future of mankind, don't you think?" —murmured and stretched for a yellow-haired, pointy-fingered, stoop-shouldered, solipsistic future. "It's wonderful and so truly wise in the eternal sense of the word to sacrifice oneself."

Chuck was wonderful, wise, true. Journeyman pharaoh

and apprentice Nazarene, a hard worker, a Fuller Brush man of power and love, he had learned through ambitious adversity to alternate two profitable sales methods for his installment plan purchase of a personality: arrogant and aggressive with men, clinging, poetic, and wombschmerzy with women. . . . "I've suffered and I'm tired"—so that they might soften to comfort him, possess the man who destroyed the men, learn without risk of challenge the facts of their bodies which they have been boning up on in movie magazines, stroke the head and measure their own beauty, forget themselves in cunning remembrance of the dreams of their future. Having written poems of atheistic challenge to God (God never replied), having abandoned Methodism and really lived, Chuck slicked down his hair with water to emphasize the diabolical points and parchment gloss of his head. "Wisdom comes from being wise," he mournfully concluded. "Otherwise you can't get to be it."

Eva Masters' eyes on him said: A real genius, the genuine article. The suffering, the love of humanity, the disdain for ping-pong.

"And now for some hot chocolate!" cried Jean Thompson. "Everyone ready with marshmallow in it?" She bestowed plates and doilies along the table.

Our recreation-room Shelley, nourished by Dr. Ratner's introduction, thirsted only for esteem, sans marshmallow, but a toothpick and a kiss for the teeth. Two solutions to the question of Chuck: Love and submission, scorn and struggle. I chose the second for a double reason, that Eva was hot for him and that he was stupid. The first helped me come to the second. Lost while I thought! Sunk in this empirical metaphysics as I mashed my marshmallow in grainy chocolate, I looked up only when Juicer, a man who understood philosophy and recognized his friend's danger, said: "Say, Dan, you know what?"

Lost!

"What?—what?—oh, I was just thinking."

"I was just thinking too, Dan." The gentleness of my great fat Lucille-looking friend! His tact! His sacrifice in the risk of bearing tidings! "I was just thinking, Dan, maybe while we drank our chocolate we could go find Eva and Chuck and decide—"

His eyes shone with grief for me.

Marshmallow foundered in my cup. Reeling with Revelation tobacco, fear squealing like a mouse in my throat, I fled from the recreation room past tray-carrying Jean Thompson, through the laundry room with washing machines opening their mouths at me and the rollers of mangles waiting like inquisitors, into the furnace room with its whitewashed walls, its puddles of coal dust, its debris of ashes, and the great organ of the furnace creaking and churning through brick and steel. Good Juicer stayed behind to suck his pipestem and meditate.

Into the dark of the hold! Into the maw of the dragon! I stumbled over a hamper of ashes and sprawled with the whitish dust choking my nostrils.

"Be careful you don't hurt yourself, Daniel," said Eva from the corner near the boiler, the pilot light its smile in an asbestos face like that of the Sphinx. Even now I recall the sweetness of her voice from her head pressed against Chuck Hastings' thin chest, loose hairs streaming over her damp forehead, hot and mussed, her mouth half-open in surprise and sleepiness and a strange new softness dreaming in her face. She was held in the hold. Her blood perhaps truer than her plans and her scheming little pupils, she said gently, "You can hurt yourself that way, Dan."

"Infections. Those ashes from the furnace," Chuck declared in triumph.

"You want my handkerchief to wipe yourself, Dan? There's just a little in your nose."

No more St. George, no more Achilles. A poor unpretty Menelaus, I sneezed out the dust, my nose twitching and my eyes running. The red peeping mouse of fear was done with me now; only this, the gray mouse of the rejected with its skinny, panting ribs and its pale, working muzzle.

Outside, the wind howled, flung dry snow; I left Eva and Chuck, their eyes on the seat of my pants. I closed the basement door to seal them off.

In the laundry room I found Pattie Donahue with her cup of chocolate. "Why hello, Dan. Are you looking for the Gentleman's? A sip of hot chocolate?"

Flagrant with shame, I demanded, "What are you doing here?"

"Oh, I don't like crowds. I wanted to drink my chocolate all alone by myself. Here"—and she handed me the cup. "You know, Dan," she said, "I really don't like parties. Look, a tennis ball." She stretched to reach it from the shelf.

Why, oh why, Eva? Perhaps she was as eclectic as I: to test the possibilities of another, to temper love in fire, to claim the rights of freedom, perhaps even to make her father happy, having chosen a fellow hypochondriac instead of a *foreign element*. Love may find us unawares even in our joy in hate! I felt the basement vibrate with the grumble and work of the furnace. Remember the look of longing and sorrow as she stretched a white arm forward with the handkerchief I never took? Remember the gift to all men in that softening mouth? *I must understand and forgive,* went the music and the words. After all, it was an Xmas party, the X pronounced: Forgive her! forgive her!

"I write poems too," said cute Pattie Donahue, bouncing the ball and not looking at me as it went plop, plop, plop, plop.

11. *Larceny in the heart*

Snow churned at the frosted windows.

I said that I emerged from the furnace room blinking and peeping like a mouse. By the time I left Pattie among the laundry and approached Juicer, who read my face well because Lucille's unreadiness was an even more slippery rival than Eva's readiness, I was no longer a feeble nibbler with a dejected tail, out in the cold alone. We stood with Stanford Leary and paraphrased ourselves and roared—out in the cold together. We knew, Juicer and I, that this laughter came to us for Stanford's jokes and our immortal souls, meaning our tears. Filled with cider and chagrin, we were no longer either skinny sneaky rats or soft sleepy ones, but big tough hairy gallopers who knew what we wanted and pounded at the pantry door like police to be let in. We had warrants, which were our youth. I exaggerate about the toughness: still there is truth among the brave talk. (We were miserable. We were proud.)

I asked small-pawed Pattie Donahue for a date. "If you're not too busy with your dancing and going to football practice. Occupied taken up, I mean. Scrimmage, I mean."

"It's ballet not ballroom. Not social. I go to watch Lewis

Snyder sometimes"—*O, I knew*—"for he makes up for the lack of weight with speed, quick-thinking, swivel-hips, and innate talent as a left end. His father played for Texas A & M, you know, a college fellow like my father. Now he's high man in his bowling league."

I understood Pattie well enough, and in my self-sufficient despair and courage I reminded her: "My father never had a degree, never even attended college."

"I know"—making her little cranberry mouth. "I knew, Dan"—that unbreakable mouth curling and tempting as it forgave itself the little white politeness which followed. "It's the innate man that counts, not so much if his father went to college."

Huddling homeward in the winter night, Juicer and I, two innate men, discussed some questions of love with a new sneering maturity after our gawking and balking on Lucille's lawn only six months earlier. "What's eating Pattie Donahue?" he asked me. "Do you suppose?"

"Oh, she's probably only sex-starved for love and affection."

"Yeah? I don't figure it me that way."

"What do you think?"

"She's hard up," steamed the breath from his sore, harried face. There was a moon with a nimbus, and each mooning street lamp had its nimbus, and our nostrils were clogged. Cold, cold, and heavy-footed in the snow. Hard to be big about things.

The knowledgeable Lewis Snyder leer stood for our first realization that intelligence is a part of our bodies, not a Woolworth toy. We shivered with the December midnight winds on the suburban boulevard; frozen slush lay broken in the gutters and over the poisoned grass. . . . We had been lucky to have books when we first realized how dark was life (sex-starved for love and affection, see?), books to make plane geometry of the heart—to know it all, as my mother said: "You think you know it all, you, Mr. Know-it-all." The bookish rules are beautiful, but merely permanent. We were learning that it is impossible to step in the same joy twice, nor the same trouble, no two girls alike, no two bellyaches saying ditto to pain. Hogs of truth, we diversely slipped and found ourselves with the short fast legs of greased porkers. After such growing pains we could no longer read the same, never again remembering what we read instead of seeing what we saw. On Eva's upper lip I saw a brown two-haired mole like a wet bug with stick-eyes, not Alice Faye's beauty mark with Clark Gable in San Francisco's plaster earthquake. Juicer smelled fish on Lucille's breath, finding her the more beautiful (that is, desired) for being no longer an angelic harpist with capillaries full of tinted air. Someone was vainly working his battery to start a car—*roo*huh, *roo*huh; it died; the man sat mourning over the wheel. *Roo*huh, it said again. Nothing. In a fury he abruptly pounded the horn. It gave only a dull peep.

A few last flakes of snow drifted down.

I said: "Is Chuck Hastings like us? What about Mr. Masters, Eva's father? He hates me." (Beep.)

"Ah," said Juicer, "they want what we want. We all *want*."

I believed you then, Juicer, and I believe you now. . . . I huffed the night air: "What about the girls?"

"Lucille and Eva and Rosalie and Lucille and Pattie and Jean Thompson?"—his heavy line of an upper eyelid thick above the pupil. "And Lucille?"

"That's who I'm talking about. Whom. Eva Masters, for instance."

"They're all like us, Dan, they got different gadgets and maybe they get the cramps once a month, but they want what we want. Lucille too."

"Maybe they don't know how to want it."

Maybe, we thought, *we don't know how to want it*. We

had what-with, we knew what-for, yet the snow drifted down upon indecision. "Hey!"—a ball of snow slapped against a freckled birch tree near us and scattered in powder. "Wait up, hey!" Pillared by frost, our tongues salted with cold, we turned toward Tom Moss as he approached in his dry low tread, enveloped in sheepskin and a woolen cap. Awed by him because he seemed to have no body to be frightened in, we trusted each other because we admitted to fear and sorrow in our bowels and kidneys and aching throats. "Talking about the party?" Tom inquired with a dusting gesture at the fuzzy thinker's knob of wool on his cap. "See that Buick wouldn't start? He's *mad*. What do you think about the party?"

"Yeah, the girls. . . ."

"Right. Check. Continue, fellas."

"They're afraid to let themselves go," Juicer said.

Long consideration. Basic matters were invoked by our way of kicking slush. Behind us, the Buick still didn't start. I sighed and spoke the truth: "They're afraid to lose it."

Tom listened politely, peeping at us from his sly eyes, and then put his elongated head with its woolly knob between ours to say, "Well, you wouldn't want to marry a girl who didn't have it anymore, would you? *I* sure wouldn't, the bitch. Listen Juicer, would you still think the same of Lucille, *respect* I mean, if Lewis Snyder took her down to the park in his father's Nash?"

"Oh yes he would!" I cried out, my tongue still hurting where I had bit it in tripping over the bushel of ashes in Jean Thompson's basement. "Juicer's not narrow-minded, are you Juicer?"—with the rage of my despair for Eva and hatred of Chuck. "Juicer knows that the spirit is the important thing, and if the girl likes you even after she kissed another guy, that means she *really* prefers you, her soul I mean, and then you're sure she loves you, don't you, Juicer?"

"Yeah," he said.

"—and don't be narrow, boorj-wah, and counter-revolu-
tionary," I finished miserably. They knew all about Chuck
Hastings.

"Trouble is," Tom said smugly, "the girls listen to you
talk, but they know what's what. Listen, don't get mad, it's
a good little line. Trade secret in the field. You got to beat
the competition. Lust comes first, haha. I talk just like you
to Rosalie Fallon, that's how I know."

Heyday for Tom! He knew his truth. Juicer and I scuffed
in silence, hunched against the wind, our scarfs tickling the
heavy ideas but the fringes crushed against our hearts. Sore
and chapped, we still believed in that stairway to the stars
when we kissed our beloveds (someday); Tom was content
to wait until they built the escalator—modern science. Rosalie and he would ride stately up together, but catch their
umbrellas in the cogs when they tried to get off.

"They know," said Tom, "how the butter will get to their
bread. Girls. They're saving it so they'll be worthwhile.
Listen, it's just like Lewis Snyder says, the women around
here are expensive types. What a line that Snyder has!
Course he got money, his father's Nash, but the line helps
too. They're educated, see? Why should they give it away
for free when it's worth something?" Abruptly sad, he repeated what it was worth: "Money—big dollar dinners. A
Nash." He looked chipper again: "They're pretty smart,
aren't they?"

What it is worth, I then thought and think now, is joy.
But Tom knew the suburb, economy its principle. *Reserve:*
this an epithet our mothers used in high praise. Economy
of love, the weapon of what we call bitches, was the all's-fair
of their deprived war: Keep him guessing, worry him a
lot. . . . Love as a tool signified that men are objects. "She's
a nice girl, well-off, a reserved-type girl, I give her
credit. . . ." Sometimes girls grew up to passion—the flesh
is strong; sometimes they learned from the Guardian Trust,

the savings bank sponsored by the school, which fell dead in 1932 while bloated with our dimes. No matter, they most of the time thought; only be careful, be more careful next time, take no one's word until you see the inside of his pockets.

Juicer and I wanted to turn our pockets inside out and run abandoned to love, dripping lint. Tom Moss carried a black pigskin snap-shut purse and picked out the coins with two fingers, pensive and cautious, when he bought Rosalie Fallon a sundae. He would not let her see, but by the metal click and intimate embrace of a patented fastener, he would lead her to believe. He would imply, click-and-jingle. And, she would want to know, since a defenseless young girl must learn to protect herself by her lonesome in a hard hard world, what about your father's pockets? Click-tinkle?

But oh how those last sweet details of chocolate syrup can be found in the indentations of drugstore glass! And what Tom missed when he left the chocolate for noisy exploration in his purse! He missed the jukebox jazz—tup-chugga-boom.

"Still, maybe you're right," Juicer said to Tom, shrugging. If you're working with suckers you got to be a con-man"—what heresy in the cult of Wolfe, Poe, and Khayyam! "I don't care."

"He's right all right," I said, "for what he's working with. Rosalie."

"Oh every confidence," said Tom. "I have every confidence I'm right. You fellows may be brilliant, but someday you'll see it my way."

"Yes, why?"

"Sure sure," Juicer murmured. He told us of the moral defense of the confidence man: A sucker can't be taken unless he tries to trick you first. You make him believe he saw the bean under the shell while you coughed; he edges forward to slap down his money with his lips licking and gleaming and a righteous indignation against gamblers in his greedy eyes. You can't con a mark unless he's got larceny in his heart. (The bean is no longer there.) "So Rosalie—sure, I suppose. But not Lucille or Eva, huh Dan? Not Lucille or Eva? Not Lucille? Not Lucille?"

Before we separated that evening, my tracks leading alone up Hiawatha Avenue past the darkened houses squatting and scowling in the snow, leaving Tom stimulated by cynicism and Juicer morose after another failure with Lucille, I told them: "I have a date with Pattie Donahue. Well, good night. I'll show her."

"Who?" they asked.

"I'll show him."

"Who?"

"Chuck Hastings," I said. *Me,* I thought. Eva!

Thoughts of the evening alone with Pattie made me sweat, like all thoughts of the important future and also like thoughts of Euclid Masters' dislike of me, which must somehow have good reasons in a man clever enough to become the father of Eva. This, my perspiration, annoyed me as I kicked through the slush of unseasonable spring on my way to call for Pattie. I had just showered; my hair was still stiff with wet. "Don't spend more than a dollar tonight," my mother warned me. "You're not going to marry her, you can have just as good a time, enjoy a movie for fifty cents."

"*I* can, but maybe Pattie can't."

Small-pawed Pattie Donahue was going through a *stage,* as my mother called it in the light of her studies of the Sunday supplement to the *Plain Dealer,* or *complexes,* the term full of the dignity of science which she later learned. (What To Do About Your Child's Abnormal Psychology. Are the Martians Coming? To Neck or Not To Neck: A Modern Dilemma by a Well-Known Authoress.) Also a

scholar, Pattie yearned for the summers in monastic se-
clusion among the white-flanneled boys at Chippewa
Lake, with a private tennis court, a shelf of cologne, and a
brainful of edification from her mother's book club. "I love
nature," she said, quoting her favorite writer, whose name
escaped her at the moment. "It's a lady, I remember that.
. . . The sunsets, the peace, the sky it makes you think of
God," she sighed. "In the city all you do is shop and run
run run around all day until the stores close and you drop
from sheer fatigue, and then you never see the sunset, does
one? And the moon! You go to a movie."

She had forgotten that Loew's Granada had a sky with
real electric stars and, waxing above MGM's latest and
greatest, a genuine Westinghouse moon. "A lovely fixture,"
my mother said, "worth the price of admission alone."

"You never see the moon at movies," Pattie complained,
"except maybe a dance, you go out on a porch, a terrace,
at a ball I mean, you go out on the veranda I mean, at the
Clifton Park Country Club, the club I mean for a drink—"

"A Coke?"

"A drink, a cherry punch with alcohol, and you see the
moon if it's out. Oh it's lovely, so. I mean inspiring."

She sighed. She had been carried away by a vision of
how the real world should be. The moon would always
hang full and the men would huff lovely words into a girl's
pearl-like little ear and she would clap her hand to her
heart, squeezing it a little, very gently, to make it swell
so prettily, and say, "Oh Rhett, you do talk!"

"What about Low-ee's Granada?" I asked, merely hint-
ing that I would like to sit in the dark with her—old rebuffs
aching like scars in damp weather. "The moon's always out
there, a half one anyway, rain or shine unless there's a short
circuit."

"I forgot," she said. "Yes. But anyway I have like an
idea you're kidding me. Now don't tease, Dan."

"As good as the original, better. Tell you what—"

"You're too old to be funny now, Dan. People won't think you're serious, and I'm people. Remember that."

"But I *am* serious," I said. "Want to? The new Edward G. Robinson?"

"Oh, I don't know," she murmured. Pattie had stretched and squirmed into garters and elastic and stilts, on high heels too early for her bestial grace, a charmer too early, rabid with perfumes, a forced flower, a hothouse darling. She was premature, ripped untimely, expensive. I wanted to sneeze when we spoke, and this gave a dangerous edge to my thoughts. "I'm afraid, Daniel Berman, you're not really serious, what I mean serious," she slyly murmured. "I have it like a little idea of mine. . . ." She put a high price on herself because more sure of prices than of values. "I'll tell you what, let's just talk, Dan." She yawned. She had a sweet furry little pink tongue. Her teeth clicked shut —she finished yawning.

"But what do you want to do tonight, it's Saturday, Pattie?"

"Oh, just talk. See the stage show at the Palace. Have a drink at the Tavern. A sandwich at Jackson's where the football players. Call a Zone Cab home. Nothing. Just like be together and talk things over, Dan. That's the kind a girl I am when I like a certain somebody."

My mother's warning about new spendthrift habits made my fingertips itch. Drained of invention by mourning for Eva, I could conceive of no answer to my mother's failure to treat me with the dignity of my age except that of sneaking a five-dollar bill from her purse, like the child of ten, that felonious sly lover. Already I imagined her reproach when she found out: "Hah, a thief! Going on seventeen years old, I got to lock up our valuables in a key, **my own** son a thief!" I would be the first thief in the family if you don't count Uncle Max, and who counts him? ("Little me is people too," Pattie said. "Now you be nice and serious, Dan.")

Lacking imagination in the depleted moral vitality of the jealous, I decided to spend all my money on Pattie Donahue, who was not even worthy of Eva's plaid shoelaces— that faithless wench, that bait for Hastings, oh I hated them both.

"You're getting prettier all the time, Pattie," I mewed, sniffing. "Is that Green Grass?"

"No, Night de Noel, my mother's." An ear pricked up to be smelled. "I've often noticed you, too. You're rather nice for a high school boy."

"So you want to take in the Palace? All right, I don't mind. It's terribly crowded on Saturday."

"No, let's go to the State."

"Okay."

"No, the Hippodrome, where the smart cinema-goer congregates."

"Yes, Pattie."

No. . . . No. . . . No. . . At last, fortified by these assertions of will, teased by my over-easy submission, she tried her lipstick once more before her mirror as we sat alone in the parlor, rolled her lips with a decisive smack, and announced, "How often do we have a night like this in January? Let's drive out to the drive-in."

"But I didn't drive a car, Pattie. My father won't let me use the Peerless until it gets a little older."

"A *Peerless? No* one drives a Peerless anymore. Well then, if you don't *want* to. . . . Anyway, the drive-in's probably closed for the season. . . ."

We appeared in a taxi that evening at the Jackson's Steak Sandwiches, known to football and basketball celebrities alike; we alighted like sports-page royalty and ate our real ground meat inside the shack, no trays screwed to our windows at a glorious tourney of convertibles, roadsters, and toasted buns. The coat-of-arms of Jackson's: A Gov.-Inspected Burger rampant on a field of Chili Sauce, and the device with fleur de parsley entwined: *In Hic Pickle Chips*. "The works," I magnificently commanded the waitress in her black satin bloomers and cape with the red satin lining —THE JACKSON'S STEAKBURGER GIRLS, LEAGUE SOFTBALL CHAMPS. . . . "The works!" I cried with a fling of my wrist in its frayed cuff (my wrists, my father's cuffs.)

"Dan," said Pattie Donahue in a wee me-saying voice, "you must not be profligate for poor little old me, really you must."

"Profligate, where did you hear that word? Nothing's too good for a date of mine on Saturday night, Pattie! There's lots more where that came from, that's my state of mind, Pattie."

"In a book, my mother's. . . . But I didn't *want* the pickle chips, Dan."

We enjoyed the works several times over, pickle chips, Jackson's Special Relish, and my profligacy which tempted Pattie off the narrow path of her mother's warnings against heartburn. She recognized the waitress. She knew the mustard-slinger behind the counter. She told me tales of steakburgers past, revelry at the Jackson's halberd, and of carefree Sundaes and chocolate Mondaes to come. "Jackson's is the nicest spot of all," she commented. The exercise of these maneuvers purposed something, of course. "I often come here with Lewis Snyder. Wasn't he wonderful though in the All-Scholastic game?"

"Maybe. I wrote it up."

"It's nice to be editor of the paper, though, too. I bet you see all the games from the press box with the real reporters."

"What do you mean, real reporters?"

She touched my hand and touched away. "Oh, *you* know, don't get mad. I mean they get *paid* for it, they wear felt fedoras. . . . Should I come out for the staff? Do you think I have talent?"—her touch touching me.

"Oh yes!"

"For journalism?" I looked to see the buffalo in her round little nickels of eyes, but she went on calmly, sucking at pickles: "Little me won't pretend like some people I could name, poetesses and people who play harps and such people. Now please don't ask me who, Daniel Berman. I don't want to be a gossip, my mother says. You either have talent or you pretend. That's the way I look at it. Me, I don't have any talent, but I'm sweet my mother says, and that's like a little talent in itself—"

"Oh you're talented," I cried.

"Yes? You really think so, Dan? Well, Lewis Snyder says and I agree with him, you're either born with it or you don't. Now he has like a born talent for pass receiving. Jever did you ever hear of the Statue of Liberty play, for instance, starring Knute Rockne and his Notre Dame boys?"

"Sure, I read it in a sports book. Well, they're backed up against the four-yard line, a minute to go, six points for the game, and the adversary—" I stopped as her nickel eyes sparkled like dimes in defiance. Her fingers chimed against rings as they reached for a loose cigarette in her pocket. It was a swagger coat.

"Lewis Snyder!" she said.

I knew whom she meant.

Over my shoulder towered Star Right End Lewis Snyder in a thick purple and yellow varsity sweater rolled over his belt. Star End Snyder gazed down at me with the contempt of a first-stringer, and then jerked his head back over his shoulder toward his two friends, first-string jocks also, to bid them watch while he made scrub of me. Hitherto hardly worthy of his notice, my dress-up civvies now drew the great fleshy lounge of his disdain, me in a tie and white shirt while he carried high on his sweater the colors of

Lakewood High, royal purple and angry yellow: "I know you, Danny-boy, Berman," he said slowly with the deceptive mildness of controlled strength.

Suddenly I knew what it felt like to be Chuck Hastings. In pity and terror I gaped at Lewis Snyder and knew what it looked like to be Dan Berman. Fury not ashes in his flickering nostrils, Pattie not Eva dabbing her mouth with the napkin in which my steakburger had come wrapped, pickle chips not kisses on her lips. . . . Pitying him, fatal with larger pertinence, I took my revenge against all the Chuck Hastingses of this world, all the meaner for my pity: "I guess I know you too, Lewis Snyder"—striking at myself with self-knowledge and cooling gravy.

He glanced over his shoulder to his waiting friends. "I guess you don't know me that well, Berman," he said. He moved so that I could feel the itch of varsity felt against my cheek as I sat. The wide muscles across his stomach creaked with unaccustomed misery in a man brawny from gridiron triumph. "You think you know me pretty well? Think so?"

"Well," I argued, "we went through school together. I used to give you my geometry homework. I always thought you were a wonderful left end"—but not frightened! I knew he was really a right end! "I guess I know you sort of," I said.

Again the jerk over his shoulder: "Maybe you want to know me better, eh Berman? Is that it?" The nudge at my cheek with his woolly tendoned belly stated: Get up if you're a man. Come on outside, bub. He had intercepted a lateral pass in the Shaker game and gotten an A-minus in French by copying from Juicer.

I patted a piece of bun. "That's all right, Lewis, I know you well enough." Hatred of Chuck, despair with Eva, these alone would not have given me strength. I was learning now the power of pity and the brutality of seeing an-

other man's point of view. These responsibilities thickening the phlegm in my voice, I turned to Pattie: "Would you
like to ask Lewis and the boys to sit down with us?
Pattie. . . ." I added. "We could push a table together."

Her piff-paffing laugh the palm!

"Oh but Dan dear, but we're going to be going soon,
aren't we, Dan?"—and her eyes, quarters now, half-dollars
of impudence, inflationary, clinked mine over the table and
clubbed Lewis Snyder's brittle ones like two knobbed
maces.

Her laurel titter! Tarara my praise! The ticker-tape ac-
colade!

Spake Lewis Snyder in the immolation of despair: "Come
on, Pattie, I said we're going right now."

Spake Pattie Donahue in the brazenness of the successful
speculator: "Maybe you're going, I said I'm not, Lewis."

Said Daniel Berman in the blood-rush of triumph and
pity: I said nothing.

"What do you mean, you're not?"—Lewis.

"I'm going with Dan Berman in his taxi. Maybe we'll
have another steakburger, works, before we go. I think I
might have a piece of one, they're so good"—a beautiful
glutton, her avaricious mouth open.

"What do you mean, he's a taxi driver now? Anything
for a dollar. How's the journalist, boy?"

Pity, pity. . . . I was Chuck Hastings, I was Lewis Snyder.
"Fine thanks," I said. "The *Times* won four prizes at Kent
State All-Scholastic. And what are the chances in the
Lorain game next year?"—I was also Dan Berman.

"No," Pattie persisted, "but he can take a girl in a taxi
when he doesn't have the Peerless. A girl hardly even has
to ask him. Why, I don't have to walk a step—"

I'll carry you for that, I thought.

"And the nice thing about a taxicab if you're the kind
of fellow doesn't care about spending like a couple dollars

on a girl, it's you can talk without worrying. Isn't that
right dear without interruptions? One thing I can't stand
it's one-arm drivers in traffic. Don't you think that's the
cause of ninety per cent of accidents, Lewis?"

The sweatered belly sagging, the fine athletic tendons
foundering, the trained face aghast. His season was over.
Forgive us all, Lewis, for not being adversaries worthy of
a star right end.

"Come on, fellows, we're getting out of here, I guess
Jackson's is just a place for school kids"—a hitch to the
roll of his varsity knit, the championship furnace-room
ashes to him now.

"Whose car did you come in, Lewis? Phil's? Fred's?
Give me a call someday, will you? Boulevard ni-yen see-ex
ought ought, you know. You write down the number. You
remember. I'd love to see you someday."

The vain flapping of defeated shoulder blades. The
broad slumped back in purple and yellow. The pride of
Lakewood High brought low.

"Slong, Lewis," said Miss Pattie Donahue to the limp
buttocks loosely embracing each other between silent sad-
dened friends.

We munched without a word. I spread mustard on a slice
of bread. "Me," sighed small-pawed Pattie. She sighed
with a satisfied hunger, tested prowess, and satisfaction in
risks well-taken. "Me," she admitted once more.

I was stunned by a victory I had not earned. I was filled
with confused admiration. Maybe eating would help.

"Another steakburger, Pattie? Cherry pop?"

"No, I just said that. I alway say. I always say a good
right end is worth a fullback anyday. I always say like a
—"

I was exhausted.

A few minutes later, finding her eyes now nickels again,
worn and rubbed, a mire of reasons, I suddenly realized

that she too had secrets. Marveling in the shock of this meeting, I wondered what profit lay in her game with Lewis Snyder. Was I worth such a display of esteem? Did snubbing Lewis, sheik and right end, entail rewards of its own? Where in the future—since we all knew that I was absent from Pattie Donahue's future, and Lewis Snyder or someone like him came closest to a presence—did this event take its stand? Small-pawed, pouting, she practiced for some kill. I recalled Eva with Chuck in the furnace room, my jealousy a link with Pattie and Lewis, my deep indifference to them making it workable and a tool. . . . "I'd like a dip of potato salad, one scoop please," I asked the waitress. Pattie was an economist with a secret nature; her glacial moneyed eyes melted, and I almost loved her for this rich slime of planning and becoming. With the sense of the uncanny—something recognized, then denied, then terribly known as truth—I suddenly felt that I was looking into the eyes of Euclid Masters thirty years earlier.

"When I have a date with a boy," she said with these new eyes, "I like to have a date with a fellow. I know what I want." Significantly, the small-pawed touch at my wrist heavier now: "Now you know how much I care. . . ."

I clung for stability to my status as an editor with notes pinned on the wall for him almost every day. My typists, my reporters, my staff. Me. My manful surname, Berman. (But who is Berman, who am I?) A practiced one in prefabricated love, Pattie could construct with her tinny words —"like how much I care"—something near the sensuality of Eva's putting on my jacket in the quiet and dark of the five o'clock school when she had walked back and forth before me, saying: *"It fits, Daniel Berman, it's warm inside."* That's who I was! Eva wore my jacket, Pattie touched my hand!

"That was very interesting with Chuck Hastings," said Pattie Donahue, "that discussion you had. . . ."—and I

saw once more before they vanished the clever scheming
eyes of Euclid Masters in his youth, the marsh of desire
and hunger and the sucking sands now dried into concrete.
"You really told him off," she said, "you smeared him
down behind the ten-yard line."

"Tougher than football, dialectic," I said abstractedly.
"You need guts and brains." Why did she press the reminder of her victory and mine over Lewis Snyder? If she
lent me this importance, how did she intend to collect on
the investment? "You need a firm foundation in modern
philosophy."

"Fight too," she said complacently, "and that old Lakewood High School try. Chuck isn't really so much if you
ask me. Once he called me up, Boulevard ni-yen see-ex
ought ought, but I was too busy. . . ."—busy eyes over
me.

We took a cab back to her house. I worried about having
enough money, then stopped worrying. She showed me
her treasure, the locket about her neck in which a strand of
white hair lay preserved in a twist. "Put the locket back,
Dan," she said. I reached it around her neck, and as my
arms went around her, her own arms came up about me.
The privacy of a body! The loneliness and triumph of a
kiss in a moving taxi! There was a secret, almost tender
smile at the corners of her mouth as I kissed it and kissed
it again. There must be secrets, I would have thought if I
could have thought, for her lips to be so warm, for her arms
and schoolgirl breasts to struggle and yield so through a
coat. . . . Thus she kissed me while the meter ticked away
the last of my mother's five dollars. "When you're fdone,"
she said, pronouncing the f for *finished* to tell me that she
meant what she said. It didn't matter. She drew warmly
and smilingly away and lay against upholstery, only my
hand still touched her throat in which I felt no pulse. *Eva!*
but it did not matter for the moment.

"Pattie," I said.

Eagerly, her eyes shining: "Really, Dan, you're a wonderful speaker, I mean you express yourself so well."

The meter ticked through our bodies' fragrance while taxi wheels throbbed over the ribs of a steel bridge. The light at the end of a crane in the valley winked up at me. I failed to wink back. It winked for the war about to begin. There was night work already. The lights of the Flats shuttled and flared; a Republic Steel furnace blazed; the entire industrial valley lay below the bridge in purple false daylight. Pattie's swaggering breasts had tickled me through her swagger coat.

Rearmament outside; Republic Steel and diplomats. Within a taxi homeward with Pattie Donahue, I knew only that for a swift moment she was a warm bird to my hand. Then she showed me the locket and its strand of white hair, emitting a sigh from her soundtrack; and discreet before death, which is as unmentionable as undies in the suburb, I asked her no questions. Finally, drawing nourishment from her lips and in some sense joining her in the lifelong scheme against death, I had the right to ask about the curled memorial hair. Even Pattie lived in mourning within her chirping exterior.

"Oh *that*," she said, "it's only mine."

"But it's almost white."

"Yes," she murmured, "it was like a little experiment. I dyed it with peroxide."

Dizzily I plunged from the peaks of love and death. I said: "You mean you bleached it?"

"Yes," she whispered, flushing, "I mean bleached"—and in pleasure at this adventure in deep feeling she threw back her head to laugh. It had always astonished me to discover her laughter; her lips seemed to form a whole, some flexible and unbreakable metal, but then she laughed and shattered that perfect mouth into the fragments of joy. "It was just

like trying something out," she cried as the taxi pulled up
to her house, "and I wear it around my neck, Dan!"

I said good-by to her on her front porch under the
spacious and specious sky of winter's false spring. She did
not let me kiss her again, although she put her eyes next
to mine—her quickened eyes like those of Euclid Masters.
They were not really coins, those eyes of cute Pattie Donahue. "Don't be ridick, Dan. . . ."—her small mittened
hands patting me away. She was a sort of marsh, with im-
penetrable marshy eyes. We see our own reflection in clear
water; I saw nothing in Pattie's eyes, and only a shiny bub-
ble of decay in those of Mr. Masters. Some primitive peoples
believe that the reason you cannot see your shadow when
looking into a swamp is the crocodile in the mud which
gobbles it up; therefore beware of looking into marshes. "I
mean gnight, Dannie. . . ."

I came home, my parents asleep, my pockets empty, to
find something to break. I was ridick. I snapped my fountain pen between two fingers, the plastic shivering with a
pop, the black ink spouting on my bed with my unseen
but crashing blood. Poor Lewis Snyder! Pattie's cute mouth,
it was true, had at least broken in laughter.

I soaked up the ink with bits of Kleenex. I let the water
run but did not wash, searching the mirror for the lies in
my own eyes. Already I had smudges of deep thought and
late hours. Tom Moss, Lewis Snyder, Chuck Hastings,
Euclid Masters, all these crocodile friends just like me,
might now too be discovering themselves out in my judgment as I looked for myself in theirs.

Eva! Love me anyway!

12. *The giving of credit*

I₸'S A BEAUTIFUL BUILDING, ISN'T it?" I asked when we saw the Taj Mahal in the newsreel.

"Yes," my mother replied, pensive in her last year's Persian, her chin resting meditative in flesh and fur, "yes, it's a funny name but"—always on the lookout for her son —"yes, I wish it was yours. Still, probably not much income. But a nice propitty. Yes."

Yes!—a fine beginning for a story. This is a yes-and-no part of the story. I tell it as a tragic joke, which is one way of saying *yes*. Let us give my parents credit: that's an American compliment, high praise derived from the Dun & Bradstreet division of the language, true all the same. In our suburb we wore an invisible armor clamped over us while we still sucked our thumbs for love and greedily watched our parents' movements. We learned to sit up for praise and not for the joy of sitting. Even the muscles and creases of our fat legs, nourished by vitamins, grew stiff in this early watchfulness. (Squawk! Bad taste of cod liver oil. *Brief* squawk.) The armored weight, this longing for power and this fear of it, plus the bad taste of health, had jumbled all our marbles. It was a heavy well-behaved madness, however, a credit-giving madness, in most cases protected from the risks of mania—the crippling without the

161

stumbling. The armor lay invisibly on skate-trained legs. We had plenty of playground space.

There was balance in life on earth. The papers said that mass murder was being prepared and also that Irene Rich stayed young thanks to grape juice. We believed the Welch Grape Juice Company, but Miss Rich disappeared; we did not believe Hitler, and mass murder appeared. How could I then have extrapolated when I was only beginning to invent plane geometry?

The houses of our suburb, built without the awareness of light, possessed it anyway because of the fact of money, which signifies space in the suburb. The houses, separated each from each, were bathed in sunlight on brick like powder on a girl's cheek; the light penetrated to the pimple-carrying adolescent blood as much as the powder did, despite the sudden smile of sun on brick, while the desire of blood foundered in comfort, sleep, and ambition. (Not Juicer and me! We moped in hideouts, smoking butts, eating peanuts, drinking talk.) The concept of *neighbors* enveloped the necessary amenities toward other houses. The nonsingers chorused their nonsongs. Economical, I like everyone else held back my limited quantity of good-will from my family, not wanting to waste it where my place was already made. It is a rare man who laughs in his kitchen as he does in his office.

My father was such a rare man. Carrying the groceries in from the Peerless, heaving them up the stairs, smelling of green vegetables, he would answer his wife's how-are-you with a: "What, you crazy? A dog felt like me he's dead five times. What you got to eat, something hot?"

"Irish stew with lokshen," my mother would say. "Cooked carrots. Toss salad. How's business?"

"Don't ask. If I open a funeral parlor, people stop dying" —his head rolling back in laughter and his hands pounding at his thighs, the fat of power on his chest and belly. Lung-

ing in double-breasted serge, the coat low and funneling
behind, the knees slightly bent, he would shrug away his
laughter finally to say, "So who wants a success right away?
You want a hardboiled egg for brunch, don't you? Wait till
it cooks. Where's Dan?"

"Reading again," my mother informed on me, "doing
nothing. Remember the time he broke all the clocks in
the house?"

"Sarah, that was ten years ago."

"So? He's a big boy, nice built, and then what? He gets
all sheiked up to go out and spend my money—"

"*Our* money."

"He spends it, don't he?"

I stood in the doorway. "I'm here."

"What have you got to say for yourself?" my mother
demanded. "Defend yourself."

"Hello, Dad."

"Son."

Although not so ethereal as cousin Sheldon, who pronounced chamois cloth *shamwah* instead of shammuss or
shammy, I showed tendencies to indecision and even wrong
decisions. "An intellectual? Can't even decide what end
he wants to eat the banana!" I also dodged my mother's
questions concerning the future: "What's wrong with a
doctor? It's a nice living, and you like to read you can
read the magazines in the entry when there ain't no
customers patients. Don't you want your little wife to have
an iceless, a vacuum, a convenient kitchen?"—questions
with a shove, they were.

My father concurred, a man who loved, in a room, looking glasses; and in a parcel of property, solid fixtures. "Why
not?" he asked. "From a doctor you can branch out. You
read about Silberger the wizard of the hotel business, the
Hotel Wizard?—that's what the *Press* said in Milton Widder's column. There was this fellow Silberger, in 1928 he

was just a room clerk. He borrowed fifteen thousand from
a Doctor Levy—it happened to be his brother-in-law the
dentist—he saved his money but you don't get rich saving,
a smart man. He had a head for business for a doctor, a
dentist. Ten years ago he was a nothing, a doctor a dentist,
now he's a two-hundred-and-fifty-thousand-dollar building
in Los Angeles City and that's only the beginning. A restaurant of the same name with dinner music with the meals,
good dinner music, classical. He got three switchboards in
his office alone, radio sets in the doubles, ear phones in the
singles. Milton Widder called him the Hotel Wizard in his
column in the *Press*. In less than ten years he did that: if
you don't like business you don't have to put the property
in your name, but who doesn't like a nice parcel, looking
glasses in the lobby? I met this Doctor Levy in Miami
Beach, you think he fills teeth now? I'll say he don't. He
lies on the beach in the sun to rest up from playing gin. He
can lose a thousand a week if he's happy and he don't
care. *That's* the kind of doctor a dentist I want my son to
be. . . ."

"Why a teeth-puller?" my mother demanded. "Why not
a doctor an allergy specialist?"

She cared for names; my father was a lover of things.
If he bought a Chinese buddha, it was because he liked it,
not because it came all the way from Chinatown in San
Francisco. "It's worth the money, a nice fixture. A fixture
like this in the store, you should put it on a dining-room
table a bed table, an ornament decoration, it costs five-six
dollars a piece junk. Here it costs fifteen dollars but you got
something, a door it opens, a Chinament he's sitting inside.
Worth every cent.

"E-v-e-r-y s-e-n-t," spelled Mother. "Even a general
practicer, why a dentist? All right, so you keep nice hours,
but you're only a D.D.S."

"He went into partners with a Doctor Levy—" He considered: "A dentist." He paused a moment. "He went into partners with this Doctor Levy, they're the talk of the town. They're *very—well—off.*" He paused for emphasis. "This Doctor Levy blesses the day he met him, and he never even went to high school. Silberger, not Doctor Levy the dentist. They call him the Wizard of the Hotel Business. That shows."

"A physician all right, you're a surgeon, a professional. You're an allergy specialist with all the little needles and two receptionists. But a dentist? You rinse the mouth with Listerine—"

"It was a nice hotel, good location, all inside wiring, beautiful, it had looking glasses in every room and a whole lot of looking glasses in the lobby. Clean too." He loved things, looking glasses for style and the regard that judges; my father loved mirrors in gold frames with nice curly icing on them to give form to the judging grown soft in America.

"You know Doctor Morris Sanders," Mother asked, "you know Moe Sanders, you know Moish? He started from the bottom a doctor, he worked himself up to specialist—"

I thought of Eva Masters, her telephones, her lawns, her little luxuries accepted and genteelly unenjoyed. Even the salad oil her mother made, snitched on the edge of a rapacious finger, had frightened me as it teased my tongue forward, strange to my palate. They all rode horseback. They belonged to a country club (two years arrears in their dues). At her mother's soirées the women spoke of cloth and style, Florentine prints and *the new collars,* Sicilian lace and this year's skirt, the fashions springing afresh each year out of the subscriptions to their magazines. "Antique jewelry is the latest thing!" a silvery voice rang out. "Modern is passé," another replied. They used French words and pronounced Morris *Maurice.* My mother called Dr. Sanders *Moish.*

"Look at Moish, he worked his way through medical school playing the clarinet in an orchestra, and met nice girls too—"

"To the point," said my father, "we call it the point in business. There's money in property. Course you got no security, but who needs security?"—the poet speaking, the explorer, the specialist in dreams with inside wiring. "America is the land of opportunity because you don't need security. You want to be safe, sit on a stool and add up figures? I don't want it altogether. I can get like that a dozen Fenn College graduates to work for me."

A magician of desire, he transformed the dreads of a chilhood in Kamenetz Podolsk into second mortgages and three-week options. Risk too is a comfort, a permission from the world, a responsibility to it. His slanting yellow-flecked Tartar eyes were delighted: "I did it for *you*, I need it myself? For all the kits. Why do you think I stayed in the store while your mama was having the kits? Do you think I trusted the help? Andy could eat all the macaroons he wants, but I don't want him loading his pockets with quarters. You have to watch. Your mother don't understand business."

This was a thrust at her habit of giving birth on Saturday, the busiest day. One of my brothers was born during the Thanksgiving shelled nuts, cranberry, and turkey season. The hospital telephoned my father at the store to tell him. If he had even thought to suggest remaining with her for the birth, she herself would have sent him away. Business before pleasure, before parturition.

"Your father did it all for you," she said, "and now you just want to go to college you don't know what-for, not even a doctor. Ida's Molly, she won't even go to the toilet without the Book of Knowledge. She comes back, her mother says, 'What color?' She says, 'I don't know—*that's* an intellectual. . . .'"

"Listen Sarah, let me tell it. We're talking about business."

"I'm listening, Jake, how hard can you listen? We're talking about medicine, a professional."

"This is a man-to-man, Daniel and me, I don't need you for a minute, Sarah."

"You mean a mother who gave her life blood, the calcium pills from her teeth, you don't need? I'm just advicing be a physician, it's a good steady thing."

"Now you listen, Sarah—"

"Just listen to me, Jake—"

I listened without attending, neither wizard nor professional, sulking before the ingredient of failure in this success of aspiration for me. I disliked to connect success and love (still do). As I had seen the eyes of Euclid Masters in Pattie Donahue's marshy nickels, so I heard his moribund voice in the careen of passion between my mother and father.

"Even the dentist made a fortune in real estate," said my mother.

"Even the professional wasn't too good for business," said my father.

"Ain't he got a good head on his shoulders?" demanded my mother.

"He got a head," my father admitted.

I wondered what Euclid Masters, like my father in ways hidden to both of them, idealists of excess, would have me become in order to justify the element of adulation in his hate of me. Americans all!

The morning following the evening with Pattie I told my mother that I had taken five dollars from her purse. "Why?" she said.

"Yes, because I wanted to tell the truth," I said—the answer to why I told her.

"What? You took it, why?"

"Yes, because I wanted to spend it."

"—I mean why you tell me, you want to aggravate me? How much can you enjoy to spend five dollars?"

Here was how much: "A sandwich, a hot drink, a taxi, another taxi—"

"A taxi!" she cried. "When I schlep myself uptown from downtown on the streetcar? You want to marry that girl, I bet she got yellow teeth from not brushing the tartar?"

"Who?"

"Who! The taxi one, thief!"

I could not explain at breakfast or any other meal that I had spent too much money on Pattie Donahue exactly because I did not like her very well. She could not understand that I spent the money on Pattie Donahue because I loved Eva Masters, although my father, nodding and sipping from his farina with raisins in it, had a nose for such complications: "I thought it was that other girl, the one from the boulevard near the Lake Shore Hotel. . . ."

"Bathtub dirtier! nogood! thief!" my mother cried, turning to my father: "You tell him," she ordered.

"You already told him, Sarah," said my father, swallowing cereal.

"Look at him. To look he doesn't go out spending my five dollars or carouseling with that Montague boy, he just browses around the house all night. I get up I say, *Go to bed*—he says, *I'm hungry I'm not sleepy*. Should I believe? The thief's hat is burning, his face is guilty. At night he's not sleepy, then when should he be sleepy? When." She held her stomach and leaned toward me, her forehead slightly damp, like a sweating pear. "See, I just felt an attack, a stomach, just like. Right here in the middle. You give me the Summer Complaint in wintertime, you! Thief!"

"Leave alone, Sarah," said my father.

"Yes," I said. I agreed with my father.

"I should leave alone, he sits like a honeybear on a guitar, I smell smoking on his breath. And did he brush the teeth today? And what about my five dollars?"

I said: "I'll pay you back, Ma. I don't care."

"He doesn't care. . . ."

But my father, who didn't care about money either, except for its color of possibility and old cloth, its smell of pockets and sex, who loved prisms, chicken skin, radishes, and the striations of things, looked at me and said: "All right, all right, I remember when I was a kit, I was just like him. Wild." He had courted my mother in green shoes, his hair wilted by water. I came to Pattie in a rain of dandruff, sallow with jealousy, changed by desire for Eva Masters into a monster against my mother's money. "He told you about it himself, he wanted it the worst way, he said he'll pay it back," my father murmured. "I give him credit."

"I don't give him credit, you know what I think? I think he's full of complexes. All right, a show, a book, you got something already, but a *taxi ride*—even Doctor Sanders takes the streetcar, his car's in the garage the Olds, and he's no general practicer."

"Listen," advised my father, "he'll get over it. It ain't complexes it's a stage, wildness. You learn. He's only a little crazy. You're only young once in a while—"

Being taken at the eye from eye to eye, I watched from one to the other to see if either might find out my need. Having lost my Eva, why did I look for love from Pattie and an illicit spending among the high school sharpies? For the same reason that Louis the Sixteenth, who feared poisoning from his Jacobin baker, still could not stay away from pastry. Yes, he even got fat on it, waiting for the strychnine to strike him down. I munched while fearing poison because my need for love was greater than my dread of poison; from the beginning in our suburb we find that love is not love without a hidden bitterness, so that we even learn to search out the poison first in the hope that love will come with it.

"Look at me, I was wild once," my father said.

"No! I won't get over it!"

"He can be wild now, pretty soon he'll be a real estate man—"

"A doctor, you mean," said my mother.

"A realtor I mean, and he'll have his fun, listen—"

"A specialist with his own office in the medical building—"

I cried out: "No! Stop! I won't get over it! Stop! STOP! I won't, I *won't* be what you tell me"—whatever that might be. I bearded my father; I watched his heavy black beard prickle along the spiked flesh of his jowls. "You can be what you want," I yelled, "and *let me be.* . . ."

The confusion in his yellow-flecked Tartar eyes, slanting with good humor and the body's pleasure, whirled suddenly with the self-pitying glaze of deception, unfocused, looking blindly backward down the long corridor of age. Ponderously sarcastic, he said, "I suppose, son, I have the right to think—"

"Who cares what you think?" I cared, but I had to care more for myself in that moment. "I know!"—that I had the right to make my own mistakes against the stupid wisdom of age.

"I suppose you know it all—"

"Mr. Know-it-all!" screamed my mother. "You call him something, Jake."

"Let him talk," my father said. "I can still listen even if he's my son." The smoke in my head was dispersed with surprise—what had he said? He said he could listen to me? I gaped forward; I breathed through my mouth; I looked at him in silence, suddenly filled with love for his paunch of desire and health, the sleek gleam of power in his smile-wrinkled Tartar eyes—what was it that made Americans of both Euclid Masters and my father? The hunger for success which they shared, their definitions trivial? The dreamwork and event mere mask for the wish? No, no, there were differences between Euclid Masters and Jacob Berman, although opposites meet in the American dream as in other dreams. What then? Subtle economies in their ways of spending each other? But there are human economies and commercial economies, and the recreation of my father's flesh must be another thing from Euclid's pause for scheming prolonged unto death. "Let him talk, let him tell me," my father said, the seams of his flesh like the grain in meat. "I'm a greenhorn, I can learn—"

"Nogood! Going on seventeen and look at him! Thief!"

"American," my father said, the truest epithet of all. "Go on and tell me, Yankee."

I felt the lost and lonely abandon of having slept through an entire day, waking at night to find that the world has gone on without me and that something from life which may have been its best part is forever lost. I knew again the uncanny childish fantasy of being where I was, only one hundred years earlier, Rip Van Berman among the restricted bowling leagues, waking to discover in my suburb how gray the stone in that time, how small this oak, how unborn these parents.

"A kit like that? a thief?" asked my mother.

My tongue pressed against my teeth, darting hard, darting free.

"What? I'm listening to you, son. . . ."—tender, tender.

I screamed: "I hate you! I hate the store and the buildings and what you think of me. I hate hate *hate* you!"—now I have a sense of the distinction. My father's heavy hand slapping me out of my rage and into tears is known in another way from the shriveled fingers of Euclid Masters nagging a card in solitaire. My father, an economist with the disdain of saving which is the saving grace, knew both how to draw and to build on the credit of love. Much tribute is owed my father, to whom I screamed and sobbed: "I hate you all!"

He slapped me and then, himself, went out to the garage to wash down the Peerless with the garden hose, thus disguising the run of tears, yes, from his joy-loving yellow-flecked Tartar eyes.

13. *"Not pre-eminently virtuous and just"*

BAYING LIKE THREE DREAMY
pups at the moon of power, subjecting our ambitions to
Love the Bunsen Burner of all our alchemies, we were no
longer sufficient unto the glandular uncertainties of our
age. This is not very complicated. Tom Moss, Juicer Montague, and I wanted to get laid. "The proof of the pudding,"
as Juicer sagely remarked, "is what all the shouting must
be about."

> *Love loff luv,*
> *We knew its name*
> *if not its deed.*
> *They're not the same.*

It was a duty of research which I owed my fantasies
about Eva Masters. In my submissive but vengeful heart,
it took part in a dialectic in answer to the low Socratics of
her father, Euclid Masters—my heart full of desire to submit to victory over itself. It was the unclipped coupons
from bonds of anger toward Chuck Hastings. In addition
there was envy of my own father, perhaps, and the smart
of his hand on my face. It might be so many things toward
my mother that I hesitate to suggest any; they are all possible—probable—certain—ridiculous.

For Juicer it was a felling of plump monsters fed until bilious on dry diet with Lucille. It must also have been everything that it was for me—his father, his mother, his age.

For Tom it was a sharing of all our articulations. Call him Oedipus Rex, too. His skinny armor clanked behind us.

Also it seemed a keen way to spend a Saturday evening. ("When a boy gets to be mature," ran one of my mother's adages, "you got to make sure he keeps clean. Cold showers are supposed to be invaluable, Mrs. Gornstein told me, until they get married anyway." But those cold showers are merely invaluable, not efficacious.)

It was a street-corner conspiracy with origins even earlier than the Last Supper, when my mother had said, "Eat," and I had answered, "Eat yourself. I already ate"—obstinacy and disdain because the maternal thermostat could not regulate the mysteries glowing in my centrally heated pants. Carrots and peas, roast beef with crisp fat, gravy, sliced mushrooms, mashed potatoes, more mushrooms and gravy, still more gravy (when the mushrooms were gone) to put on the more mashed potatoes—all this only made the mystery of life more imperative. Good food. There was also salad. Cucumbers sliced lengthways like pickles. And pickles. I studied my father, the familiar of pleasure and power, as he gobbled another slice of apple pie, first mashing it into cream with his fork; I wondered if at any moment an adult—a father, say—could escape the memory of joy in the ecstasies which I imagined. Would it change my own eating? my sleeping? even my pungent dreams?

I had a piece of pie myself, but it was too sweet to finish in that hour of expectation.

Leaving home, I wore my covert suit with the zipper fly and the five-pointed handkerchief as brilliant as the wise man's star of destiny in my lapel pocket. Hair slicked down to pin-feather wisps behind my ears, armpits Mum'd and

socks Foot-ease'd with potion and powder, gym-knits shorts
and new T-shirt inspected for snags and smells, all these
solicited the approval of some lucky salesperson of love. I
wanted her to be pleased! Juicer, sweating already, wore a
striped blue shirt stained with salt at the armpits, as was
his father's double-breasted blue-serge jacket; I disapproved, just as I disapproved of Tom's spare yokel leanness,
dry as old biscuits. Perhaps they were critical of dapper
Dan also, too celebrational for their moment of talion,
me a Byzantine priest, Juicer an overluxurious Roman, and
Tom a sly hell-fire Calvinist descended for a night in town.
"What you think this is, your wedding?" Tom asked. "Getting married to someone?" We judged ourselves fondly.

"Yeah? Well, it's more like that than a funeral, you
jerks—"

Their mournful eyes lent no support to my argument.
Nor did mine, though the linen star at my lapel shone
bright with Dad's initials. We were responsible to the universe of pleasure. We were as dutiful as ideal grooms. Both
shame and a fine false-hearty fret lay on our overheated
faces. "Cleanliness is next to godliness," I had admitted to
my mother, "but only *next*."

A bittersweet caramel evening, the candy of decay in the
suburban air melting up from leaves this week discovered
sodden under warm snow: the sweet softness in a warm
early spring with the debris of winter still scattered in
puddles or brewing heaps: the sewers running with the pur-
loined recollections of desire and oily slush: radios suddenly blaring from windows surprised open: dogs nosing
in hedges, their rumps twitching, their hair bristling for the
smell of warmth or the smell of cats under the swollen and
shapeless February sky. And someplace Rosalie Fallon
drawing plump figures on the dining-room table, Lucille
Lake refrigerated by her harp in the perpetual winter of
patience, small-pawed Pattie Donahue scheming in her

diary for new investments and the possible profit of love.
And Eva Masters languorous on the arm of her father's
chair while Chuck Hastings described the setting sun over
the Golden Gate and drank chocolate with a marshmallow
intended for me squashed in it. . . . We three parodied our
parents' contentments while our parents chopped up the
record of the day's disasters which had not reached us.
The smell of wet ashes in the alleys, the smell of impris-
oned blood in our nostrils.

> *This was serious,*
> *Fatal,*
> > *funny:*
> *Two dollars of love*
> *is a lot of*
> > *money.*

"Nice night out," sniffed Tom Moss.

"Nice? Epochal," murmured Juicer Montague.

"You got the address?" I asked. "World-shaking." Perhaps the world was shaking, but Tom, Juicer, and I were
ashiver.

We scuffed each other into the streetcar which would
carry us downtown. Our dimes clinked into the box and we
submitted to the grind of wheels against rails. Our solemnity spoke for respect for streetcars in the past; the perch
and slap of our barbered loins on wicker argued new purposes to this evening commutation. A lady looked for a
seat and I gave her mine, then hung from the strap with
the swollen patience of a salami on the butcher's hook.

"What does this remind you of?" I asked Juicer.

"Nothing," said Tom.

"Wolfe. 'The Killers' by Ernest Hemingway, why? Nothing," said Juicer.

"We forgot to get transfers," I said.

We transferred into the cross-town car that would take us among the swarming Hungarians and cheap hotels of the Flats near the river. "Here, you hold the address awhile," said Juicer. I slid the card into my pocket. It had been recommended by a college boy on Juicer's block who had made a gesture with his circled thumb and index finger and a jabbing hand to indicate great value received; it had been confirmed by Lewis Snyder the sheik. *Lucille,* Juicer breathed. *Eva,* I breathed. Breathed Tom: "If it's more than three dollars, hell, it isn't worth it. What do they think they are?"—outraged in imagination by the thought of overcharge.

Juicer and I, thumping hearts, felt already overcharged. We talked of vice like young priests, with a purely ritual knowledge, interested in our sins but our blood too hot to feel the chill of fear. Or if there came a chill it was a pleasurable one, followed by flushes and a crowded sleeplessness. But solemnity and grit, where was desire? The slothful city stirred in its murky waters. The streetcar carried us on.

"Rgh," swallowed Tom in the throes of some stifling meditation. He wrestled with it a moment, fine lines appearing in the muscular knots at the corners of his mouth, and then repeated the comment.

"Me too," Juicer agreed, "I feel the same way myself." We expressed our joined concern in elaborate electioneering scowls. We comforted each other.

"Lewis says this girl really loves it," Juicer insisted hopefully. "She likes it. She's terrific."

"Really sexy, eh? It's great that way."

"She doesn't mind," Juicer said, his hands hanging between his knees.

We were morose. We were fantastic. We were ready to soar in the arms of a paid employee.

"You pay before or after?" Tom asked, receptive to the lesson in sin that, whenever we paid, it would be after.

Custodian of the key, I looked in my palm at the card for the New Rome Hotel, the Rome Hotel Hoor House, as Lewis Snyder called it: "Just ask for Black Lil. That's what I always do." Tom, who had finally procured the card from Lewis after Juicer's recommendation, gave it to us to guard in trust because of the possibility that his mother might look in his pockets.

"It's pronounced hor," I said.

"Hoor," Juicer said.

"Hor!"

"Hoor!"

Hor hoor. . . . hor hoor. . . .

"Bad woman," said Tom Moss the mediator.

"My mother says hoor," grumbled Juicer.

"That's what *she* says," I said, unsubmissive to authority.

"My mother never says it at all," Tom remarked with a certain amount of pride. "She's too refined. Lewis Snyder says Black Lil is the best—she's terriff."

The streetcar swayed over rail and brick through jungles of neon, through wildernesses of smoke and noise and Saturday-night wiggling. Finding love difficult, we had studied magic and hypnotism: how to draw objects through glass, how to see the future with Professor Nostradamus of the Academie Française, how to recite charms over a frozen girl's back. Wonders had we seen, Pattie, Rosalie, Lucille, and Eva, and we needed a wonder to make ourselves as old as these knowledgeable creatures. "Every confidence," said Tom. "I have every confidence in Black Lil since we come on the recommendation of Lewis Snyder. Let me hold the card awhile."

"Yeah? I kept it when you were afraid to, just a card—"

"Let him, Dan. I wish we were there already."

"Oh so do I! . . . I mean, in a way, so do I."

The city labored in night shifts and pleasure, as did we. The red false dawn of the mills preempted the distended sky above us. Happy voyaging dupes, our veins full of paint and our eyes myopic with rut, our mouths full of words and our hearts full of reticence, our pockets full of money, our memories full of courage, our new shoes full of feet, our ears full of slippery slivers of orange wax, the seats of our pants full of regret, our buttons full of thread (plastic buttons, real cotton), we wondered whether we really wanted what we wanted. Pampered and sniffling, we went adventuring across town on the streetcar. "Penny transfers, lads?" asked the conductor.

Alchemic boys in creaking pants,
We mimicked the paternal stance

Of mighty love and spiced success,
Which comes of saving from excess.

We leaned our pimples toward the past
And knew our futures would not last.

We swam with dread in novel seas,
Gave up the town's economies.

For childish boys, let love suffice.
But then let love be fierce and nice.

"I don't care what she asks, that Black Lil, I'll just give it to her," I said.

"Yeah, it's worth it," said Juicer.

"But what if she asks too much, a gyp?" Tom inquired. "I don't want her to make a fool out of me."

We looked at him in commiseration. "Dan and I are fools," Juicer said, "we admit it. But we're not stupes."

Arrived. Bricks like some monstrous tomb and shade-drawn apertures. Up a stairway into the maw.

The heroes of passion shuffled into line past a bellhop's cop-spotting eye. *Okay you, okay you, okay you.* We waited amid the taste of dust in a room without windows where the grins of our compatriots discovered the three little Dutch boys volunteering for service at the dike. We attempted the loll that conceals on sofas; we sweated and breathed with difficulty. The drill master who nominated us for service, one at a time, had the pleasant habit of a fat man, resting his warm hand inside a loosened belt as he stood. We did not lose our ignorance all at once that night. In quest of a magic gesture which would spin us through the revolving door to power and love, we felt our virginities creeping away almost unnoticed in the air of that brown hotel room with its brown bituminous haze. We were blotted by suspense and forgetting to exhale.

"You," said the fat guard standing next to me. "You with the no-part in your hair, yeah you, *next.*"

I obeyed.

No daughter of Gomorrah with a stiff neck in spangles and the ripe fatness of mutton about her haunches was Black Lil. She chewed Spearmint and practiced elementary public health. She examined us with the puerile caution of a Board of Education nurse. She might have been a nursing mother, which surprised us who had the image either of all Truth and Beauty (Lucille, Rosalie, Pattie, Eva) or of some sagging machine with dugs of rope, burning for degradation. The breasts of Black Lil, Secret Vice of the Football Squad, swung like taut sweating gourds; her thickened body, that of a woman with pregnancy on her mind, took us all three (separately) with laughter and a certain amount of appetite at this slaughter of the innocents. It could be a taste like any other, such as for strawberry ice cream. Her skin was as hard as that of a fresh plum. Afterwards she humorously chased us, not even picking our pockets, saying, "Git." And: "Come around again when you save up the pennies in your piggy bank, y' hear me now?"

On the long rolling streetcar journey back, Juicer asked finally: "How did you do?" We had been rocking half-asleep in the meditation that what we did was not so much as it had seemed at the time: *The pastness of the past.* We had been ripely musing in this and in no thought at all.

"It was great," I said, "really great."

"Me too, I really made her happy," Juicer said.

"Boy," said Tom. "Wow. She helped me take off my shoes." In respectful silence we all thought that was real hospitable of her.

We fell again to our sorrows. In my heart I addressed Eva, saying: Love me anyway, despite sin and Chuck. Juicer and Tom must have been engaged in a similar forgiving of trespasses in their heads. They also wondered what Black Lil was writing in her diary about us. Poems? Epigrams? Just what? Abstracted, full of sermons, itching, we descended the streetcar together but hardly said good night as we turned off in different directions. We were all sad. I was sad.

We fled to our mothers' homes like three long-tailed lonely high-foreheaded spermatazoa, our nuclei in a turmoil, our chromosomes sizzling.

14. Red Masters, the West Side nihilist

ONE NIGHT AS I PONDERED weak and weary over many a quaint and curious volume of forgotten lore, suddenly there came a rapping: rapping, aye! but more a tapping at my chamber door. "Ma!" I yelled, "that you?" Answered me only the tintinnabulation of the vacuum, vacuum, vacuum cleaner on the parlor floor. I scraped back my chair and gazed for very dread into my death's head from Kresge's, both of us slack-jawed, my scrapbook and my ping-pong trophy softly croaking, "Nevermore."—Well, it happened almost like this, although the occult personage was a breathless, carrot-haired, big-toothed raven who said not, *Nevermore,* but *Hiya, Dan.* My lips had, in fact, been mumbling over a poem to Eva Masters with a certain critical faintness, as of overindulgence in trochees, when I heard a bap-bap as of blunt-nosed bats whamming against the drainpipe outside my window. "Ho," I cried, and leaned out. "Ho, watchman, and what of the night?"

"Hiya," said Red Masters from the grass below, his healthy face grinning up at me, illuminated by the light next door in Mrs. Farren's kitchen. "Give me a hand, will you?"

"What do you mean?"

"To get up, stupid. You think I want to slip and break

182

my neck? Came to talk to you, not shimmy for the fun of
it. Skinned my knees already."

"Wait a sec, you can get in the front door."

"Naw"—the conspirator's scorn. "I got to talk to you
privately. It's about Eva, so hoist now, hey?" This was her
younger brother, freckled, skinny, and jittery as a child
actor in the role of Puck—Red the Precocious, just entered
high school, not James the Sad Neurotic from college. I
locked my feet in a drawer full of poetry, leaned out, and
yanked at him from above. The maple creaked; I groaned.
With a scramble he piled headfirst onto the rug near my
desk. He bucked the wastebasket full of parts of an old
alarm clock and my discarded thoughts, and I fell beside
him in a shower of manuscript. Paper clips hissed and a
disembodied spiral notebook retched out a month of
ballads. "Who's that?" Red asked from the floor, indicat-
ing a photograph above my desk of walnut-stained maple
with screwable drawer knobs. "Lou Gehrig? Kay Kayser?"

"What do you mean, it's Lord Alfred Byron, can't you
tell by the clothes? Get your big feet off my epic."

"Well, it could be Richard Halliburton. . . . It's not my
big feet, it's the boots Ma makes me wear." But with no
resentment he added: "It ain't easy"—without moving
from the floor after this brief prologue about poetry—
"since Dad hates your guts. He really has it in for you. I
never saw anything like it before and I read *Abraham's
Irish Rose*. You should hear him. A girl has to listen to her
father once in a while, since he made her what she is today,
and I quote his very words. Dad stinks."

Having gathered up the papers and tenderly installed
them in their drawer, I turned upon him what I hoped was
a fevered and sleepless eye, full of quotations from my
own soliloquies: "And what about Chuck may I ask?"—
the lid, I fondly imagined, drooping, disconsolate, and
world-weary.

"Hastings?"—a stiff-kneed whicker. "Oh, forget about

that Hastings lug. Eva says he's stoo-pid. Her very words. Chuck Hastings? Goshall, she likes you better, Dan!"

A definitive poem on unfaithfulness almost in grasp, I protested against this rifling of my chagrin with a facile grant of eternal bliss. I betrayed my disappointment. "It didn't look like she thought Chuck is stupider than me when I just by accident happened to see them together in the furnace room at Jean Thompson's that night—"

"Listen Dan, I tell you she likes you a hundred times better." *Hunnert,* he said. "His kisses don't fire her to undying passion, see? She told me not to tell you. They don't even illuminate her soul—"

My mother shouted from the front room: "Hey, you talking to yourself again, a boy going on seventeen?"

"I'm working," I yelled back, "homework. . . . Yeah, you were at the part about her soul."

"Listen, I'm only fourteen though very advanced for my age and all I can tell you is she likes you better. How do you know you're not meant for each other? Possible, ain't it? That's a fact. Probably one kiss from you is worth a dozen from him, maybe more. Want to see her tonight? She doesn't know I came to tell you, but she's waiting for you at the Korner and Harris Drug Store just by accident until nine o'clock in case you wander down to buy a package of razor blades. Got me? You shave yet, or just once or twice? Don't tell her I told you, she'd murderize me— you ever take a look at her fingernails? Once I got an infection when she scratched me, had to soak in Epsom salts. Just wander down there, see, for some Gillette's Double Edged, for a Hallmark greeting card, for some balm for your sorrow, and a Coke and fate will bring you back together again. Whatever you do from then on is your own business, far be it from me to mess around"—an intriguer rogue, a cap-and-bell jester with the big tragic words and freckles soaked in lemon juice. "She's sitting at the table by the Vitalis and Listerine, hear what I say? That Hastings is a drip. Wear a scarf instead of a tie. It's fate, see?"

"Yes, why?"

"Go!"

We went. We vlooped down the drainpipe like two messages in a department-store tube. I pressed the hand of this quick carrot-topped Mercury, my furthermore raven with the nicked buck teeth, and was off to a rendezvous with destiny—his big sister. He wagged his head with pubescent incredulity that anyone could so sprint for that pining sibling, but tried to discover virtues even in his own sister as he looked after my face smudged with slush from the gutter. I hurdled Mrs. Farren's fence for a short cut.

Eva and I shared a hot chocolate at the Korner and Harris Drug Store. After wetting the paper napkin against her tongue to rub away the dirt on my cheek, she pressed her lips together and murmured tenderly, "That Chuck Hastings, just don't you be jealous. It was a little investigation for the sake of my poetry. You have to experience life, Dan, you should understand that. It's the newest way to be a great artist, and besides I was curious. One thing I learned: he's not a genius, I didn't feel anything when he kissed me. It was like blowing up a balloon. All hot air, that fellow. Maybe he was really in San Francisco, but you're more sincere, you're deep, Dan, I found that out. Even if you're two years younger than Chuck, you're a lot more profound. You were right what you used to say. . . . I forget the exact words. Now I appreciate you."

"Yeah?" I said, hard to please. "Tom, Juicer, and I had a little experience Saturday night—" I said nothing more but made a cynical face until my nostrils ached and I had to let it go. "Maybe it's too late," I muttered.

"Oh Dan! Do you think it's *ever* too late? I mean for people who. . . . Tell me about yourself," said Eva, "I

want to hear you speak again, your words, your voice, your
very thoughts. Would you like some of my chocolate from
my cup? Mother says I'm old enough to go on a diet, isn't
that grand? Would you like me to be svelte for you? I'd
do it only for you, Dan."

"Svwhat?"

"Svelte. It's the feminine thing to be."

Consoled by high combat with the dragons, Pattie Donahue, my parents, and Black Lil, I let my true love pro tem,
Eva Masters, pour me a libation of hot chocolate with
marshmallow in it. I returned to her a taste of the marshmallow in our good-night kiss. This was a historic moment
because it represented the first in every young suburban
American's long struggle with girls who speak of diet when
he wants to speak of love. "No bananas, no potatoes," she
said. "But vitamins are slimming, my mother says."

"Tomorrow, Eva? I asked. "At the Korner and Harris
Drug Store"—significantly—"*our* drugstore?"

"It's the carbohydrate that does it," she said, being the
feminine thing.

Back home, I shut the door of my room to try to salvage
the rhymes in my wreck of a poem on infidelity. Perhaps
with a little touch here, a little touch there, it could be
altered to a subtle obscure neurotic ode concerning the
vanities of love and the flesh. If only she had let me remain
disillusioned two-three days more, I would have finished,
but ah! the inconstant female of the sex. These were my
four walls again. Back to the prison of Art. "Well, how
was it?" asked Red Masters.

"What? What?" Sitting cross-legged deep in shadow on
the floor near the box which once had contained my stamp
collection—long since abandoned to carbon copies of
neurotic odes—he nodded his head and grinned at me.
"Where did you come from?" I demanded.

"I decided to wait." He jerked his head toward the drainpipe. "I'm getting good," he said, "shinnied right back up. How was it? Am I right or am I right?"

I warily agreed. "But aren't you going to get home late? School tomorrow."

"Ah, I'm in dutch already. Doesn't matter *what* I do. What a mess. Listen, Dan, I'm on your side in the struggle against familial opposition. It looks like I'm entering the phase of adolescent rebellion against parental authority. We psychic siblings have to hang together. My brother James says it's essential to all progress, so I'm going to be tardy tonight. Did you kiss her so-long? Did she tell you what Dad says about you?"

"I want you to know I appreciate your interest," I announced, wondering if he could have sneaked a read at my poem about Eva, regretting that it was a mere first draft.

Said Red: "That's all right. Secrets. Lovers' whisperings. I just want you to know you can count on my utter discretion, Dan. I'm no stool pigeon. I may come from a neurotic home life, but no one'd ever catch me squealing—break my mother's back if I do. Dad says he'll lock Eva up if he has to if she keeps on seeing you. I guess you're out to corrupt the flower of her youth. Got a cig?"

"You smoke?" I asked, horrified.

"Don't you?"

"Sure," I said negligently, recovering, "but not in the house. My mother's allergic. Prince Albert in the can, a pipe."

"Okay, I'll wait. I never roll my own, I buy them. Well, he says you're dirty, see—that's my Dad talking—and you got pimples on your nose, and you sneak, and everyone knows your father's a shopkeeper, and you're not fit to dance with, see—"

"I don't think he likes me very much," I said. *Yes, but why?*

Precocious Red Masters, the child of age and an old

child, had lost the stiff arched back and pouting belly of
earliest babyhood; the high fling of that childish rib-tossing
had been internalized to a quality of mind—he refused to
move sideways in the house of crabs. His chief occupation
was to listen, secreting abstract generalizations and wax in
his ears. Sometimes he hit upon a particularity, a thing of
sense, a thing his sporty conscience could work on, and
then over his mouth flashed the sudden smile of sun on
brick. In me he recognized a brother despite my down-
curved nose and my father with a hard *t*. Gangling, big-
footed, and eager, he walked the streets in conquering
dreams; they were mine as I too prowled. How he touched
the strange girl on the bridge and she looked into his eyes
as the moon fled through autumn clouds: they were pure
dreams and classic ones. How in his rage at injustice he
pulled down the walls with his hairless fourteen-year-old
hands: they were blind dreams, dreams Samson would understand. How he walked, walked, walked, and finally became a self, that wonderful being which I already was and
yet was not. He expressed opposition to Euclid Masters'
solitaire and the gentlemanly ideal by aping my unruliness,
which seemed to be heating the warm decay of his family
into a sputtering disintegration. He threw stones at my
window to tell me the latest. He came, this handsome
traitor to the suburb, tap-tapping at the drainpipe, cap and
heart in hand, big white teeth in his mouth: "They don't
like your face, Dan. Oily on the nose. Evil nostrils."

"I perspire," I admitted, "real sweat. I really appreciate
your mentioning it, Red."

"It's not your fault," he consoled me. "What's important
is not the face, be it red, white, or blue, but what goes on
inside. All faces are created equal, that's the American
dream."

"You're lucky, faces I mean, Red, you're going to be a
killer when you grow up."

"What-do-you-mean, when I grow up? I'm very mature for my age. Listen, even Eva said she could really go for my type. Your face is okay too, Dan, I always say it's *interesting*. Listen, I always tell Dad you can't help it—"

"Thanks, Red, you're a pal. How's your father's stomach?" He had had another attack the evening I came to take Eva to the *Times* spring party at our faculty adviser's house. Thinking myself a gallant in the best tradition, I had brought her a red rose from Winkelmann the Florist. "One rose!" Mr. Masters had raged to his wife and Red when I left. "A rose, eh? Only one! That's enough! They save their money for other things, you can count on that. . . . Do you think he's trying to turn her head? A rose? Waxed paper? Eh? eh? Oh they're born clever like that, aren't they? They think of things like roses. . . ."

Eva was growing up and losing weight without her diet. In this unease with her father she became, astonishingly, almost a woman. She was learning from her own need that pain is a necessary thing—very young for such knowledge. Thinking of Euclid Masters, love and hate from her, fear and pity from me, we walked to the party and wondered whether we should begin meeting secretly. "That's called going underground," I said. "It's up to you."

Whether from scruples against scheming or a desire to twist the knife—I cannot tell even now—Eva wanted to continue meeting me at her home. I arrived half-deaf, all ears for belief and with a mastoid of dread, not really able to imagine the words as she bathed and dressed for my coming, flushing in the foolish dream that someday Euclid Masters would learn to look and to speak in the world of persons. It seemed that only the umbrella hump of his back knew that I was there. While I stood in the parlor waiting for Eva to come down, he played solitaire, shamelessly cheating as if alone while I peered over his shoulder. He could never win often enough to conjure me out of existence. Eva made us wait together while she made herself beautiful for us before the mirror, her mother whispering and wringing her hands.

Mr. Masters' condition—it was a *condition*—got worse each time they had an argument about me. I was sorry for him, feeling myself profoundly unworthy to disturb his peace of peristalsis. "The doctor gives him pills for his hypochondria," Red politely informed me, "thank you for asking. And how's yours? Your father, I mean."

At that moment my father was eating in the kitchen, chopping up onion into a salad, adding bits of green pepper. Then salt. Then oil and vinegar. And black pepper. Euclid Masters, whom I wanted to love, went on morselating intravenously.

"Maybe," I said, "if I talked to your father he'd see I'm not so bad. He never even *says* anything to me"—deeply suspecting that Euclid Masters must see those unnamable secrets that prevent us from condemning a failure to give us love. "I don't think he could be so bad after all, with Eva and you for family—"

"And James," Red pointed out. "You should get to know my brother when he gets home from college."

"Yes, he couldn't be such a bad man with a family like you," I reasoned, leaning toward Red Masters in my room while my parents discussed business in the kitchen and the melting slush squeezed through the rivets in the drainpipe near my window. We were vicariously united by gratitude and adventure. His spite against his father helped him to look at me. I still remember the boy who was easy with his big sister's boy friend: Red Masters and I discussed parents and love with the pure feeling of platonic brothers-in-law. Long may he live in tenderness, vehemence, and high spirits!

"My father has a mind made of boogers," he said.

15. Arrogations and Ingratiations

Do CHAMELEONS CHANGE THEIR skin? Yes. But is the flesh underneath the same old flesh, or in the shape of it the same? And is that stunning new spring skin a merely unmottled repetition of the old one? Or is the color really invented anew? It's time to return to Eva, who was fast growing under conditions of warmth and inner pressures from a lover of verse in general to a very complicated young lady, that is, a lover of poetry in particular. Paring herself against her parents, she met those difficult family moments about me with chagrin, partial comprehension, and self-surprising courage. She studied my photomat snap in her purse and the leather-framed portrait of Euclid Masters on her dressing table; she squinted and wrinkled her nose to the candid in tennis togs of big brother James, asking of him an explanation for conflict between two individuals who had in common, after all, that they were men of a sort. Receiving no mystic reply by neurotic power, she turned back to Euclid and me, sighed, yawned, confided in Red, washed her stockings as the college girls do, and prepared to meet me at Dairy Dell for a sundae.

"Eh? Where are you going?" Euclid Masters asked.

"Out," she said. "Back at nine-thirty," she called over

her cologned shoulder as she opened the door. "To see Dan," she murmured, closing it. Courage: she added these words to prickle his slack-skinned chin before the door clicked shut. She glanced back at Euclid Masters' stiffened silhouette through the parlor curtains, his locksmith face a key in profile, metallic, subtle, eaten by use, well-counterfeited to itself—a key turned in locks which devoured it in the darkness of unsuccessful openings. His face hung in the window as she moved softly away, a key jangled with strange coins, thrown in old drawers, hung on rusty nails.

She touched a damp finger along her eyebrows and admired her depth of feeling in her mind's notebook. "Hi."

"Hi, Eva."

"I have to get home early to fight with my father," she told me. "I don't want it to last too late, there's a *dictée* tomorrow."

We met at the corner and maneuvered across the greasy walk for the most favorable angle from the streetlamp. This was not mere vanity; like good suburban Protestants —neither of us had gone to any of the popular Sunday schools, however—we suffered from an exaggeration of the moral importance of beauty as a sign of grace. In conventional piety, aided by repeated voyages into the local color of evening, we evoked the scenery of our mind's eyes: "Look the leaves—they're flowers in the light—glorious the way that green whitens and silkens"—Eva's sermon.

"A storm, don't you think? This dampness means a storm, the first thunder of the year"—metaphorical Dan in finger-wetting prophecy.

A late child, hurrying home under oak and birch along the boulevard with his mother, put his scrabbling fingers to his mouth to tease her, pulled his lips at random and said: "Bbbl-bbbl."

"Red's a friend. He has our own interests at heart."

"He's all right for a kid brother. James would like you too, if he only got to know you."

"Your mother wouldn't bother much. She'd get over it. It's your father."

"What do you think Lucille Lake's mother would say about you? Ever think of that?"

"I never thought about it, Eva." But Mrs. Lake was a nice lady. She looked only at what she saw. She saw me and not an idea when she looked at me. "What are you saying, Eva? Why?"

"See, you shouldn't blame my father, that's why, even though he's a callous monster."

"I know he's your father, just he doesn't like me. Maybe if he's only a callous monster about me, maybe then we can make him see—"

"Oh Dan darling, what should we do? What should I do?"—sinking softly into my arms without breaking the slow undulation of our stroll. She had mastered the art of the caressing walk. "Dad doesn't understand, but he's my father. And I can't give you up, Dan!"—knowing somehow that surrender to him would violate all the laws. "What can we do?"

"Your father's really interested in the question," I said.

The March evening surged about us with its scent of a new season, old leaves, and automobile exhaust. Warning eyes flickered behind lawns from the frame houses puffing from their chimneys along the boulevard, the bulbs of maids' rooms at the eaves the jewels in their foreheads. Beyond, at the lake, long low freighters flashed warning lights and slipped into harbor with their loads of red ore from Duluth, or out again with machine parts bound for Buffalo. It was the time of rearmament. I had won a senior debate, arguing that useless spending for armament would bankrupt the nation. Who needed guns and tanks when World Peace-

ways could tell us how to get along happily together?
(Euclid and Adolf were not listening.)

"And Jack Mamble?" I asked after a silence of communion in poesy. "And Chuck Hastings?"

"That's all past, Dan. I've learned my lesson. Women
have the right to vote, when they're twenty-one, I mean—
why can't they sow wild oats too, and reap the whirlwind?
They learn that way. They learn. Oh I've learned, Dan—"

"What do you mean?"

"It's *you* I appreciate now, Dan. I really do." And she
offered up the sophistical argument about how it was, indeed, a compliment that, with all her wide experience, she
had finally found me best. Not Jack or Chuck. Me. Dan
Berman. Deepest soul and best at kissing. I was superior
again. I felt like the cake last prodded in a baking contest, champion after all. My icing shivered before the prick
of this idea: Miss Betty Crocker Masters' Choicest. It was
not very pleasing.

"Pattie Donahue?" I crackled vengefully.

"Who?"

"Hue," I mysteriously intimated. We omitted Black Lil
for the moment.

"*I* think," said Eva, "if you want to know what *I* think
about it, that you have your little old eye on Lucille Lake.
You devil you."

I admired her intelligence and her consideration of me,
and to it I responded: "Course, who hasn't? But Juicer's
mad for Lucille, as you all well know, and I'm Juicer's best
friend."

"Well?" Eva urged, kindled by the precedents for per-
fidy, forgetting in her love of scandal how important I was
—she was using me to destroy the peace of her family.
When I said nothing she broke out with an apology: "But
that Chuck Hastings, he's nobody's best friend. Just his
own. Kissing him is as good as licking a postage stamp."

And because she understood that a sensitive chappo like me might harbor jealousy of a postage stamp, she added: "He's no genius either, that Chuck."

Among the glossy black plastic tables with chromium pipe legs and red leatherette seats, before the Dairy Dell juke box all light and music, served by a chubby soda jerk, suave and eunuchoid, whose apron advertised his many flavors, we wide-ranged over the kaleidoscope thoughts, prayers, and nightmare ambitions of high school lovers. We talked, we lectured, we gave advice freely. Dairy Dell was our temple, our confessional, our consultation chamber. As in a nightmare, Mr. Welch then came bobbing into view, grinning gummily, sniffing out disaster, buying cigarettes. He unpeeled the pack and watched us, and only after I caught his eye and commanded him to die did he turn away. His fleshy adult back under the overcoat breasted the evening. He walked backwards, desperately fending off my jabbing will with his armor grin.

"Mr. Welch," I said as he escaped with his life. (Mr. Welch defined the difference between a spy and a scout.) "But you were telling me important things, Eva."

At the behest of modest Red she told me that he had once been judged the best junior high school swimmer in Greater Cleveland, or rather, in the waters nearby and in the pools. I repeated: "I like him. . . . I like him. . . ." Friendship with Red restored weight—the ballast of social structure—to the hallucinations of a love of Eva in which her father's keylike head rattled into view at every handholding or kissing moment. Red was a place where blood agreed with us—this is necessary even in love. Red had a hard time. Eva told me of an educational stunt invented by Euclid Masters for his youngest son. He had taken Red into the back yard with two glasses of water. Into one he had mixed a teaspoon of soft vegetable loam until, swirling, it blackened the water. The other he left untouched.

"This is your mind as it is today, son," he had said, indi-
cating the glass of clear water. Tapping the muddied dark
of the other with a spoon, he had added: "This is the mind
of your new friend, Jacob Berman's son, eh?" From this
glass he poured a few drops into the clean water.

Eva blushed for the scandalous pleasure, for dread, and
for pity of me. I admired Euclid Masters' gift for metaphor
and felt—as we all do when we call out strong feeling—
that there must exist some truth in me to which the sick,
the tired, the depleted Mr. Masterses of the world respond.

"And then what happened?"—like a child following a
serial story.

"The clean glass got dirty. It only takes a drop, you
know." As she said this, I saw the mud spread like a dis-
integrating pellet through their pure tap water. "Red just
walked away. He couldn't say anything. He told me he
wanted to break the glasses."

"Is that what he said?" I considered this. "No, no, that
wouldn't work. . . ." I saw Red swimming vainly away into
the house, drowning in indignation, impressed, leaving his
father—whose frozen face parodied his own long open
athletic one—bearing the glasses high and pouring his
libations on the cropped grass. Saying: "Eh? eh?" And
Mrs. Masters watching from the breakfast-room window.
And humid-eyed Eva upstairs watching from her bedroom
window. And all those eyes-on-stalks in a house of sea animals moving slowly from one to the other in the long dark
corridors of hatred and forbidden desire.

As if reading my thoughts, Eva touched the back of my
hand—she constantly touched me when she talked, sometimes seeming to stretch in the current about us—and she
said: "Take me back now. I'll make us a hot cup of chocolate. I mean a warm cup of hot chocolate."

"At your house?"

"At the house. I don't care," she said. I chose to be led,

submitting my freedom to my wonder at a girl with such economical touchings who could nevertheless feed me love spread like sweet butter over her father's ill-will. Eva was not so foolish in life as that other Dan in me asks her to be in this sad vaudeville about her. Tender and frightened, very young, she held to self-knowledge in the learning, and could live with both fright and tenderness. She liked me. She loved her father. Eva admired herself—first things still came first. "At the house and I don't care," she said. "I want some hot chocolate with wafers. With you."

"Yes, but why?"

Leaning together in stealth on the porch, we looked through the window into the parlor where Red sat cross-legged on the floor near the radio, where Mrs. Masters knitted with her busy lips counting the stitches, conversing with herself, and where Euclid Masters read aloud to his family in his hypochondriacal old man's voice.

Mrs. Masters might have been thinking while I squinted and crouched with Eva on the porch: "That's grand. It would be grand if we had some succotash to go with it, or a can of baked pumpkin." She looked through her husband to thoughts of meals which would make him love her, love her, love her, while her hands twitched at the needles making James the pair of collegiate socks recommended by her knitting journal. Euclid Masters was joined to his wife by a piece of paper.

Red scowled and rubbed his wrist at the scar like a tiny white worm where his mother had stuck him, years ago, in pinning his gloves to his sleeve. She did not want him to lose a glove, careless about pricked wrists. And Euclid Masters was joined to his sons by fear and exclusive ambitions.

Reading aloud to his family from the memoirs of a former President, Mr. Masters hoped to communicate his humors and his moral synthesis. He succeeded only in providing the nasal murmur within which, like secret lovers in an adulterous bed, their secret thoughts darted and played. Euclid Masters was joined to his family by shame, by pretense, by spoiled hopes. He was joined to his house by a first mortgage.

Eva touched my neck with a cold hand in the damp weather. We went in. I stood shivering slightly in my steaming clothes at the entrance to the parlor. We had interrupted the reading. Stupified by surprise and gas heat, they stared at me. "You know Daniel Berman," Eva suggested softly.

Red came up with a start. "Dan! hiya! I didn't expect how are you? Sit down, hey? Give me your jacket"—his hobgoblin head awag in the joy of surprise at that age.

"How about some chocolate, everyone? Don't get up, Mother, you stay and talk with Dan." In some testing of me, her family, and herself, Eva again left me alone with them. In some deep examination she left us: perhaps only in the ambition to show me that, despite literature and fear of her parents, she could still make fluent chocolate on a chill March evening. And if this was not courage, it was at least practice toward it.

"What's new, Dan?" Red asked, a hobgoblin child with big nicked teeth, a pants-rolled and skipping person.

"Oh, nothing," I said, plotting to make Mr. Masters look with favor on this genteel lie: "Nothing at all." I suspected that he found my pleasure in novelty, in any change, in the brightness of all event, a signal of the rootless alien. If I said nothing happening, perhaps he would rest in peace and *like* me. His locksmith eyes of splintered metal glinted over me in the smile and caress of a rasp: no smile at all.

"Maybe I should help Eva," Mrs. Masters said.

"Sit down. Sit down, Dan"—Red, my friend the raven, nimble Mercury my pal.

I sat down slowly, hoping that age might reconcile us. I sat down with backward glances, hoping that a conservative approbation of cushions might reconcile us. I sat down like Jean Thompson, on the edge of the sofa, hoping that modesty about the size of my buttocks might reconcile us. The anthropometric eyes of Euclid Masters took my measure with foreknowledge, as a blind salesman might learn to look at a customer.

"I guess I'll go don't you think to help Eva?" said Mrs. Masters.

"You stay. Don't get up, Deborah," Euclid Masters commanded, and she obeyed.

I looked for help to the gas flame spitting from absent tiles in the fireplace. A pile of *Saturday Evening Post*s on the magazine rack lay just out of reach, their edges slightly curled by heat. "You were reading something," I said, "I'm sorry to interrupt. I didn't mean to. You can go right on if you want to, Mr. Masters."

"I don't want to, eh?" He was coming unthawed at my words, not to meeting me but to the sputter of his fury.

"Oh, it wasn't important—I mean politics," Red told me. "History, I guess. A biography sort of—it's just good for us, that's all, Dan."

"Daniel Berman, eh?" Euclid Masters asked me with his eyes half-shut. "Well. Isn't that more or less a German name? eh?" His eyes flicked open. The importance of gestures, those of human beings as well as those of crustaceans frozen in the ice of the butcher's window, returns with the recollection of that moment in the crab basket. I could have blocked up my ears and heard him as well. While his wife's round mouth popped invisible bubbles, his eyebrows jerked, his finger tips plucked, his ossifying nose twitched at the cartilaginous tip with an unspent sneeze. And all the time this pincer-crab-key, this clever disabused old man, this father of Eva for whom I would have died: —he shuddered with impatience to be at his business: "Daniel Berman, eh? Berman. Certainly a German name. Isn't it? Yes. I think so. In the family how long now? Did you say? Two generations? Three? What?"

And we sipped cocoa to the slow movement of this theme and its variations:

"The lack of a sense of quality—thank you, Eva darling —is an absence which cannot be felt by those groups which have never known a tradition of gentlemen. I use the word advisedly. I presume that we Americans made our choice when we made the Revolution, for in severing ourselves from our tradition and accepting the responsibilities of power, inevitably we were obliged to use the labor of Central, Southern, and Eastern Europe. We could also hope to temper these blades so to speak in our own fires, couldn't we, Red? Do you follow? For the moment we will leave out of consideration the accident of slavery and all the misfortunes that have ensued, another aspect of the same issue. Sit still, please. I say therefore—I admit willingly—that ours is a civilization which puts a premium on commonness, on rudeness, on rough-and-readiness, if I may express myself in such a manner. . . . Yes? eh? you see?"—the scherzo now, his hands fretful in his lap while his sentences rolled on, his platitudes and his groping arthritic fingers at peace while he cried out shrilly: "What? oh! you see?" In the mirror over the gas fireplace he glanced at himself, spread a hypochondriac hand over his heart in the heroic pose, and saw a room and a world full of grotesques. A gargoyle, he let his droppings fall to us from the gutter, and imagined himself the architect of a cathedral. He looked at my face in the mirror—a face with adolescent disturbances of blood and beard marking it with indecision and the demands of this condition—and he said to the glass image of me: "Well, Daniel Berman, you—if I can call you Dan—from the point of view of one of the new people of the world, whose interest it is to smother the past, what do you feel about history? eh? Traditions, I mean, from the point of view of *your* people—"

"I don't understand," I said, "and I don't think you're right about gentlemen—and about the new people, I don't—"

"Oh don't misunderstand me! I'm just watching. I am merely a single isolated observer. I don't say it's wrong. Perhaps we have no public choice. That may well be. I only argue that we can still choose, for ourselves at least, between the gentlemen and those who want the power—*their* kind of power. At least that. If nothing else. What I choose to call gentlemen. I know you must think of me as old-fashioned. There, I admit it, Dan. Then what? After I admit your word for me, Dan, what do you propose next? For *me,* I mean. You must know more than I do about it, young as you are. *Your* kind, you see? What I am telling you is that it is a choice for our privacy, which is all we have left—"

"Father," Eva murmured warningly.

He turned from me to her. "All the while we sleep, daughter (*they* don't sleep, do they, those people?) they are planning what to do with us, not consciously perhaps, but in their way of doing for themselves, buying cheap, selling dear—"

(How well did Euclid Masters sleep?)

"—figuring, figuring, planning, buying to sell and selling to buy again—"

I saw the spattered rust of waste in his eyes. In his voice of emery and metal I heard the specious vitality of despair, the depleted heart of the sick, the boredom of ignorance-in-the-know: the Euclid Masterses of the world.

"—They have their stunts, their quick fingers, their pleasures—they know how to capture us with their fool's tricks, ingratiate or arrogate—"

I said that Euclid Masters was joined to the others in various mechanical ways. He was joined to me by a common seeking of fortune understood in uncommon ways, a clear recognition of enmity complicated by the love of battlers for each other, and by the suspicion which my existence renewed of forbidden possibilities. "Don't expect Dan to agree with you, Father," Eva said.

He shuddered once more and stared away when I met his eyes in the mirror, like a man caught reading over a shoulder in a bus.

What can I do? I thought.

Nothing.

Nothing opens that lock.

He was afraid of possibility, that man, and there we deeply wrestled in disarray; he let me move backwards out the door, flushing and bump-ankled with shame for him that evening because he neither arose from his chair nor said good-by like a gentleman; but now again he watched my going in the mirror.

16. *The salvation of spendthrift economists*

WITH THE STUPID WISDOM OF age my parents told me that my friends would not always be my friends. "You'll grow out," my mother said.

"You'll maybe move to another city in your business," said my father.

"In your profession," my mother said.

Right! Some of those who were then my friends no longer are. Wrong! These friendships are not ended. The new year enters as a baby, goes out as a graybeard, but enters again as the same new baby. There is a presentness also to the pastness of the past. A new thing invented never becomes decrepit in the eyes of its maker, and love is still a new baby.

"There'll be some changes," my father insisted. "The N.R.A. looked big. It didn't last."

"Castles in Spain! Smoke in the head!" my mother said. She meant: Every man his own Marquis de Sade. . . . Only God can make a tree; He seems to devote his best energies to it, leaving to inefficient parents the job of making children. And then we cute kids sacrifice our parents in time for Easter or Passover, leaving to future ages the responsibilities for atonement and resurrection. Our speculations in sin and evil free us for tenderness; cruelty leads to guilty kindness (unlucky we!). Other loves are possible, however, if the body stays hopeful and the morning dawn remembers to blush prettily, beard against fresh cheeks—then the fried eggs and buttered toast.

Back to 1939. Automobiles had lost their running boards; Hitler stamped his foot in front of the French ambassador, who thought him vulgar (*"M. Hitler s'est faché en disant...."*); in addition to Juicer Montague and Tom Moss, Red Masters had become my friend. He suggested that Eva and I elope, hoping for an appointment to swell a progress, brace the ladder beneath the window. He volunteered to send a part of his allowance each week to whatever strange clime of a Grand Rapids or Cincinnati where we would hide out from Euclid's dogs. His imagination kindled by a painting in the Cleveland Museum of Art, Red liked to imagine Eva like Odalisque on a couch, rump angled heavenward, while I paced, composing epic verse, and the unhappy pursuing hounds bayed beneath our tree house. Occasionally, between stanzas, languorous Eva and fugitive I made forensic love. The leafy refuge shook; our eyes burned. Below, Euclid Masters howled murder and his mouth was wolf-black with fury.

"That's a nice word picture, Red," I said, "but real life isn't just poetry and love-making in tree houses."

"No," Red admitted, "you're right—fantasy is my stage of development—but in real life my father is still a real crud."

Red and I walked amid the suburban spring smells, wiggle-rumped dogs, call of vacuum cleaner and telephone, whir of pruning shears and snip against branches; we spoke of our philosophies. We thought the government should cut down its spending. No more boondoggling. After all, our parents' children would have to pay. We crossed through the bumper-to-bumper honkers of the boulevard. Juicer was a genius, but Red was pretty smart, too. He approved of Harold Ickes, but not of Harry Hopkins—judicious. At the age of fifteen he also understood about the important phenomenon of time. He no longer believed in the little monkey inside the clock who pushed the hands around and said tick-tick-tick because it was all alone. There was no monkey; there was a machine which said tock-tock-tock because it was all alone so much by itself. And time is remorseless.

"But why does your father hate me?" I asked. "Does he have reasons? I like reasons."

"He hates you, that's the reason," Red replied.

"It's not my pimples, my parents?"

"He doesn't like you, he hates you."

"I keep Eva from studying?"

"He just does, that's all." We exchanged ideas and found common ground: Some words are unusually expressive, not enough people care about the truth, Jan Sibelius composed that other nifty tone poem about a swan besides *Finlandia,* and Euclid Masters was a pain.

"Hates me, Red?" I had trouble accepting this peculiar treasure of a fact.

Red carried the tops of acorns in his jacket pocket to ward off the rheumatiz (from his grandfather) and the psychosomatiz (from his big brother James in college). He did not believe in superstition, but knew it for a fact that the mind affects the body and his father hated Dan Berman. "The very ground you walk on. You poison the earth. You corrupt our civilization. You brought commerce and usury into the West."

"What's that—usury?"

"I don't know. Maybe it's how you talk too loud in a restaurant in West Palm Beach."

"Red, I swear, I never was in West Palm Beach."

He was full of grief for the wrongs done me daily. His fine, slightly protuberant eyes—so like Eva's, so like Eu-

clid's!—reached sadly for mine in midair. "I know. It's
unfair, Dan. But that's the lay of the land at our place."
Quoth the red raven: "Forever more, Dan."

This impressed me, that Euclid Masters could hate me
without caring about me, that I should have so little to do
with it; it brought into the springtime of that year some of
the awe of congregations for useless miracles. The clock
ran without a monkey, or imported a monkey only because
the specifications called for rubies, radium paint, and ring-
tailed grinners; Euclid Masters put me in his clock without
a reason, and along the shale and shore of Lake Erie I
wandered to know why. I climbed the cliff to Homewood
Drive. I found a soggy tennis ball on the playground of
Taft School and heaved it up to Clifton Boulevard.

In Europe the death agony of six million Jews had
begun. A boy my age named Herschel Greenzpan had shot
a Nazi third secretary in Paris. Before the Greenzpan boy
disappeared into history, he helped me begin to define myself. But what—as my father said—what do we know in
Lakewood? Depression, recovery, newspapers; school, ambitions, habits, hopes; Juicer, Tom, Red, and girls; our
change of life—our pubic yearnings into philosophy and
the suspicion that *others exist*.

I loved ice cream. I loved Eva. I loved the Truth. As
through a glass darkly, as through a suburb protectedly, I
began, just began to see that actual Herschel Greenzpan
and living, breathing Euclid Masters were also a part of
my Truth. In fact, the Truth was really a sum of such
parts, terrible and sweet.

The Truth—*All*—was what I lusted after. What was
All to me? A new flavor of sherbet and Sherwood Ander-
son, a new triumph over my parents and the smell of an
alley, a new dialectic with Juicer and a blouse on Eva, all
and over it all, a spilling from my throat of important songs
with trivial words. I was Stokowsky in corduroy, with the

difference that he aloofly goosed an orchestra while Eva and I democratically felt each other up. We were in love; love was in us; the body's sweet squeaking was the melody of doors opening.

On the day that I tried to tell Juicer about *All,* it rained. There was thunder—it might pass over—but then the sky shook itself like a laden, bestirred tree. "Do you mean the Whole Truth?" Juicer asked.

"No, *All,*" I said.

"I call it the Whole Truth," Juicer said, "me."

"All, Juicer, all!" With cautionary high finger I aped my momentary archrival, Chuck. He too spoke of deep matters, and though I knew him for a slug—he drugged us—his raised index finger made psychic, threatening sense. And so I raised my finger at Juicer. Floom-boom of sky, barometric April furies, mystical April me, that foxy foolish loony lorn Daniel Berman.

On this day it rained. On the next day the sun burst out, daggered with April, and I forgot my philosophy in a retrospective exhibition of touch football in the street. I soaked the cuffs of my pants in the sparkling grass, but scored three touchdowns, receiving a number of long passes onto the sidewalk. Winning at games or business or love is the best personal support for a philosophy—and a validation of some merit, besides. We warmed our faces in the clear sunlight. The seer of All and the grand maestro of the Whole Truth then ate hot fudge sundaes. "Ramakrishna, Kahlil Gibran," said Juicer.

"Did you see how I broke through the hedge to catch that last pass?"

"Yes, you got burrs on your socks."

"You too, Juicer, so don't sneer, it's not very Yin and Yang of you."

We plucked at the clinging vegetable beasties. I flicked mine at him. He flicked his at me. Shrunken-headed porcupines from woolly aborigines at each other; prickly pears from anciently jovial friends. Pop, stickle, and pluck in a drugstore; back and forth; the white-coated pharmacist, selling Serutan, frowned and threatened to spell us backwards unless we behaved like gentlemen. I licked my spoon of hot fudge and returned to business.

"Ramakrishna tells all about the physical side, how to make her happy, they say, Juicer."

"They say, Dan," he said sadly. "I hope you figure out how to make her father happy."

"It's not in Ramakrishna, the eighty-four Indian positions," I said. "I wonder if there is a position." And if I could take it. And if it made functioning with Euclid Masters likely, happy, or possible.

"Abject," said Juicer.

"I do object."

"Ain't what I said."

"I heard you, I was only making a deeply meaningful pun, Juicer."

But when I called for Eva at eight o'clock, her father, untouched by puns or philosophy, looked at me with the fierce hurt that is told of infected dogs, who turn their great sad eyes to the world one last time before going howling off into madness. I looked at him, lifted my hand, wanted to say something. What to say? There was a strand of hair in his eye which must have itched and scratched, but he did not touch it. He did not brush it away. He was already too far gone in pain and trouble to give his body any ease. He walked away without answering the words I never spoke, the words of comfort or brotherly communion. I had lifted my hand. Red said he found gestures—"talking with the hands"—an alien habit which confessed a brutish inarticulateness in English.

"Ready," Eva said with her gloved hands still and svelte at her sides. "Back soon, everybody."

I held the door for her. I was busy opening doors in those days, and learning that if you stand in a doorway it's likely to slam in your face. Nevertheless, stubborn as most inventors, I stood and waited. I had recently invented love, the flesh, and pride in my loneliness: how could parents, procreative by decree, understand this? I passed nights without sleeping only because they slept; the red-eyed days were a secret triumph, mitigated by Murine, thus acknowledging a droplet of society in my burning tear ducts. This suburban nihilism served the process of willing myself into existence. I completed the cardinal act of my father and mother, who gave me matter and helped me huff life into it. . . . So plunged my deep thoughts deeper while the world slept, spinning a familiarly used element back to unknown sources, like bath water in a drain. I lay awake thinking, thinking, thinking of the sleeping world. I waked before dawn and walked the equinoctial streets only because I wanted to be alone, a solitude relieved by the clairvoyant ambition that Eva might have the same impulse at the same moment in her dissimilar delicious damp bed. I spied milkmen, cats, abandoned toys, no Eva. Gentle Eva slept on, untelepathic, in violation of all the rules of clairvoyance. (I had made them up. Love conjures. Eva slumbered.) I petted a lost kitten and carried it on my shoulder along the shale cliff above Lake Erie. The comfort exchanged with that strayed and deluded poor puss meant— what? That all was not lost, the dawn not absolutely wasted?

Yes, that all was not lost though the dawn was absolutely wasted.

Yes, that the dawn was not wasted though all was lost.

Mnaaow! said the grateful kitten.

Now! Now!

There is a seven-syllabled Fuegian word whose precise meaning is: "They-stare-at-each-other-each-waiting-for-the-other-to-volunteer-to-do- what-both-wish-but-are-not able-to-do." And *there* is the criticism of all our suburban delights, a generous condemnation because the contaminating Euclid Masterses have even forgotten the true good of wish. What did Eva and I want? At least we wanted to want; we yearned.

Before her birthday Eva hinted to me, "You know this nervousness I had lately? Well, it isn't neurosis after all, it's a thyroid condition. Of course it's good for the poetry, but I had trouble sleeping. Now I have pills," she murmured, fluttering her eyelashes.

"They say it's the salt," I said. "My mother says it's the fish we don't eat. We should eat more fish and iodized salt, I guess. Has the nervousness gone down say ten per cent after the first week of treatment?"—the suave estimation by a man who might someday be a professional, receiving money with averted eyes and a stethoscope pressing against the copy of *Time* in his overcoat pocket.

"They're these dear little pills," said Eva, glamorous as an actress or a championship swimmer, "but I have to carry them in an envelope onvolope. I don't have anything to carry them in." What flair to those nostrils! What fine fettle in those eyelids! "It's a shame to let these pretty little pills get all crummy in my little alligator purse."

With the insight of a true lover, both abandoned and calculating in his passion, I remembered to buy her a finely wrought Florentine pillbox in that same Miss Mabel's Stationery and Imported Gift Shoppe where I had earlier found a copper candlestick and a snowstorm paper weight with an arms-out histrionic Heidi welcoming the sluggish elements. "Oh!" cried Eva, throwing her arms about my neck, "it's cunning and very nice indeed, really lovely, Dan. It's just what I wanted, and very useful, too. How do you ever think of such things?"

"Oh it's nothing." The blush ran hot under the frames

of my glasses. "I write them down in my little notebook—
the one you gave me for Safety First Day."

"But that was just a little *token,* of my esteem for you I
mean, but this is real Italian silver from Italy, isn't it?
Isn't it?"

"Well," I admitted, "real Italian silver from that Miss
Mabel's place I told you about. It's a little discovery of
mine. Juicer buys all his leather goods there, a letter opener,
a memo pad. Do you like it?"

"Oh it's cunning," she would say in approval, like a
lovely girl from a fine family. "That's icky," she would
say like a sorority woman from one of the best academies.
"That's very delicate indeed," she would say like a young
lady gifted for shrewd discriminations. "It seems to me
rather ambivalent, I mean levels of meaning, don't you
think?" she would say like a plump little intellectual who
had read her brother's books, her clear bulging blue eyes
showing faint veins like healthy turnips, the pulse in the
bluish flesh of her soft neck thumping for emphasis and joy
in the present tragic world-historical epoch with its declines
and falls and difficult forecasting.

"How can I live up to you?" I groaned in one breath-
mixing moment.

"On the contrary," she said, "I would prefer to be worthy
of you than the other way around."

Her grammar jiggled by passion to primary feelings, she
played the Love Theme from Tchaikowsky's *Fifth Symphony* on the baby grand as she spied me coming up the
walk. Unlike Rosalie Fallon, who loitered with her delights like sugar cookies for sale in the baker's wagon, and
unlike Pattie Donahue, who fled beckoning like the go-
away-closer mechanical rabbit in a dog race, and unlike
Lucille Lake, who studied her beauty in the shimmer of
ambition among the careen and jangle of her harpstrings,

Miss Eva Masters was a shy and wholesome creature who lived only for poetry, her brother's tic, and kissing with her mouth open.

Pits in his face, eaten from within. Pits of frown and defiance in mine. The humor of Euclid Masters dissolves to one last caprice: he speaks in obliquity, his words darting up from the solitaire display of pink kings and violent knaves: "Going to college soon, are you not? Columbia University? Or maybe Chicago? Big cities? You like big cities, the nervousness, all that pushing? Thrive on that sort of thing, do you? That the place where you fit?"

I lift my arms grown suddenly heavy, but his breath hurries on without accepting this tribute or taking notice that my breathing is broken to a sigh. I sigh, I lift arms.

"Don't like the quiet life here, do you? Some families five generations, some more. Six ourselves. Originally from Boston, old Amos Masters. Maybe you ought to go to New York, eh? Feel at home there? A one-generation city? Eh? Eh? Am I right?"

"Mr. Masters and I have been thinking, Daniel," begins Deborah Masters.

Euclid Masters wants no help, no questions, no answers. He speaks to a phantom which he addresses by my name while he fabricates his solitaire luck, peeking at the cards from under Postum-colored lids grainy with the desolation of insomnia: "Know your kind, don't I? Daniel Berman? Am I right? I am right." He plucks his card from deep within the deck. "I know I am right."

"I think you must really speak more distinctly for Mr. Berman, Euclid." I'm a Mister already! She murders her husband with boredom as she has herself already been murdered by one of boredom's anxious corollaries, bewilderment.

"I said I'm right in my little effort at summary, Deborah."

"Well Euclid dear, if you could just stop playing a moment—"

"Solitaire is my hobby, isn't it? I can talk at the same time." Suddenly he has a duck's muzzle. The pink bill can nibble me to death. "Mr. Berman understands me, doesn't he, Mister Berman? Save all our feelings? A great mistake otherwise?"

"Well," I say, "well, I don't know. I mean with all due respect for you and Mrs. Masters, Mr. Masters." I look for his eyes to find what I am in them, but the thickened lids and the shadow of portent make them too dark for me. He is not an animal though he populates my bestiary; he is a man, alas. He quacks like a man—he treads swamp waters on webbed toes—but he is as malicious and unhappy as only a man can be.

He turns up a three of hearts. He turns up a three of spades. I ask: "I mean what do you think I am, Mr. Masters?" I am sincerely interested. I value his opinion. I want him to look at me.

"What you are, eh? Perhaps your personal qualities? That's not the point. Not the point at all. Your effect on me, my family."

Who? I think but do not say.

"Your sense of self—your self-respect, eh? You think I should care. Child. Poor child you are. Child but already grasping. False pride perhaps? Amazing people—you're an amazing people. Ask yourself if you can. Think. Frankly?"

I think: I can't take commands from him. Suggestions, advice, criticism, I am proud of my susceptibility to them. But the question is one for Eva and me. *We must duck this quack*.

"Man to man? May I? Eh?"

"Yes, of course, Mr. Masters."

"Eva. Eva. I want you to consider a father's wishes. She's my daughter, eh? You understand that much? So far?"

Eva has come downstairs dressed for our movie. It is Saturday night. We expect Franchot Tone to be swell in *Mutiny on the Bounty*. We may miss the newsreel of smiling Roosevelt, keenly participating in plans of his own; morbid Neville Chamberlain, assenting to others; and Grantland Rice at the track. We don't even mind missing the Sing, with filmed balls bouncing onto the words of Somebounce Wherebounce Obouncever the Rainbouncebow. We hate to miss the Prevues of Coming Attractions, usually the starkest and best part of the evening to us hopeful sorts.

Eva is wearing a dress which hides the pulse of her throat but, in return, betrays her arms. She has powdered her biceps. Her waist is narrow and girlish; her breasts are hard and high—no, they are not hard. She is slender but her breath is suddenly difficult. "This is very interesting," she says. "I asked you to have more dignity, father. It is very interesting. I'm so interested that I am absolutely, I am positively speechless." She considers the implications of this statement. "Why I—why I," she says. "See what I mean?"

"Reasonable man, Eva. I'm a reasonable father. I permit you to talk it over."

Leaning against each other, half-drunken for loneliness, blind with tears for ourselves, each other, and our parents, we rush out the door. The birch which was standing there a half hour ago is still alive and green. I turn from the doorway to Euclid Masters. I think I say something like: "It doesn't do any good to talk like that, Mr. Masters." Perhaps I only say: "I won't bring her home too late, Mrs. Masters"—which means the same thing.

Perhaps I say both or neither, but anything I say means: "You have no right. You have no right."

Eva and I hear him over his hand of solitaire spread on the table behind us: "No? no? no?" Confident.

When I think of that time, all her little falsenesses and pretensions vanish, as the price of a gift is of no importance when we receive it from a friend. She insisted that this giving take place at her house. Merely spring-laden, love-laden, filled with anxiety and hope, I did not carry so many burdens as Eva. At home? At *her* home? No, I said. I did not consider so many matters as she. "Put yourself in my position—"

"Maybe I'm not in your position," her teeth gleamed at me.

"Maybe you will be," I ominously threatened, probably meaning something.

"No!" she said. A young woman is rarely so obstinate as when she is considering loosening her clothes.

"But in your house if someone—"

"Yes!" she cried out. "I want to be home." And inexplicable tears were suddenly passed from her upper to her lower eyelid, saying to me, *Because, just because.*

She blinked and watched, this darling to whom I belonged; she watched and blinked, her tears revolving, turning and turning in the light of an April evening in Lakewood Park. We stood behind a memorial rock set there by the Daughters of the American Revolution and I supped at those tears, kissing and wondering, made drunk by Eva's sweet salt, leaning against a plaque which said LAKEWOOD CHAPTER ON THIS SITE IN 1885. . . . "Don't," I said to Eva, doing.

We belonged to each other, hands, lips, eyes, fiery sensations down below and shivers of agreement all around.

Yet we found a use for these things. We were economists still. My portable inspiration, her gaze rested on me in order to call forth my thoughts in rhyme. I supped in salty brine, unseasick. I rhymed her tears, perhaps; that is a heavy charge against me. But not heavier than that of making tears of my rhymes, mistaking one for the other, and then mistaking her schemes against her father for love of me on that site in 1939.

"Why there?" I asked.

"It's so lovely by the fireplace."

"Why *there*, Eva?"

As I said, she insisted that her gift-giving take place at her house on the evening when her parents visited her uncle late at the other end of town in Shaker Heights. She used this and me and her tears separately to the one great purpose, herself. But oh that quickness about the heart! She really meant me. She selected me for the first clacking descent on the great rollercoaster ride. She really and truly meant me! She put her arm in mine, her swagger coat open to the spring breeze. She urged my hand up and down her sleeve as we kissed in the shadow of Mr. Taylor's Buick. In the black shadow of a blue Buick, Eva and I turned pink, our brains congested and our vesicles lambent. We overprepared like mad. Years later, I still remember the furry arms of girls in cunning angora or adorable cashmere, girls who approached away or fled closer like fine plump cats, purposeful in play, sly in promises, leaving me finally with eyelids smarting and finger tips richly tingling. Good advice suggests gratitude to those who unto their own selves are true! And we answer yes, must.

It was at her house that my gratitude first occurred. Pressed against the edge of a couch like two crushed cushions, happily mussed, tearful with suspense and loving exasperation, smelling sofa stuffings and years of sitting, driven together and each profoundly busy with his own business—flaming youth! high school lovers!—we were grateful to each other. "You all right, Dan?"

"You, Eva?"

"I'm all right, Dan."

"I'm all right, Eva."

Crumpled and dim Eva's voice. Honey of hands. Sapping, surprising tenderness. That birch tree just beyond the door —were its leaves green and looking? was its bark white and peeking? Let all birch trees, fathers, ambitions, and dreads tend to their private work. We rode the great ride and outdistanced the world. Alone for a time.

And thus after a moment: "*Stay.* Just like that." She lightly touched my face, skillful and proud of it. She shivered with patience and independence, a shiver of surrender to her being woman and to me, signifying triumph through me over the future and the past. Birch at the door, Euclid's portrait in oil over the fireplace, arrogance and hope, fear of immolation. She stretched in my arms. Faintly her breath quickened, slowed, deepened against me. Softly her body swelled against me; commandingly.

"You, Dan?"

"You, Eva?"

"Stay."

"*Stay.*"

She was traveling under orders, but to her credit she entered the spirit of a voyage. For a time she forgot the orders and traveled. Eva tried to give me what I had counted as valuable even from Black Lil, and succeeded fairly well, considering that she did it merely for what she called love of me—that is, the thought of her father clearly in mind, of her elder brother, and of the imperative bargaining in that market where Pattie Donahue and the other nifty kids shopped. That she possessed a mind large enough to include love of me and notice from her spinal column along with those other responsibilities is a recommendation to mercy. Lakewood does not encourage such luxury in its strict gardens.

I now think of Eva with a warmth which I lacked when I thought I loved her; I'll not forget her because I am inclined to agree that I did her wrong; I signified beliefs which she must later come to deny, and thus brought her oversoon to belief and overold to denial. Did she enjoy?—that is hardly a question for such serious lovers. Did I enjoy?—yes and no, a qualified yes and an unqualified no. Inevitably, of course, detumescence and Lakewood's busy whispering at the walls. After coy heats us, all animals are sad.

But if you ask my feeling toward her now, I can give the answer of vindication: yes. If she does not say the same, she can at least admit that the future is hardly likely without the past. "I like you better than Chuck," she said. "Hastings, I mean."

"I like you better than Rosalie Fallon. I mean Pattie Donahue," I said. I did not mention either Black Lil or Lucille Lake. To atone for this sin of omission I committed one: I said that I loved her.

"I don't care," she said.

There were tears on her lashes. Then there were her hot tears on my mouth.

She returns to me now with a state of being which we must lose with age, the luxuriance of blind solitude, that lorn ecstasy of skinny boys who climb trees and carve invented initials in the bark. We recall only a moment of this youthful loneliness, when we created our abiding image of love, and this instant stands for the hours and the years. Now I remember Eva with her head thrown back to kiss me, her round observant eyes peeping under her lids, her pink tongue peeping through her teeth, her busy pulse self-regarding and as alone as mine in the unreachable places of our blood. She grasps all of my memories but little of my past: she retains the nostalgist in me. Her mouth, which seemed ready to explode in both tears and laughter, fell away under mine. Freeing me of pity, she made me ready for tenderness.

"Would you like a kitten I found? My mother won't let me keep her."

"Dan, you really like me, don't you? It's not just love, you *like* me?"

"Yes, Eva, I think so. Do you like me too, Eva?"

For answer she kissed someone. I feel sure it was herself she kissed, but not only herself, the sensation running along the capillaries and writhing nerves of her lips to that sponge of a brain in which so many schemes waited to be squeezed out, and down through her spinal column where so many longings and willings really lurked. Why her tears? Why my tears? I also kissed someone, and kissed her too, and still do.

17.   *Reverse endings to the good joke*

UNFORTUNATELY, THAT IS ONLY
part of the story. It happened like that, but it also happened
like this. (Did you wonder why so sad, why so lonely, why
so childishly isolated?) Both metaphysics and biology,
scrambled in the suburb, have trouble meaning what they
are meant to mean. There we were—dark house, alert
flesh, hopefulness. We each commanded worlds at our
finger tips on that mohair couch which rubbed our skin
blushing, raw. But at the moment when she had nothing
to lose but her feignings, Eva said: "No."

"What?" I hiccuped at the cool tremor and the decision
of the word.

"No."

We had taken that one step beyond the penultimate
step, and yet Eva spied a last berry of purity which she
could guard. Physically? Even physically. Sex is very
complicated for children and adults—adults and children
will understand me. Sex is not always fully sexified. The
cherry can masquerade as a puckering cranberry, a pickled
beet that had not ever been depickled. Eva's purposes
were served by a pre-expiatory, interrupting, reservating,
precociously adjourning, suburban economy. Here I must
withdraw, I shrink—this is a delicate subject.

220

Anyway, Eva's determination was laced with knees, elbows, and high command. In Lakewood we always took nay for the voice of tradition, authority, and virtue; everyone said nay but the milkman's horse. Eva wore, nonetheless, a sad pout beneath her swollen pout, a dark and ardent animal mug below her chicken-wire muzzle.

"No," she said.

I heard her talking. Since neither heart nor body can be held fully responsible for this sound (this closing nasal palate mark, this refusal, this awful retreat), neither hatred of her father nor love of me, neither duty toward her brother nor love of me, she must also have signaled by it her choice of suburban economies in place of celestial harmonies: "No." She trivially added that she loved me.

I said yes. I shook my head yes over her. I shook her cool arms yes.

"Yes?" I inquired. I was tied clawing against the mohair like a sacrifice on an anthill. There were ten thousand reasons to say yes. Itch, hope, fear, giggles, scratch, huff, puff, jig, joy, and nine thousand nine hundred and ninety-one others. Her cool knees had yearned, spread, cleaved like the prongs of a magnet. *Clap-to!* now went charged knees. The steel filings were released. No further charge. "O Eva, yes!" I said.

"No," she said.

Each of us spoke the truth, I suppose, she more assured in the denial of my *yes* from her stiff crumple-knees breathing in the crevices of cushions than I in the affirmation of her *no* amid the rising warmth of well-creamed skin and the last of the Christmas cologne. A certain disengagement occurred. The fabled single animal regretfully reverted to two. A dilemma found its return to discourse, and we felt that wonder at the absolute's responsibility to the world *which is* that always confounds lovers. From hot blood and dizziness we sighed and heaved back to politeness on furniture. We went to the bathroom, Eva first, then I went, each one carefully locking the door. There we reached and straightened, buttoned, zipped. There we thought of things to say.

"Are you hungry?" she recited.

"Eva," I said.

I had washed with icy water, shocked to my shrunken center, jumpy. I had combed with water, too. Her cheeks were flaming with mohair and with my first prickles of beard. She was sorry. She had rinsed her mouth but still had a taste in it.

"I always have a nice time with you, Dan," she said, turning away, "even if we only stay home and talk." She turned toward me, her eyes flooded but this time holding back the tears. "Dan, listen, I just can't help it, it's just because I really can't—"

"Yes, some cocoa would hit the spot," I said.

She frowned as if I had somehow failed her with curt cruelty (I had). But it's hard to keep my eye on that sublime far star which is the source of all light and heat—the real thing—when the hand pointing to that star makes jangling, distracting, charming gestures. Supple Eva was double-jointed. She could bend her thumb to her wrist and her father to me. How then to be kind? Starlove, starbright, only star I saw that night, it lay far away and the girl who seemed to be pointing was interested only in her subluminary, planetary gestures. She too had reasons on the mind. And surely, star-preoccupied, I was not enough interested in *her*.

Nevertheless, our spoons chinked together for the pure tenderness of which we were not capable. They say that the innocent are pure! No, we had polluted ourselves for the sake of an economy of spirit, not yet learning our way to the desire and pride which are joy's innocence. We wronged ourselves! We had to learn! We were tender in regret.

When Mr. and Mrs. Masters returned from their visit, they found our spoons intimately linked over hot chocolate in the kitchen. Eva and I were having conversation. We were speaking of the picnic of the *Times* staff next Sunday at Luna Park. To communicate a certain shame and re- morse about previous matters, Eva was putting pieces of cake into my outrageously open mouth. We were probably smiling. The kitchen was bright and the tiles were glisten- ing. The pantry was ajar and Red's box of Wheaties was showing. He had pasted a photograph of T.S. Eliot over the picture on the box of the Champion who always par- took of the Breakfast of Champions. ("It keeps me young like a bull," declares Tom Eliot, star poet. "I shall hit the ball with bases full.") There was also Ovaltine on the shelf, and Postum, Choco-Dox, and Sanka—the better to make you sleep, my dear. And a flyswatter, the better to make the flies sleep. Dormative qualities were much in demand that year. Mr. Beck, foreign minister of Poland, had gone to see Hitler about Danzig and come home needing a pill. Fretful Eva essayed a smile. It was something past mid- night by the electric clock above the refrigerator. Last year it would have been giggles o'clock in the morning; tonight it was half past regret, a quarter to yes and no time left.

The enemy entered.

There was sweet cake in my mouth. Eva was feeding me.

Thickly bundled against the out-of-doors, Euclid and Deborah Masters hung in the doorway to survey the debris of butter, bread, marmalade, breakfast cups, yesses, and noes.

"Mr. Berman?" said Euclid Masters.

"Oh Daniel Berman," said Deborah Masters.

"I believe you have not quite understood me," Mr. Masters said.

"It seems that you haven't understood him," Mrs. Masters said.

Oh! said Eva's silent mouth.

"We talked about this all the way back from Shaker Heights," Mrs. Masters said. "That's a lovely section. Red is spending the night with his cousin."

Euclid Masters held his hand across the English wool of the lapel of his overcoat as if he had a pain beneath the buttons. He waited for my reply. Again I thought I saw a hair across his eye.

"I don't know how to answer you, Mr. Masters," I admitted. A soft flutter of his eyes, almost flirtatious, indicated that my presence among his breakfast cups was more than sufficient answer. It was far from breakfast time. Rage—fear—hate. Calmly he sorted out his feelings by counting the silver. But it came in a bundle, rage and fear and hate. Wrath in his flirting eyes, and a hair—Do Not Disturb.

"I asked Dan to have some chocolate," Eva said.

"You don't know how to answer me, eh? no?" (I had heard enough of no for that evening.) "No?" he said.

"No?" Mrs. Masters asked.

"N-no," mused Eva Masters. Her sigh seemed to regret not having said yes to me.

"Yes, that's right," I efficiently summed up, "it's really up to Eva and me." With a specific nostalgia I added: "We're not doing anything wrong." And garrulously: "Of course, if you'd rather we drink our chocolate at Clark's, well, I don't mind—"

"Is that the point, Deborah? eh?"

"No," she dutifully affirmed.

"Perhaps it would be best if I spoke out directly," Euclid Masters said. "I have tried to spare the feelings of all of us." I stopped meeting his eyes because I felt my heavy guilt in obliging him to say what he meant. He did not want to tell me his little truth. As he moved for the first time closer to me under the kitchen light, I looked to see if he lacked a shadow, which is said to signify a great deal; his shadow followed faithfully, signifying little, but growing large away from the light (a giant, a god, a father) and small as he approached (a dwarf, a fat insect). He had a shadow which behaved like others despite his deifying hypochondria. I made of it what I made of him. I did not judge its size or thickness, but it fell between me and the light.

"I didn't mean to make you angry or hurt you," I managed to say. "It's just, I think, that Eva, I mean Eva and me—"

He was close enough to touch me. His dry commercial hands held each other for strength. I could hear how breathing changes during a season of suppressed anger: long hard sighs, whistling their chagrin to the source of inhibition. Listen well to this whisper, which says softly, with the sweet phlegm of asthma: *I hate someone, something. . . . I hate you. . . .*

I must have met his stare with the idiot wisdom on my face of a gambler, a Jew, or a Negro in the presence of those who fear him (hate him). I tried to look at Euclid Masters. I was blinded by avid darkness. Again my eyes were felled by the deep instinct of submission to those who do not like us—all their false reasons are so much less imposing than those they cannot know which belong to each of us in secret. *We* know, we judge ourselves; a foolish enemy can give the lie to our writhing efforts at virtue, purpose, value; and he throws us into despair. My locksmith friend unwillingly aided me, as does any strong hatred, in the self-destroying will to self-judgment. We stood in silence, in our contest of silence in the kitchen. I recalled the high sounds of company in my parents' home, the fine mist of tea and the smell of rubber from the heap of galoshes in the hall, and my mother crying out, "Your feet are wet like dogs, drink tea. Even an Englishman he drinks tea from a cup. . . ."

But this was no friendly steaming kitchen place. Pots

and oven and silence and dry wrath. Someone had shut
the pantry.

"You understand my position, Mr. Berman," Euclid
Masters said at last, with no smile at his use of the mister.
"I have a certain authority in my own house, eh? My own
daughter, eh?" Her eyes darted sideways like those of a
little girl crumpling herself at the foot of the bed, frightened
by an abstract noise made particular in her ears. "I am
going to state very clearly now, Mr. Berman, exactly
what it is that I forbid you to do. I want my daughter to
hear me tell you"—but he did not look at her. "Listen. I
now forbid you—"

My lungs grew full and heavy. My throat swelled. I
wanted to make a noise like a hurt animal, and I did, but
soundlessly, for a lifetime of politeness made me say instead: "Oh."

Since he had expected defiance at this point, and since
instead I had met his eyes in anguish and belief, he added
only: "This thing is making me ill. You have no right to
make me feel like this. Why do you want to do it, Dan?"

"I'm sorry," I said, "I'm *sorry,*" again with the conviction that those who disliked me must be making true
final judgment, for why else such strong feelings about me?
I trusted strong feelings even when I could not see the sense
in them. Euclid Masters was not a rhetor; his arguments
and his character did not make his beliefs attractive or
credible; but he embodied in his skeleton and in his
actual sick Euclid Masters flesh the argument which tells
the most severely at that age: *he believed what he said to
me.* This conviction gave him dignity in my eyes. In a
time of fakery it even flattered me.

Clutching his lapel like a tragedian, he said: "I am going
to ask you straight out, eh? to stop seeing my daughter."

"Why?"

"And to stop speaking with her when you see her."

"Why, Mr. Masters? Tell me why."

Our gaze languished against each other. Eva and Mrs. Masters may have thought that we were aware of discomfort. We were not. Finally Mrs. Masters said, "He asked you why, Euclid."

"I said stop. Just stop. Stop, that's all. Stop it. Stop it."

"Why, Mr. Masters?"

"You oblige me, boy."

Idiot-faced, I stared.

"You," he murmured, fervently looking through me to his vision of me, "don't you all act alike? Haven't I met your kind before? the tribe? in business and every place I go? the law offices? even the town on the coast where my father used to take me sailing?"

He was making a speech. He was remembering his childhood. He meant what he said. In my new covert suit chosen to give virtue to my longings and the desire to please to my fears, my knit tie too tight so that Eva's father might like me, even my thighs and armpits specially scrubbed earlier in the evening so that my propriety would not be a sham, wanting Eva's father to approve my unseen places and unknown dreams, shy, deeply courteous, and reaching toward him while my fingers tugged at the seams of my pants, I pitied him for the need to put his hatreds in the form of questions. I watched him with broken stillness in my noisy heart as he said:

"You think you can make a fool of me? my entire family? a boy of seventeen? you?"

I wanted to apologize to him. I wanted to say that I was sorry; to say, Go ahead, Mr. Masters, tell me what you want to tell me; to say, I'll listen, you don't have to ask. I give you my permission. You're old enough to have confidence. Tell me if you have to. . . .

"The brethren?" he suggested. "Miami Beach? the movies? the New Deal?"

From behind her mild maternal bosom and soft middle-aged flesh, above the dignified budding of a string of uncultured pearls, within a face worn and tender with love of her own children and of all children, Mrs. Masters loyally echoed her husband, saying, "The Jew Deal."

"Mr. Masters," I said. You're old enough to be my father, I thought.

"My wife just says things right out, doesn't she, Eva?" And now the heavy burden of illness and discontentment was suddenly lifted from his brow. He put his head toward me. "Sometimes I'm grateful, eh?—my wife and her ways —that she makes it possible for me to preserve my tact." His eyes winked into mine. Joyously he smiled into my face.

I wanted to wink and smile back. I was pleased that he felt good about something, especially about something his wife had said. I have always loved a loving couple. A glimpse of Eva being whirled into the circle, her mouth panting and horrified, full of teeth, returned me to the duties of a swain. "Oh! oh! oh!" she said. My failure to strike out at him in this moment, an agreement with him which only now I begin to identify, an agreement on the metaphysical terms of a pun, finished Eva for me and me for Eva. Romantic down to the elastic of her dainties, she expected me both to be the forbidden and to deny it. She wanted me, for the sake of her ideal of pirates, to walk the plank without a map of the treasure. "Oh!" she was saying. She wanted me to be Bad. My calmness, a consideration if not an acceptance of his accusation because of the spirit of faith in which it was offered, changed my neckerchief back to a Prep Department cravat.

Euclid Masters again stretched and smiled. His fingers patted his own palm. He enjoyed the yawn. My silence spoke, I believe, for a greater sympathy with him than for Eva, not for a lack of daring. Piety did not detract from the courage of Moses before Aaron and his calf of gold. For the moment Moish Berman rejected an abstracted humanity for the sake of a suffering desert devil.

Mr. Masters slipped out of his coat. Once more he could dwell in his own house. I imagine Pilate so sighing, stretching, and putting off his cloak after a hard day's judging.

"And another thing, Mr. Berstein—"

My name was fun. He stretched on his toes for comfort in this kitchen whose food he could not digest. He came down straight with the floor. He knew that his wife and daughter followed the gesture, toe down and heel up; heels down; toes down. He knew a kind of pleasure in his diseased guts. Whom had he judged? Yes, Berman and Masters, and why?

He had five toes like me! On each foot! And a tiny, apparently useless one, important for balance!

He paused to watch me as I thought: This is being grown-up. I was, I really was his antagonist, my status a partial victory. If I were to continue this way, would it answer him sufficiently? Did I have this option toward a man who, while he could not strike me down, he could *not,* he could and did carve an abyss on all sides from which, far away, Eva, Mrs. Masters, and Euclid himself grinned at me. From across the abyss my childish unconcern ebbed away, rage replacing it. The linoleum, the insulation, the brick, the cement, the earth cracked under that kitchen; I dived into it—the washed glacial upheavals, the trampled Indian earth of the Western Reserve—and then arose once more through element and product into our suburb. My stomach and knees sent up the message: *oof.*

He repeated: "Mr. Berstein, there is one other matter I ought to mention—"

No option during earthquake. You have to move. No option before those death's-heads across the abyss. You have to answer the grin. My stomach going flimsy, my heart knocking to be let out, my body told me that the choice of which motion, this one or that one, can be freely made; but it is the demand of survival that a decision be taken. Does weathering the attack give an option to sail before it with a smile, making a high smiling swoop in history? No. Mere persistence, mere survival. No option for a flight without earned wings, which gain their soar in a use of winds. Decide. Move and decide.

"If you will allow me, Mr. Berstein, I would like to state—"

No. We can make statements later. Freedom itself implies obligations—the freedom of explosion—when the prisons come steely about us. Yield to him, yes; then yield to anger, yield to hate; then fly right. No further option.

"Say what you want to say, Mr. Masters. Speak up!"

"All right, Mr. Berstein—"

"You don't have to say that. My name is Berman, if you want to call me that. You know it, Mr. Masters. Berman is the same style anyway."

He made a secret little mouth, *ah.*

"Go on, Mr. Masters, I didn't really want to interrupt you. If you say Berman I know what you mean. I already know what you mean about my name."

Ah, the dry lips grinned.

"I'd much rather listen to you. Please go on. To tell the truth, Mr. Masters, your name seems funny to me, too. Because it doesn't mean anything." That pleased me, it did. "Speak up! What did you want to tell me?"

Ah-h, indeed, it grinned. His wife fluttered behind him in the silence, and I caught a glimpse of her head disheveled by peeking. No one spoke. I waited. Perhaps Deborah Masters pushed her husband. Eva was pushing. No one spoke. Perhaps only at last I threw back my head, wrestling with disbelief. "Then that was all?" I asked. "You just wanted to use my name? That all you can do?"

He soothed me. "Oh, please, really, Mr. Berstein, don't think that's all."

"Berman," I said.

"Mr. Berman," he said.

It was difficult to answer a man who no longer even recognized a question. We stared at each other in the kitchen, undistracted by kitchen things. To go on my way would not be sufficient answer to Euclid Masters. (Both of us were patient now.) But to go on my way over him, through him, maybe that if anything could oblige him to ask himself a question again. I had chosen the proper option in his trivial joke of names. I no longer needed his questions, but as a fatality of remaining human, I had to act as if I did; there are many Euclid Masterses in the world. He had an obligation toward me—to become real. Still, the seeming of a Euclid Masters partakes of being. I cared for him.

"Dan," said sweet impatience behind me. "Dan, you mustn't forget me. Get back on the subject, Dan. Yes, tell him what we mean to each other," Eva told me.

"Eva?" I said.

"Tell him what we mean, Dan! Don't let him do this!"

No, I had no right to care for him.

No option.

No other right but hatred.

No, no, no.

And I tried! I wanted to hate him as some men want to find faith.

"Dan, why are you just standing there?"

And the whisper from Mrs. Masters: "Euclid, I think you should finish explaining to the boy now."

"Tell him, please, for both of us, Dan!" This was a fierce Eva whom I would never know.

"What?" Euclid Masters asked.

"What?" I said.

I didn't know or couldn't tell it. I struggled to find the Personnel Manager in geometric Euclid Masters, the hypochondriac, the locksmith, the horny crustacean, Jehovah, Aaron, and petty Pilate the Economist-in-chief. Speak up! Last chance, Mr. Masters! I saw only a man who was not level with himself.

With hatred of us all, Eva proclaimed: "Tell him I'm going with you to the picnic on Sunday!"

I did not know what she meant to me in the crowd of her fathers. I watched his eyes fall against mine: the fatal pity of the Inquisitor. "Enough for today, please, Dan," he said in a low voice.

Tell me now, Mr. Masters.

"Tell him, Dan!"

"I. . . . We . . ." The parents passed over each other the glance of property owners before the trapped trespasser. I tried to obey Eva. "We mean a great deal," I said. "To each other, I mean."

You have a minute yet, Euclid.

For perhaps the first time this evening, Euclid Masters turned his eyes wholly from me to his daughter. He interpreted for himself the rage in Eva's stance, and at last, with a high good humor that could no longer be contained, he laughed. Hatcheting the locks, this locksmith laughed. Ignoring stitches, cricks, false stomachs, and asthma, this hypochondriac doubled over with a pumping laughter. He cast off all accouterment, said good-by, and there swayed Euclid Masters, himself, twitching and hawing. The pantry door fell open and showed the boxes and cans of bedtime drinks. Euclid saw and laughed. Flogging his moribund geniality, this man unleashed upon me those two dread weapons against a seventeen-year-old: first my sympathy for him, then his contempt for me. He slapped his thighs with a clicking sound that recalled my own father's fat clopping; he stammered out: "They mean—they mean—a great deal—he means—to *him*—" He choked but hallooed his doubt: "Eh? eh?"

Yes, yes, I admit it. There was an abyss, and only across it could he believe in me. I existed, yes, as nothing, as faraway nothing and Berstein, as the abstract form of threat to such a man. Poor Euclid, this made him laugh. During the time of his incredible humor he convinced me of the chasm yawning between everyone else and me. But the moment was not wide enough for his purpose. With no school but his own failure, he could not unlearn me of bridge-building, of my election to a pleasure in construction over vacant places. From years behind his blow, still stinging with assault in this altitude, I think out to his grave: *Laughter should be enough, yet sometimes it is not.*

Speak up!

In the spring of 1939 Euclid Masters had his moment of dominion in that suburban kitchen. We all shrank beneath him. Then anger, like a slight hunger, lengthened Eva's neck and lifted her head above the satisfactions surrounding it. A mistake for which she needs to be forgiven is that she took my boggle for fear of him. It was a stare compounded of everything but fear: wonder at being able to call up such hatred and such laughter, a pride in his crippled love which made such feeling possible, a secret riding with passion, whatever its object. Nothing further? You find this not enough, Euclid? Then I thought he had said my name. "What, Dan?"

But it must have been someone else, some hoarse other voice.

It was Euclid.

"What, Mr. Masters?"

His lips had vanished against each other. I leaned closer. I could not take my eyes from this crustacean suddenly become a crescent-mouthed shark in his house of crabs, a chain become bells, a triumphant man.

"Say something, you, Dan!" Eva turned toward me a face contorted by hatred and self-pity, chin pointed by the mouth busy in itself, neck trembling, the fine beat of pulse broken up, eyes narrowed and darkened to those of an old woman. All the physical energies compressed, she seemed to shrink before me, sharpened into a single motion of querulous shaking and dry heat. With this great last mobility of childhood, her hiss of breath floated above us, light as a rotten nut. "Are you just going to stand there?"

"No, Eva. Yes."

"Do something!"

"I see, Eva."

She was making a choice because I failed to strike at him in some epic way. I obliged her to economies even more fine than the pity with which her trembling reproached me under the name of cowardice. She found her way to use the old man and me as tools against ourselves, forgetting that this was just what her clever father wanted of her, this and her consequent forgetfulness. *No*—from another abyss and the more patient assault of time.

"Why are you just standing there like a dead man?"

"Don't get mad, Eva. I wanted to stand up, that's all, you shouldn't call me names."

You owed us all more, Mr. Masters. You had another option. No, Euclid, it was not enough.

Cried out Eva Masters with tears of chagrin and despair from the perfumed distance of her corrupted imagination: "Just the same, I'm going to the picnic Sunday with Dan Berman. I am!"

Again Euclid Masters put his face close to mine, turned it slightly sideways, screwed up his eyes deliciously in a close-mouthed grin, and asked me: "Just the same?"

18. *The tunnel of love*

CROSSING THE STREET TO OUR
appointed place of congregation on that bronze-aired,
penny-dry June afternoon of the *Times* picnic, Eva gave
me her arm in such a way that I had to take it high and
touch, indeed, a tender more-than-her-arm. The swelling
fragrance of breast beneath sweater, the straining ripe-
ness of unripe girl, this could decide my palm and de-
range my senses; it could also serve the last paltry snack
of ennui and decision—Eva giving charity before retiring to
pity.

"You look nice, Eva."

"So do you, Dan."

"Nice. I don't like to look nice."

"Well, maybe you just can't help it."

Why should she care for my palm and my desire after
I had flunked in her parents' kitchen? Ridden by the need
to judge herself, how could she add my peculiar self-
judgments to the evidence of her history and future? Oh
but she was pretty anyway! A flower growing straight in
the shade. "What you thinking about, Dan?"

How her father's dialectic would work upon Eva and
me I could not predict, obedient at first only to the arguments of her softness, her fragrance, and her cloudy

235

magnifying-glass eyes. We no longer skipped. My hand, as it pretended not to touch her as closely as it did, was offered an idea soft with portent, furry with angora. Left soft arm, left firm and soft breast. Sweater.

"Is your father angry?"

"Daddy? Oh, maybe he won't speak to me for days and days"—suddenly the child's brilliance of fever on her eyes.

"Oh, you poor Eva."

"That's all right, Dan, please it is. Hiya, Tom! Why Juicer, hello!"

Like cute spring minnows, we nipped apart at the touch of greeting. Flitting and agile, quick with light, we inquired, touched, noted, judged. The girls vibrated in approximate resonances together to classify lunch and sandal, brush of hair and hubris of brassière, while the boys spoke louder and more loud the words of assurance and greeting, all of which want to mean, *I see you.*

"Juicer, where you been lately?"

He looked hurt and swollen, having gained weight in unhappy eating. There was a bluish lap of flesh at his chin. "I saw you in school, Dan, didn't we? You've been busy. Girls. I understand."

"He understands," Tom said, "since I explained it to him a hunnert times if not more. It's natural. He ought to get it by now. It's the time of life we're in. Especially you."

"Must be," said Juicer.

"The hormones are starting up," Tom said, "but you got to be careful."

Juicer refused to look at me. His eyes on a low-slung lady in magenta Western pants asked if I swallowed a hormone for forgetting friendship.

"There's a book tells you how to live right, be healthy and strong, otherwise you get prostrate glands," Tom said. "I sent away for it in a plain wrapper."

I would have touched Juicer if I dared. Instead I kicked his Keds lightly. "Juicer, let's do something tomorrow," I said. "It's no school, how about it?"

His upper lip pulled forward and down over his front teeth. Shame. Pride. The breakup of our gang. "Well, I'll see if I'm not busy with some girl. Maybe I'll have a date. I was thinking of asking Lucille." But he grinned and paldom was righted again, and he said, "Listen, how about the burlesque show at the Roxy, hey Dan? Nekked wimmen."

We churned and jostled. We touched and explored. Tom informed us that he too had a scientific interest in observing how nekked wimmen wiggle and stomp. "I owe it to my future wife. She'll want me to make her happy. I intend to marry a modern woman who will give me my healthy, unborn children. Statistics prove it's better to be cosmopolitan."

We exercised tact. Secretly Juicer and I believed that twisty and twirly there's a happy girlie was part of being cosmopolitan, but only part. When puritan Tom took up his rare cause, he took up a *cause*.

Then we let three streetcars pass, a group decision by request of small-pawed Pattie Donahue, as we awaited Lewis Snyder. In the morning sunlight below the STOP sign swam familiar particles of dust, yet when I looked more closely not one was truly recognizable—so strange becomes the banal when our way of looking is in the way of changing. In months we had grown inches, bones for the day and fat sleekness for the night. Juicer, Tom, and I admired with the pride of creators the economical girls: Rosalie Fallon, who ducked and jiggled in the calm banana-breasted carnality of the Siamese maiden in a travelogue; virulent Pattie with her metaphysical mandibles; svelte, frugal, and rapacious Lucille, the busy-eyed, diamond-eyed harpist; profound Eva, self-regarding and hyperthyroid. With the haste of those who live by beauty, they joined in a covert glance at us which said, *I've to hurry, otherwise old before I find my way.* . . .

Pattie Donahue put her sideways giggle between Juicer and Tom and me, her face a mask of coquetry and ice, and then asked the world's most foolish question: "Why are you looking at me?"—her nice hands opening. Her sign said: Trespassers Will Be Violated.

"Looking? What do you mean, looking?" We had been taking something from her for our Vesicle Trust Savings Bank. Hairily we heaved and rippled our intellects to confound the girls. "I guess I'll write a tone poem," remarked Juicer, "the words and music, typewriters in the chorus, see? Our modern age, see?"

"Aah, that's old stuff, Juicer. George Gershwin already did the modern age, you know, the one that went—I can hear it in my head but I can't sing it. It's strictly passy. Listen Juicer, what you got to do is *after* the modern age, something really new." (Ardently, a brother.) "You got the talent, Juicer, you can do it." I turned to Eva: "He just hears a song once and he plays it on the upright, his mother's, two-handed. He's terrific."

But Eva was looking at Chuck Hastings.

"What's so modern about modern times? Just there's more dead people than there used to be"—the cynical smile of the extracurricular Sunday afternoon deep, thanks to Tom Moss, man of the futuristic. "Course there's more hormones, too."

"Say, there was this fellow in San Francisco, he said you don't have to die, you could live to a hundred"—no one knew who had invited elderly Chuck Hastings, alumnus undergraduate, not even on the staff of the *Lakewood High Times*. "I talked to him myself and that's how I know, me. In Frisco this here fellow vivisected cut up some dogs, say listen here. . . ."—Chuck Hastings, the balloonist of ideas,

soared happy with empty luggage in outer space. He had
invited himself, as prophets often do.

"Hey Eva, I want to tell you something. . . . Wait up,
Eva!"—Dan Berman.

"Tell *me* something, too," said Pattie. "Where's Lewis?"

The streetcar whined, stumbled, stopped. We filed
aboard without the negligent Snyder, sheik and left end,
small-pawed Pattie's resilient heart as unbreakable as the
plastic bathroom cup with its accumulated cosmetic of
mouth-refreshing tooth powder. "I guess he's not coming,"
she said. We consoled her. Boys accept this duty on a
afternoon with girls; 'In picnics begin responsibilities,' as
the Irish poet sang. Chuck pursued Eva and me with his
long-nosed pout and bad-breathed arguments. I studied
the important distinction between devotion and jealousy.
Jealousy hurts the belly right here, low down; unhappy
devotion riles the stomach where the belly hormones are
stored.

Chuck sucked flaps of food from his teeth and clicked
his palate in important labor, shaking his head to dislodge
the day's scruff of ideas. Circularly I exercised my pseudo-
argyled ankle in a distracted gesture I had not made up—
it had just honestly happened to me. I let them talk,
Chuck jutting toward us, Eva tranquil in her plans by my
side. We swayed thus through the rumor and hullabaloo of
the city, the hauling cries of work and the ruling purr
of machinery, these echoes of that time's pure music of
pleasure and pain. Only once I interrupted to point to a
group of small boys hovering over the Civil War cannon
in the Public Square where, transferring to an East Side
streetcar, we overheard an erudite discussion of gunnery
and whether these weapons would protect the city from
sudden attack. "HITLER PROMISES. . . ." said a headline
caught like a kite in a tree.

"Aren't they darling, I mean infantile?"—Eva.

"Kid stuff"—bogus Chuck. "Juvenile delinquency among the underprivileged is the technical term."

"No, they're just expressing their anxieties," I commented. "It's a game."

"Where did you learn that?" Lucille Lake said to me. "What do you know about anxiety, Dan?"

When had Lucille begun asking questions?

"In a book," I said, full of grief.

"Books!" said Chuck. "Personally I spend most of my time *living*. What do you think, Eva?"

"But they're real genuine old cannons," I argued, content with this trivial civic historicity in my devotion to Eva and my inner victory over jealousy of Chuck (premature).

I did not know, as we traveled through the Cleveland Street Railway System toward Luna Park, how Eva was figuring that this trolley, with its stiff straw seats and dry spitty smell, was precisely the sort of vehicle on which one should regret traveling to Luna Park with Daniel Berman. She considered several subtle and technically skillful ways of informing me. "We're all going through a stage, me too," she ambiguously murmured. Slyly her eyes wobbled over mine. I misinterpreted as love her exhilaration at an essay into distance from her father; the old order was being strapped and disciplined, then to be restored under another harness to full powers. She touched the tingling dryness where her mother's perfume had kissed the behind of her ears. "We don't know everything yet, Dan. . . . We can't go past the end so soon. . . ."

Despite my respect for Euclid Masters, I was not capable of such retrospective complications on a day of sun and water and yellow wind in the spring leaves, taffy and sawdust and the Fun House, a day of June and a day of picnics. Juicer and I had decided to take possession of the world even before admission to college gave us the right (*nubile oblige*). This was at an age when Gandhi already had a family and was considering the vows of continence, vegetarianism, and total responsibility. In the meantime, Juicer, Tom, and I secreted while Chuck molted. Tender Eva, methodical and purposeful, worked out her problem. The streetcar clicked and swayed through the blocks of Cleveland, more Cleveland, final Cleveland.

"Lewis will probably arrive by his father's car any minute," Pattie was whispering to Rosalie. "Want to bet he's buying me something?"

"Nobody else got a corsage," Rosalie said bitterly.

"Maybe candy *and* a corsage."

Spitefully Rosalie smiled. "Candy would melt and get sticky in this heat if he puts the convertible down. Fattening. Rots the teeth. But I'm sure Lewis really likes you awfully much, so maybe he'll show up after all."

Tom nudged me. "What's the diff between carsick and seasick?"

"Is that trying to be a joke?" Juicer asked, swaying.

"No, it's probably something psychological," I said.

From across the aisle came the words: "What did you say, Dan?"—another genuine question from Lucille Lake!

Tom was holding himself. "Streetcars do this to me. Maybe I should eat a cracker. Streetcars."

"Maybe hormones," Juicer said, expressing a general resentment of Tom and Science. "But I wish I had a cracker for you, Tom"—expressing a particular affection for Tom and a trust in Science.

"Streetcar. Cracker. Hoo-ow, fellas."

Unable to help his suffering, we put a brave face on it. The nausea of others is not difficult to bear. We bore Tom's magnificently. We swayed and rocked and let the streetcar carry us onward.

End of the line; the gates of Luna Park. Suddenly veiny-legged women trotted in shorts, and the smell of popcorn and hotdogs swam over gravel and automobile exhaust; we descended blinking into a sun multiplied by forenoon. The sun took up the risks of motion and salted fat; the sun was taken by its own, by food and by the secretions of play. Oily gravel spattered at our feet; flint, fierce reflectors, careen and reek of pleasure. The women in bandannas shrieked as they ran beneath the sun, their men spraddle-legged in pursuit with swimming trunks itchy under pants. "Oh don't forget the lotion, Harry!" Already, from where we stood, the scream and whir of the Loop-the-Loop enticed us, and the funny music of the caliope beckoned. Ralph Guitano and his Eight-Wheeled Rhythm Boys Eight proposed the Roller Rinkeroo with its ball-bearing delights by insinuating above the click of wooden wheels that:

> "Somewhere, over the rainbow,
>   Way up high,
>   You'll fly over the rainbow,
>   Bye and—"

"Bye," assented perfect-pitched Juicer.

KAHN BROS.' LUNA PARK, CLEVELAND'S OWN PLEASURE DOME, the neon on stilts above the gate throbbed against the measureless day. (Where Ralph, the sacred rhythm ran. . . .) It was the Kahn combine that promoted (did decree) this domain of pleasure, my father told me, Victor Kahn and his kid brother Kubla. Pattie leaned sideways toward me in a spectacular summer frock, showing one breast with its pink nipple sprinkled with pepper, straining to the starboard because it would be immoral to show the other, and generous, all too generous. "Look Dan the clouds," she intimated dreamily, destroying Snyder by sympathetic magic. "See that one looks like a face?"

"I already saw a face," I said, refusing to look, disgruntled by vague suspicions, stupified by the sun.

"Coming, Dan?" Eva asked. "We're all going. . . ."
(Down to the sunlit sea.)

Individual spines on Youth the Porcupine's back, we
stiffly stuck each other, and then softening in the first sawdust shade, we made of our piling together a scurry of
pale underrock tumblebugs. We picked up dirt in our path,
crackled and stickled, rolled tenderly together through the
coloring Sunday morning and afternoon. A cry occurred:
"Hey there!" or "Hi!"—the melody sang up in call of
greeting. It made no difference. It was Lewis Snyder that
we announced. It was the squeak of pleasure in the blood.
Dust on our eyelids gave them weight, pressed them heavy,
made of lashes a veil; dust on our noses straddled the nostrils, pulsing; dirt and sun and oil elucidated our crinkling
flesh. Even Lucille's diamond eyes darkened at moments to
show the hidden stresses and fires within. Eva delicately
ate crackerjack, popping it virtuously onto her tongue as
if it were the host. She won a whistle in the package I
bought her.

"It's *paper*," she complained. "It's from *Japan*."

"Gee, it's a genuine Japanese paper whistle from Japan,"
I said admiringly.

That should have made all the difference, but her eyes
clouded, rejected, switched me off. "Hi Lewis, where did
you come from?" she asked.

"Just a hunch, just a little hunch of mine. I says to
myself, I says two bits they're by the Dodgem, so down I
comes and what do I find?"

"What?" breathed Pattie in suspense.

"You, kiddo!"

And he carried her off on his arm, presenting gum. I
stood in the widening emptiness. Someone entered it toward
me.

"Hello, Dan, going on the Dodgem?"—diamond-eyed
Lucille with her busy unawakened smile.

"Yes, why?"

"I'd like to try it. . . ."—in her musical face the quiet brooding of coal into diamonds, hard and pure, the decoration of fire—that marriage of coal with weight, consecrated by time. "I bet you know how to drive already. I don't have much time for such things. I practice four hours a day."

"Yes, why? Yes, why?"

Juicer watched us, ponderously breathing, sweat showing a beggar's patches under his arms. He let the crowd surge between Lucille and him and did not explain the Dodgem principle, electricity diffused on chicken wire, even after I left her.

"Coming on the Dodgem, Eva?" I asked.

We admired the skill of the Puerto Rican whore alone in an electric car, steering in time to the music, magnificently swooping, chewing hard, her long sleek ears tight to her head, bumping with grace and taking a high calm turn to submit to being bumped. She drifted with a waltz and occasionally nudged someone as an obligation to possible business. Only her teeth brought down hard on gum, shaping and snapping, frazzling and agglutinating, destroying and redestroying, seemed to fret over her memories; the rest of her was elegant and gracious and had forgotten. The boys who watched over this traffic (electric Dodgem masts tapping the Dodgem power, I informed Eva) liked the girl and sometimes gave her free rides. Eva frowned, perhaps out of disapproval of free rides. The ditto mark of fuss always boded ill; my stomach slunk around a corner when she looked at me like that. I could not follow her moral circularities.

"Coming, Eva?"

"No, why? . . ."

Lax, lubber, pouch-eyed Juicer, pinched and watchful Tom, useless Chuck, toothsome, tricksome Pattie, light Rosalie, long-eyed, bronze-armed, quiet and smiling Lu-

cille, broody Eva—all prowled loose that afternoon. Plus
Jean Thompson. Plus others. Plus me, Daniel the Spaniel,
Berman el-Sermon, whirled alone in that bobbing ghost
ship—his head. He wanted to join a crew someplace for the
trip we all make. Sun, loneliness, the abstract nostalgia of
caliope music had joined to pickle him; he was marinated.
"Lucille? Pattie? Eva?" he said. "Something special doing?"

> *It is a tainted mariner*
> *And he stoppeth one of three*
> *'By thy garrulous word and glittering I,*
> *Now wherefore stopp'st thou me?"*

"Look for yourself," quoth Pattie.
"Want some ice cream too?" quoth Eva.
"It always takes a while to get warmed up," quoth Lu-
cille.
"Jeez, it's a nice day," quoth Berman, "and I wish
something would happen.

Leaning, standing, impatient, we ate our lunch out of
bags, spicy hotdogs luxurious in *the works,* green spangle
of relish and angry mustard, potato salad lubricated by
mayonnaise and pulpy with cold cooking, conversation
breathy and quick. If we said nothing, we at least said,
"Um. . . . um. . . ." My hangdog stomach reentered my
domain when Eva smiled. Why smiled? She toothily showed
buds of teeth over a sideways slip of celery—no, she was
only crunching—but hullo anyway, belly o' mine, and stay
a while, why don't you? (And if you find you have to go
again, send me a card from Luna Park.) While we
munched we listened to the know-it-all call of a carnival
barker:

"Now I tell you what I'm gonna do, friends. Now I
have a little free gift here for each and every man woman
and child who dares to take a chance. Gather round,

gather round, you heard what I said, absolutely free, I said don't block the way, that's right, pull clear there, boy, I said step up and see what the well-known firm which I have the pleasure and honor to represent"—hat respectfully touched—"is more than willing to do for you in order to introduce its new product, Sunshine City Salt Water Taffy with the Vitamines Added. . . . What? *What?* Do you mean to stand there with your upturned faces and tell me you're a man and won't try your luck to earn a Real Ingersoll Watch, a Gen-u-ine Parker Fifty-One Fountain Pen, a Free Gift for One and All in each and every purchase of a sample box of Sunshine City Salt Water Taffy, packed especially for us by a well-known maker of salt water taffy purely as a sign of friendship and confidence in our public?" (He lifted his hat in a tribute to the well-known maker.) "All *right* then, step up ladies, step up gentlemen, give him a little shove if he's a namby or a pamby, girlies. Our own lavatory scientists added the Vitamines Added. Your money freely returned if you don't win a valuable prize. That's my word on it, folks, and that's what I live by—your confidence in Sunshine City Salt Water Taffy. And now do I see a skeptic over there in the audience? You with the mistrustful smile on your face? You think you're going to get hanky-pank stuff for your fifty cents, whistles, charms, crackerjack prizes, Mister? All right, I tell you what I'm gonna do—"

He fell abruptly into dark brooding.

"Whatcha gonna do?" came a cupped-hands yell from his brother-in-law at the back of the crowd.

It rose before him like a visitation. "Thank you, thank you, sir, and I tell you what I'm gonna do. You heard how I give you my word already? Well, take a look at me. Now, absolutely gratis and in addition, I'm gonna ask you to step up where everyone can see, and then I'm gonna pick at random from these here generous sample boxes of that taste-delightful Vitamines-Added Sunshine City Salt Water Taffy, a Parker Fifty-One Fountain Pen, a Real Ingersoll Pocket Watch including the supplementary gold chain, a Free Gift of Unestimatable Value—watch me close now— and I'm gonna. . . ."

"Not unestimatable value," complained Tom Moss, "inestimatable."

"Want a box of taffy, Eva?"

"No thank you extremely, it makes my face break out unless it's Atlantic City salt water taffy. He didn't say what kind it is"—the frown between her eyes frittering with the effort of classification.

"My heartiest congratulations, Mister! A Real Ingersoll Pocket Watch with the supplementary—"

Tom, skinny as a tick, leaning near us with his mouth full of hotdog, mumbled suspiciously, "Sunshine City probably isn't any kind of a city at all. They probably made the taffy from Morton's salty water. Results in tartar decays the teeth. Who wants an old Ingersoll watch? Couldn't be so hot for fifty cents per timepiece."

An abyss between us for my having spoken with Lucille when he did not dare, Juicer stared at Eva from his anguished eyes above the glacial blue of freshly shaven cheeks. Perspiration ran among the snarled hairlets of his new chin beard; we exchanged no further greeting while, in the carnival maelstrom, we felt the noisy toy-filled bath of childhood run out down the drain. "I don't even have a temporary license anymore," Juicer said. "I drive a car."

"Whose? What kind?"—my Eva.

A conspiratorial giggle united Rosalie Fallon and Pattie Donahue. "Everyone loved me"—fickle Rosalie Fallon— "but he loved me *so much.*"

"I always kiss him behind the ear. I don't know why, but I think it's kind of cute"—small-pawed Pattie Donahue.

"That's a nifty love affair, Pattie—"

"And he drives this neat roadster, Rosalie—"

Chuck Hastings approached these two with the intensity of devotion felt by a petshop clerk before a crate of fresh merchandise. He put his head first to Rosalie, then to Pattie. I watched his rodent-eyed pursuit, and their retreat, and his pursuit. Juicer and Eva were sampling each other's sandwiches. I strolled toward Lucille, who stood alone with her strange air of not being alone: this self-sufficiency was neither a disgrace to her nor, either, the exultant freedom I knew in my shocked-awake morning walks. "What do you think of Chuck?" I abruptly asked her.

"You don't like Chuck, do you?"—the diamond eyes busy over me.

"But that isn't what I asked you."

"Do you want my opinion?"

"Yes."

"Why yes?" the smile of the princess undressing before a slave because she cannot regard him as a human being. She smiled and smiled at me, tall and slender and those hard tanned musical arms piously crossed over her not yet fully created breasts. "I feel the way you do, Dan," she said at last. "I'm human too, you know. I think Chuck is just—"

"I'm here," said Eva. Eva took my arm and blew us away with a momentum that ceased all at once, a rush and a dawdle. She sighed, leaning on my arm. "Nice," she said about nothing.

"Nice," I said within the same general context.

Patiently digesting, having learned to give ourselves a moment, we watched the auction of the handmade antiques. "Friends," whined a pair of pink lips, "friends, now I suppose you good people been handed a fast line of con once or twice in your life or lives—think before you answer. . . ." This special sale took place at the edge of the grounds, near cottages inhabited by widows triste but still hopeful in their incomes and their sagging, having chosen to wear the black under a shriek of Loop-the-Loop and its climbing clickety-click. Lulled by the auctioneer's music, pink lips in pink assault against a microphone pinned to his shirt, we stood in the shade of trees here since the time of the several Indians of the Western Reserve. "Gone dollah ten, dollah ten, dollah ten—dollah quahtah, dollah quah-tah, who says a dollah quahtah nice genuine silvah coas-tah?" He rang a knuckle against it. The song of songs for our life or lives—think before we answer! "Now who, now who, now *who* says a dollah fawty?"

A man in a checked golf cap like a bootlegger's nudged me and suggested, "It's worth at least a dollah fifty."

"Yes, why?"

"*Sold* to the young gentleman with a big heart and a love a nice t'ings for a dollah fifty," bawled the auctioneer, tonguing the point of his pencil.

"No! no! I didn't say anything!"

Lucille smiled, saying, "He didn't say anything. His heart is bigger than a dollah fifty."

"What do you mean?" Eva demanded.

Lucille smiled carefully. "I'm just making jokes. I need practice"—diamond-eyed Lucille, hard and musical.

Lewis Snyder pushed us along. "Fun, jeez, let's have a little fun around here. . . ." Eva, having followed Lucille's smile from its origin to its destination, retook my arm. We went past a booth where a mathematico-artillery genius could win a Swiss clock housing trumpeters for the hours by hitting a bull's-eye forty times with a .22 rifle whose barrel was made of exhausted macaroni. Dong! Out leap the Calvinists, blowing horns. Dong! Two o'clock. Dong! No, three. Galvanic, the trumpeters revolve back into their chalet. *Dong,* uncertainly pipes the choked mechanism from behind closed doors.

"Did you ever see those clocks strike, really strike I mean?"

"No, Eva."

"Those little men move, really move I mean. . . . My mother has one. There's Red. There he is"—the subtle tumbling bear who sometimes barked Hosannah, the nimble hobgoblin, the nevermore Mercury, Red my pal.

"Yes, why?"

"My father must have sent him."

"Why?"

"Is that all you can say?"—but I waved to him. Now no nick-toothed grinner, he turned away from his sister and me. He shambled alone and miserable and kicked the base of a water fountain. "Okay," said Eva, "if that's the way he feels about it. I'll show him."

"What do you mean? What's the matter with Red?"

"I'll show him," she said.

I wanted to defend Red, this seeming a duty unto myself, but Lewis Snyder hurried us forward. I discovered again the black look on Juicer's face which says, between friends, that there will be no meeting between you on this day. My leaning to Lucille had shown him another lining to the coat of friendship. I glanced at Tom, who greeted me among the crowd with the dull look of politeness in the eye, that glaze which argues: Outside I'm asleep and tolerant, inside I might still be alive.

"Hey you, Red!"

He was gone again.

"I hear you have a kitten you want to give away," said Lucille. "I like kittens."

"Who said?" I asked her, thinking about something else, probably my sorrows.

"Didn't you ask me why?" Lucille Lake, the harpist with eyes and a smile like diamonds, was plucking the air and saying, perhaps to me: "I'm learning to give my opinion about things. It's part of growing up."

"But first you have to give yourself, that's why. . . ."— That was Dan, that was Juicer, that was even Red Masters wandering uneasily like a lonely evening visitor with reason to doubt his welcome, with reason to doubt his reason, with Luna Park whirling about his distracted center.

"Did your father say anything special this morning?" I asked Eva. "You seem worried."

"I'm not worried at all, Dan, far from it."

"What about Red?"

"Maybe he's supposed to watch us, so what? I don't know. It doesn't make any diff anymore."

"What do you mean, Eva?"

"Don't worry, Dan. I'm not worrying anymore, I told you far from it. So don't, see?"

I looked at her but did not see. "That's not why, Eva." *That's not yes.* . . . We shoved and pushed through a crowd with the illusory orange blood of five o'clock aslant on its cheeks. "What's the matter with Red?" Slow, slow, the Puerto Rican girl on the Dodgem still graciously dodged, bumped by men but resolutely unsquealing in her hour of repose. Thompson Products had disgorged a crew of overtime workers looking especially sallow in their purple Bowling League shirts. Someone said that Roosevelt didn't really hate war. Someone else said that Harry Hopkins. . . . I would never know the rest of the connection between Harry Hopkins and the bowling crowd from Thompson Products. An ambiguous blue of afternoon shadow crept up the walls of the Fun House. The House of Joy! 1000 Laffs Count 'Em! We advanced with money in our pockets and tickets in our hands, the sun-bruised whites of our eyes as tough with thread as old money. Recorded hilarity bawled without a face from the loudspeaker. I thought of Euclid Masters, and I caught a glimpse of Red, and I touched Eva's hand through the turnstile. "Eva?" I asked. "Red looking for you or me? What's Red looking for?"

She did not answer.

She moved ahead of me, behind Juicer and Lucille and Tom and Rosalie and Lewis and Pattie and Chuck, single file like pellmell studious rats through the Fun House maze, switching our tails, tickled until we could hardly speak, laffing exactly one thousand times, our eyes squeezed in ecstasy and our sight shimmering, leaping over the jets of stale air, plunging through the cunning doorways, squeaking like laboratory rodents, honking and twisting and trapped in taffy, very far now from Norman Thomas and the Town Meeting of the Air. "Eva!" I cried. "Don't get cut off from me, Eva!"

"Why not?" Her high peal of laughter seems to come rushing back through fifteen years in the Fun House.

With luminous tumescent skeletons, with whistles and sirens and gusts of wind, with caged false animals truly roaring, with trick mirrors, with cows falling upon us from the ceiling, with apocalyptic sliding carpets, jerking boats, and treadmill staircases, with upside-down rooms and rooms askew, with reeling, catapulting, and plummeting, the Fun House of our resilient dreams and capricious hearts in crisis continued the Fun House of the Kahn Combine—gilt peeling and the sly mad ones hiding in the latrines. . . . "Very sociologically inneresting," observed Chuck Hastings. Red followed in silence like a paid mourner. Red dodged head-down behind us like a paid mourner who finds himself grieving but receives his coin anyway.

"I'm tired of insights, don't you think?" Eva was telling Lewis Snyder.

"Yes, why?"

Streaming reckless and breathless through our Luna Park day, with a thousand unleashed dreads within, we ran in a greedy, intimate pack to find out one last ride before the evening's journey home. Eva! The Tunnel of Love! Ask Red what he's looking for, won't you, Eva?—and then

tell me, *Why so sad?* . . . A shove by Lewis Snyder, that
sinister farcer, put me in the wrong cell of the silent water-
urged caterpillar of Love's old sweet tunnel. Leaning on
Juicer's arm, Eva stepped down into the cubicle behind me,
holding her dress tight away from splinters. Snyder pushed
me! Ride with the buffet, but ride all the same! (I thought I
heard the laughter and the crabwise rustle of Euclid Masters.) Our caterpillar was in motion. *Styx,* went the turnstile behind us.

Eva decided, Eva made a decision, tender Eva determined her free will within the conditions of a shove from
Lewis Snyder, Spinoza the Sheik. Eva sat where she wanted
to sit, sitting on what it was ordained that she sit—sitting
with whom she willed that she should sit. What a selection
was there, O Snyder, O fatality's left end! Eva's pouting
rump squeezed beside Juicer's spread sitting hams.

I wondered what had happened to Red, and then my
eye found him, ticket between fingers, waiting for the next
trip which he would take alone. He secretly wished us a
voyage if not a happy one, known by name to everyone,
perhaps my friend as the current took us off into the darkness. He knew how necessary it is to travel. *Yes,* he thought
out to me, *why?* We averted our eyes in agreement not to
speak and signaled our sympathy with each other—a sharing held with little knowledge. We had his father in common, however, insufficient cause for anything. We said
good-by to each other by turning away. Eva too willed her
dimming, with only the dial of her watch green in the
dark, leaving me alone or thinking myself alone.

Thus we tumbled for one final ride in the carts of love.
Hooked to each other by machinery and memory, joined
and floating, hauled and spun on the back of a snake with
a painted apple in its carved mouth, we stared forward into
a night with uncertain docks at the end of its second-hand
seas. The glint and slosh of waters darkened by love com-

forted us. Caterpillars grow up to be butterflies, but snakes only become snakes. Some caterpillars, however—Red stood there in a receding zero of light to remind me—are born to die as moths, and some snakes discover themselves to be ambitious, gill-slitted, Bermuda-bound eels. We emerged into the light again blinking, and I realized that I was with Lucille Lake. Behind me sat Juicer with Eva, behind them Tom with Rosalie Fallon. Ahead of us sat Lewis and Pattie, and in the lead, splendid in his solitary devotion, crouched Navigator Chuck.

Chuck Hastings, our executive Noah, I mean to add here, was kissing the empty air. Tom was kissing Rosalie: such is the power of the world and of the tunnel of love. Lewis was kissing Pattie: such is the inevitability of the world, of the tunnel of love. . . . Eva! Eva! My friend Juicer was kissing Eva Masters. She kissed him with a tear for me in one eye and a tear for herself in the other. Out of loyalty to her father they did not run together on her cheek, evaporated first—it seems to me—by the fires of her ambition and of her chosen economies.

My dismayed gaze coasted down my nose, then skidded, then discovered the interesting fact that at this moment, still in the shadow of the terminal bricks of the tunnel of love, I was kissing Lucille Lake. There is no justice in our lives, I thought like a child, but as I felt musical Lucille's sharp little teeth against mine, I suspected that there is perhaps something better. Enough why for a time, for a time enough *yes*.

19. *Intimations of justice in the far hereafter*

Moralité. ART IS SHORT, BUT
life is long.

There shines a star, a far point of light, a truth. We live
and die, and that star is what we care for. But there is also
the walk in the field to find the star, the map of words, the
raised arm and the pointing finger. I must not mistake my
words for truth, my star map for star light. But Dan Berman
can take the arm of his wife, take joy of the words they
use, how they lie down together to look for the light which
they see singly and side by side.

Therefore Dan offers this piratical, lying map of his
boyhood. Follow, please, the invisible path from the end
of my finger to the star.

We all grew up in our several proper ways. Well, Euclid Masters died, of course, poor man, poor monster. But
watch out! Bestial Pattie Donahue became a social worker
and does piles of good to everyone!

Let us remember that health is a series of illnesses properly understood. Friendship is a history of hatreds, religion
of denials of God, pity of cold scorn, prophecy of lies, and
knowledge of a buzzing host of errors—all these imperfec-
tions properly understood. Yes, but why? What is a proper
understanding?

255

Good grief. I make a moral conclusion out of responsibility to my medical mother and old economical friends, who sing the ad hoc song that we begin as gill-slitted fish, prehensile monkeys, and irregular dreams. We end half in memories and half in worms, runs their a priori music.

Why does Tom Moss sell new Ramblers, used Chryslers?

Why does Red Masters teach Communications Skills to skilled eighteen-year-old intercommunicators?

Why does Juicer now do what he does? (Topnotch legal research.) Why did Eva marry a Costa Rican, the third time she married?

Not even my wife, who knows most things, knows why. When I ask her, she uncovers the harp.

The good life is empirical and a way of looking. Otherwise how to know whom we are kissing?

Yes then, and why?

I mean that we have to count on surprise and discord in this life, breathe through the mouth, and expect new songs. Therefore endless! Therefore thanks for what our irregular dreams do to our monkeyshines and fishiness! I mean that true economy, friends, is an extravagance: Be good for our own pleasure—*that the why*—but be bold for the children of everyone—*and this the yes*.

Therefore look well! It will improve our judging tomorrow.

Begun in Paris 1950
and Cleveland 1952
and Port-au-Prince 1954
and Detroit 1956
Completed in New York City,
Ithaca, Salt Lake City,
and Reno 1959-1960